I0724647

# WALK OF FAME

## RAISE A GLASS, BOOK SIX

## MARY E THOMPSON

BluEyed Press

**Walk Of Fame**

**Raise A Glass, book six**

Copyright © 2018 Mary E Thompson

Cover Copyright © 2022 Mary E Thompson

Cover photo (vineyard) from depositphotos © vitalytitov

Cover photo (couple) from depositphotos © NatashaFedorova

Published by BluEyed Press, All Rights Reserved

No part of this book may be reproduced in any form or by any electronic or mechanical means, including information storage and retrieval systems, without written permission from the author, except for the use of brief quotations in a book review.

This is a work of fiction. All characters, businesses, locations, and events are either products of the author's creative imagination or are used in a fictitious sense. Any resemblance to real persons, living or dead, is purely coincidental.

Ebook ISBN: 978-1-944090-44-9

Print ISBN: 978-1-944090-45-6

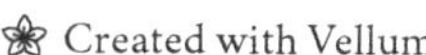 Created with Vellum

1

---

Kate Maddox waved to her fans and stepped off the stage. The cheers of the crowd rang in her ears despite the headset she wore. They loved her.

*Someone has to.*

She smiled at all the stagehands and worked her way through to her dressing room.

"Kate!" a voice said from behind her. She sighed, her hand on the doorknob.

*Almost made it.*

She spun and plastered on yet another fake smile. She'd gotten good at them over the years.

"Hi!" she gushed. She'd seen the woman around backstage but hadn't spoken to her. "How are you?"

"I'm really sorry to bother you. I know I'm not really supposed to talk to you, but I was wondering if you'd sign something for my daughter. She loves your music."

Her smile felt as fake as the songs she sang on stage every night. Songs that spoke to countless people, but not her.

"Of course. I'd be happy to. What's her name?"

"Rebecca. She's twelve. She wants to be a singer like you are. She's already started writing her own music."

"That's amazing. Tell her to keep writing and never give up on her dreams," Kate said, signing her name with a flourish and adding a heart. There was a part of her that hated hearing about kids looking up to her, but she knew it was part of the job.

She wasn't anyone's role model. She wanted to be, but she wasn't who she thought she'd be when she started singing. She always dreamed of writing her own songs. Putting her voice into the music. She did a little at first, but her label hadn't allowed her to record any of her own songs and after a while, she stopped writing them. Instead she sang songs written by others, songs that made her feel like her life was full of sex and fun.

If they only knew.

"Thanks so much, Kate," the lady said, accepting the marker and the flier Kate signed. "I hope you have a really good week off. I heard you're visiting family for a few days."

Kate nodded but didn't give any details. She tried as hard as she could to keep her private life separate from her public life. Unfortunately, more than she liked got out.

Thankfully, no one knew her real name.

Or almost no one.

"Have a good night," Kate said with a grin that made her cheeks ache. She waved as the lady walked away, clutching the signed sheet to her chest.

Kate walked into her dressing room and sighed.

"Ambush?" a voice said from the other side of the room.

Kate huffed a laugh. "Always. Are we ready for tonight's escape?"

Kate looked at her best friend and assistant. Quynn O'Hara was the most loyal person she'd ever had in her life that wasn't family. She still kept secrets from Quynn because she never trusted anyone completely, but Quynn knew who Kate really was better than anyone.

Quynn smiled, her face transforming from the steady mask that kept Kate sane to the devious woman that kept her true identity a secret from the rest of the world. Her neat blonde ponytail and brilliant green eyes gave her a studious look, but Kate knew her friend was anything but.

"I have your outfit ready and a driver waiting to take you wherever you want to go. I'm going to stick around here since it's your last show for a week. I think there are going to be more people than usual hanging around."

Kate sighed. "You're probably right. Especially since they all want to know where I live. I never should have admitted I live in Syracuse."

Quynn smiled kindly. "You weren't thinking."

"I wasn't thinking about a lot of things at that point in my life."

"Yeah, well, Christian is a part of your past. And keeping who you are a secret is something you have to be okay with."

Kate sighed again. "I know. I just don't know if I can put it all out there. You see how the media is with all these other singers. They're like vultures. It's bad enough for me, but if they knew who I really was, I'd never be able to leave the house."

Quynn smiled and guided Kate to the chair in front of her mirror. Kate looked at the woman reflected back at her. She was as phony as the smile plastered on her face on stage.

"Listen," Quynn said, flipping Kate's hair into her face. "I know you want to be able to stay out of the limelight. Unfortunately, people are trying to figure out who you are more and more. It's getting harder for you to hide."

"I know," Kate groaned. She winced as Quynn tugged at her hair. One by one the purple highlights came out, followed by the brown extensions she added to give her hair a fullness that wasn't natural.

Quynn dropped each chunk of fake hair into the bag they used for her supplies. One of the many bags that Kate and Quynn never let into the hands of someone else. Kate couldn't risk a random person getting a hold of her highlights and figuring out that she took them off when she wasn't Kate Maddox.

Quynn flipped her hair back over and Katherine looked at herself in the mirror. The clothes still screamed Kate, but Katherine was coming back.

"I need to wash all this makeup off and change my clothes."

"Do you remember what it was like before you became famous? You couldn't wait to make it big and have a huge contract and concerts all over the world. Now all you do is bitch about it."

Katherine gave her friend a sheepish grin. It was the truth. She worked hard to get to where she was. She busted her ass to break into the country music scene. And the truth was, she still loved it. There were just parts of fame that got to her. Parts that made her wish she'd made different decisions along the way.

Like her choice of men.

"I shouldn't complain so much. It would be nice to be able to just be me, but if everyone knew who I was, I don't think I'd ever be able to be me. I'd be watching my back constantly. I couldn't go to a bar and pick up a random guy for the night."

"Is it one of those nights?" Quynn asked knowingly.

Katherine nodded, stripping off her stage clothes. The tight dresses, low-cut tops, and pants that felt like a second skin were too much. She had curves galore and complimented her designers that they always hid them well, but it would have been nice to show a little less cleavage. Or a lot less.

"Where are you headed tonight?"

Katherine shrugged, but she already knew where she was going. If Quynn knew, she'd insist on tagging along, or follow Katherine without her knowing. But Katherine needed a night to herself. A night to decompress from the tour that felt endless. A night with a stranger and sex that made her forget how much she hated the way she felt at times.

"I guess I'll see you at your parents' house tomorrow?"

Katherine nodded. Another pang of guilt hit her. She wasn't planning to meet Quynn at her parents' house the next day. She had reservations at an inn. She thought about canceling her reservation, but she wasn't sure. The idea of staying with her parents for a week was less than ideal, even though she loved her parents.

She just wasn't prepared to answer all the questions she knew were coming.

Quynn handed her a makeup wipe once Katherine had her jeans and tank top on. She smeared the heavy stage makeup from her face and finally breathed. She grabbed the gauzy top and pulled it over the tank top then faced the mirror and finally smiled.

"Better?"

Katherine nodded. "Much."

"Good. I'll text your driver. You have your bag?"

Katherine nodded. She hated leaving her guitar behind, but she knew if she walked out with it, everyone would know she was Kate Maddox instead of some nondescript stagehand.

"He's ready for you," Quynn said, tucking the phone back into her pocket. "I'll run interference for you."

Katherine threw her bag over her shoulder and went to

the door. Every time she went out, she got nervous. But she looked so very different, she knew the risks were small.

She just hoped it stayed that way.

———

DILLON YOUNG TOOK A DRINK FROM HIS BEER AND LOOKED around the bar. He sighed and tipped the bottle up. It was stupid to think he could show up on a Thursday night and find someone to go home with.

Dammit.

Dillon nodded to the bartender and got up. He was halfway to the door when it opened and she walked in.

Dillon stopped in the middle of the damn room and watched her. Jeans hugged her curves and a flimsy shirt hung off one shoulder. Her light brown hair drifted behind her as her eyes scanned the bar. When they landed on his, they scanned his body as her lips curled up.

"Hey," she said.

"Hi."

"Are you leaving?"

He shrugged. "I was."

"And now?"

He grinned. "It depends on if you're staying."

She looked around then shook her head. "I could go."

Dillon put his hand on her lower back and guided her out the door. As soon as it swung closed behind them, he pressed her back against the wall and sealed his lips to hers.

She knew the score, but he wanted to make sure she understood the only reason she was leaving the bar with him was so they could make each other feel good. It wouldn't go anywhere beyond the night.

He thrust his tongue between her lips and ground his hips against hers, letting her feel the way she already affected him.

She whimpered and clawed at him, trying to fucking climb him. He didn't mind helping her at all, scooping her up so she could wrap her long legs around his waist. God he loved a woman who could handle how big he was. When she hooked her heels together, he groaned.

*Fuck yeah.*

"Are you close to here?"

She nodded and pointed to the hotel next door.

"Walk?"

She nodded again, dragging Dillon's lips back to hers. He kissed her until his balls ached and his cock tried to talk him out of waiting until they were behind closed doors.

With a groan, he unwrapped her legs and lowered her to the ground. The top of her head was almost up to his nose thanks to the heels she wore. He didn't usually find women that came so close to his height, especially ones that exuded femininity like she did. There was a classy elegance to her that had him reaching for her again and again as they walked the short distance to her hotel.

Dillon wondered briefly who she was to be staying at a hotel in Ithaca, but dismissed the thought as quickly as it came. It worked even better for him that she wasn't a local and he'd never see her again. Then he knew she wouldn't be after him for anything other than the one night.

He never imagined being named CEO of his family's vineyard, Amavita Estates, would bring out the gold-diggers like it did. If finding a woman in his hometown of Bereton, New York wasn't bad enough with his five male cousins screwing half the women in Seneca County, it only got worse with women who were after him for his money.

If they knew he didn't make any more than the rest of his cousins they'd back off, but Dillon didn't care. He just ignored them. He didn't want his cousins getting taken advantage of. It was better for everyone if he stuck to Ithaca, thirty minutes south of Bereton, for his hook-ups.

They made it up to his companion's fifth floor room without running into another guest the entire time. She tugged him into her room and let the door slam behind them as she kissed him like she couldn't get enough.

His fingers dove into her silky hair, tilting her head where he wanted it so he could devour her. She eagerly opened for him, tugging at his shirt as they kissed like they couldn't do anything without being connected.

Dillon yanked his shirt over his head, then ripped hers off. His hands went to her breasts, perky nipples pressing against the lacy green fabric of her bra. He unhooked it as he lowered his mouth to her skin, running his tongue over her breast before pulling a nipple into his mouth.

"Oh, yes," she moaned, clutching his head to her chest. She dragged him to the other side, showing him exactly what she wanted.

As he ravaged her, she unbuttoned and unzipped her jeans, shimmying them down until she could kick them and her boots off. She dropped her hands to his jeans, unbuttoning his and trying to shove them down.

Game fucking on.

He grabbed a condom from his pocket, always prepared, and shoved his jeans to the floor with his briefs. He rolled the condom down his length, his chest puffing when she fucking purred and reached for him.

His hips bucked when she wrapped her hand around his cock and stroked him. "I can't wait. I need you now," she moaned in a throaty voice that had him more than ready to fucking go.

He tugged her back in for another kiss, their teeth hitting, lips pinched between, and tongues tangling. She wrapped her arms tight around his neck and tried to climb him. He cupped her thighs and lifted her. Her legs slid around his hips, spreading herself wide for him.

Dillon plunged in with a single deep thrust. She moaned, dragging her lips from his with the guttural sound. He took a few steps and pressed her back against the wall opposite them. There was a bed somewhere, but he wasn't patient enough to go ten more steps and try to find it.

She held on tight, her thighs gripping his hips as she worked to thrust up and down on him. His balls tightened, the need to come racing down his spine and making him fucking tingle.

He gritted his teeth and clenched every muscle in his body. He rarely stuck around, but he sure as hell made it his mission to give her at least one orgasm that blew her away before he even thought about coming.

"Oh, God. Yes. Fuck. Harder."

Her throaty demands spurred him on. He pressed her back to the wall and used his hands to guide her over his rigid cock. One hand went to the wall, and he slammed into her.

"Yes," she moaned. "Keep going."

Harder. Deeper. Wetter. He grunted, thrusting into her. Her head hit the wall, her eyes dazed with lust. He clenched his jaw tighter, forcing his eyes from her face. Those pink lips, unfathomable brown eyes, and flushed cheeks made him want to come.

Her legs clenched tighter, her channel gripping him. His grunts grew louder, drowning out all other sounds around him. She gasped, moaned, and panted.

Then she fucking screamed.

"Yes! Oh, God. Yes!"

The best feeling in the world was when a woman came around his cock. He'd give up just about anything to feel that. As she whimpered, her orgasm fading, he thrust harder into her, shocking her with the force of it. Her second orgasm surprised her if the gasp followed immediately by a moan was anything to go on.

His throat burned with the need to come. His entire body tensed for a second, then burst like every inch of him was able to let go.

He yelled as he came, his words mostly nonsensical. She held on to him, milking the last of his orgasm from him as he fought for breath and tried to stay on his feet. He gave up the fight to stand and let them both sink to the floor, still connected. Panting, sweating, hearts pounding.

They sat there for a few minutes, breath slowing until they weren't struggling. Dillon was trying to figure out if he could stick around for a second round when she shifted.

"Damn, that was fun."

He chuckled. "Most fun I've had in a long time."

"How long?"

He pulled back and looked at her. Those stunning brown eyes watched him, questioning but not judging.

"Too long," Dillon admitted.

She ducked her chin and nodded. "Me, too."

Dillon kissed her cheek, feeling more connected to her than he'd been to any of the women he'd hooked up with in far longer than he cared to think about.

They got to their feet and cleaned up. Dillon still wasn't sure if he needed to head out or if he could talk her into a second go, but she answered for him.

"Want a drink?"

Dillon tugged on his briefs and nodded. "Sounds good."

They shared an awkward drink, trading small talk that told him absolutely nothing about the woman he couldn't wait to be inside of again.

Hell, he didn't even know her name.

"Want to try the bed this time?" she asked.

Dillon laughed and nodded. He grabbed a second condom but put it aside as he drove her insane with his hands and lips and tongue. When she was writhing on the bed and begging him to fill her again, he was more than happy to do exactly as she asked.

When round two was over, Dillon slid into bed with her, promising himself he'd be long gone by morning.

## 2

QUYNN WOKE up Friday morning to the sound of her phone rattling off the nightstand and smashing against the bottom shelf before it fell to the carpeted floor next to her bed.

She bolted upright, disoriented. She looked around the room before she remembered she was in a hotel room somewhere outside Binghamton, New York, pretending to be with Kate Maddox so Katherine could vanish for a night.

Quynn groaned and padded to the bathroom knowing whatever was on her phone could wait a few seconds for her to empty her bladder. She spotted the mini coffee pot on her way back to the room and went ahead and started it, knowing she'd need it to get through the day.

With a fresh cup of coffee in hand, she retrieved her phone from the floor as it vibrated again.

"What the hell is going on?" she wondered aloud as she swiped the screen to read the latest messages.

"Oh, shit."

Quynn scrolled through alert after alert about Kate Maddox and Christian Blake's impending reunion.

"No. No, no, no. This can't be true. She can't have gone to see him last night."

Quynn opened one of the many articles about them getting back together and studied the pictures first. She knew Kate better than anyone. She knew the nuances of her outfits, the things she liked, how she fixed her hair, even the changes her body went through. Quynn could spot an old picture, even one that had never been printed before, in a heartbeat.

Except those.

She flipped to another site, but it showed the same pictures. They were clearly leaked from the same source, which was part of what concerned her. They were dark, almost too dark to make out Kate and Christian together.

But on the third site, Quynn grinned. "Busted."

There was another picture of Kate and Christian. One that showed Kate smiling up at Christian, a look of complete adoration in her eyes. The look made Quynn stop. She hated how hard her best friend fell for Christian. He played her well. So well that even Quynn didn't see it coming, and it was her job to see things like that coming.

Quynn shook off her dark mood and focused on the picture again. Kate and Christian were getting into a car, his car. Most people wouldn't notice the difference, but Quynn did. Not only was Kate wearing a pair of boots that she tucked in the back of her closet and refused to wear again, but they were getting into a car of Christian's that Kate said he sold toward the end of their relationship.

It was all a lie.

Just like everything else Christian said.

But Quynn didn't know why he was telling everyone they were getting back together. He had a game, like he always did, and she had an obligation to warn Katherine.

She thumbed out a quick text to Katherine telling her Christian was telling everyone they were getting back together. She linked to a couple of pages with pictures, including the one that proved the stories were contrived.

Quynn nibbled on her thumbnail as she waited for Katherine to text back. She reached for her coffee and took a sip, not tasting it as she waited.

Quynn gave up and took a quick shower, with her phone right outside on ring so she would hear it. She got out, check it just in case she missed a reply, then got dressed.

Quynn packed up her stuff and double checked that she had a car coming to take her to Katherine's parents' house later that day. She was getting frustrated that she hadn't heard a thing from Katherine.

A knock on the door had her breathing easier. Katherine was back and they could go. No big deal. They would figure out Christian together.

"Where the hell have you been?" she breathed as she opened the door.

Christian pushed inside. "Where is she?"

"What are you doing here?"

"I'm looking for my girlfriend. Didn't you get all the alerts this morning?"

"She's not your girlfriend anymore, Christian."

He shrugged, his smug smile firmly in place. Those thin lips and shifty eyes made him look like a timid frog. He was attractive enough, but he wasn't as hot as he thought he was.

"She'll come back to me when she hears what I have to say."

Quynn snorted and crossed her arms, holding the door open with her foot. "She'll never come back to you."

"Is she here?"

Quynn shook her head. "Nope. Which you can plainly see."

He rolled his eyes like a teenager with attitude. "Fine. Then I'll have to stop by her parents' house this week so I can talk to her."

Quynn fought to keep her chin from dropping. "We're not going there."

Christian chuckled. "Of course you are. Kate always stays with her parents when she's in town. That's why you don't usually come with her."

Quynn hated that Kate shared so much information with him when they were together. She needed to be smarter than that. No more telling men who she really was. Especially not guys she'd only known for short time.

"Tell her I'll see her soon. Actually, I think I'll text her. Give her my news first. Bye, Quynn."

Quynn glared at him as he walked out then let the door slam behind him. She had to warn Katherine.

> Christian was just here. He wants to talk to you. Knows we're going to stay with your parents.

Quynn tapped her phone on her palm and paced. It felt like forever, but she finally got a reply.

> Okay. Thanks. Talk later.

"What the hell is that supposed to mean?"

---

"HOW ARE THINGS GOING SO FAR?" DILLON ASKED KRISTEN when he caught up to her Friday mid-day.

"Good," she breathed. She looked rushed and distracted.

"What do you need help with?"

"Um… It's fine."

"Kris, talk to me. What's up? I'm here. I can help. I have nothing going on the rest of the weekend."

"I know you're busy. It's not a big deal."

"Kris," he groaned.

"Fine. We need help in the fields. We're struggling to get everything set for tomorrow. We have our plans, but we need to get it all ready."

"I got it, Kris. Get your stuff ready for today. I'll find Henry and Ryan and take care of tomorrow."

"Are you sure?"

"Yes. Absolutely. Now go."

Kristen grinned and sucked in a deep breath. Her shoulders eased as her eyes closed. He felt like a shitty cousin for putting so much on her. They all worked together. She didn't need to be so stressed.

"Hey, Kristen?"

"Yeah?"

"Don't hesitate to ask me for help, okay? This weekend or any time."

She paused a second then nodded. "Thanks, Dillon."

He nodded and headed back to his office. He shut down his computer, told his sister, Andie, he was leaving for the day, and headed home.

Dillon's home was his sanctuary as much as anything else. He had one of the two bedroom homes on Amavita Estates to himself. A lot of his cousins shared their houses, but Dillon always lived alone. For a while, he thought he was lucky, but lately he wondered if it was just because none of his cousins or siblings had any interest in living with him.

Dillon stripped out of his work clothes and dragged on jeans and an Amavita Estates t-shirt. He went back out into the field, texting his cousins to find out where they were and what he could do to help.

He met up with Henry and Ryan near the first tour stop. Kristen planned out a whole weekend of activities to kick off the summer over Memorial Day weekend. Saturday was supposed to be their biggest day, with a day of tours through the vineyard and tastings at each spot.

But the best laid plans and all that…

"What's going on?"

Henry sighed. "We're just trying to figure out how we're going to do all this."

"Like what?"

"If we're going to have tastings out here, we need a lot in place. We've been talking about this, but it doesn't feel like it's going to work."

"Have you guys finished up what you're doing today?"

Henry and Ryan shook their heads. "Not even close. We've been working on all this for Kristen. We haven't done any trimming or had a chance to get to all the vines."

"Get out there. The most important thing is to make sure this vineyard stays running. I'll work on the logistics for tomorrow."

Dillon went the opposite direction of Henry and Ryan, toward his parents' house. He grabbed the golf cart his parents had and went to work.

Hours later, Dillon was hot and sweaty and fucking exhausted. He straightened out everything with the tasting and got Kristen's approval, along with Henry and Ryan's. He helped his cousins in the field for the rest of the afternoon and went home feeling fucking fabulous.

And exhausted.

All he wanted to do was take a hot shower and crash. Too bad he had to go back to the wine and appetizers tasting event for the evening.

Dillon allowed his gaze to travel over the fields he'd just

left as he headed toward his home on the edge of the property. His cousins worked hard and they were doing well, but Dillon loved getting his hands dirty. As acting CEO, he no longer needed to work in the heat of the summer, but he loved it once in a while. He'd been feeling restless. Cooped up in the office was never his dream, but as the oldest, he didn't get a choice. His dad had him assigned to the CEO role long before he went to college. Dillon liked to be outside, though. Get his hands dirty.

As he rounded the corner toward his house, he groaned. On his front porch was a woman. He didn't think he could give a woman what she needed after his long day, but he also only liked his women around when he asked them to be. He didn't do well with drop-ins.

Dillon drove closer, the electric cart silent and unnoticed by her, and examined the firm backside covered in stylish jeans as she bent low to look in the front windows. Her heavy breasts swung free when she leaned over, and his cock twitched in his shorts despite his exhaustion. Her long hair was the color of the dirt Dillon was covered in, and he wondered why the color was so sexy on her but not on anyone else.

A few more seconds and he was within speaking distance of her, but he found himself inexplicably mute. He tried to place those hips, the gentle sway of her seductive ass, the breasts that were teasing him from a sideview, and the hair that he wanted spread over his pillow, but he couldn't figure out who she was.

If she was one of his former flings, he was pretty sure he would make time to see her again, but first he had to figure out who she was.

Dillon cleared his throat and the woman jumped. She spun around and faced him, her rich brown eyes rendered him speechless as quickly as her hips and breasts had done before he looked into her eyes. She had eyes that reminded him of the cat his mother took in after finding it in the field one day, eyes that betrayed all her emotions and hid her true secrets.

*Son of a bitch.*

It was her. The woman he'd spent the night before with. The same one he hadn't been able to get out of his head all day. Whose bed he left after three rounds of the most amazing sex of his life.

And she was looking down at him, hands on hips, like gum on the bottom of her expensive looking boot.

"I was told to come here. I thought someone was going to meet me."

She snapped him out of his trance, and he mirrored her aggressive stance. "Well, since this isn't a hotel, I have no idea what you're doing here."

Her face and demeanor changed instantly. She had the decency to look chagrined and he nearly smiled at her discomfort. "Shit, I'm sorry. The woman at the inn said I could stay here for the week. I have a reservation. I thought you were the person I was supposed to meet."

Her tone instantly softened him, although the longer he stared at her certain parts made him harder with the memory of the way she'd responded to him. For some reason he wanted to protect her, to take care of her. There was a fierceness in her eyes but also a vulnerability. He could tell her initial bravado was false, and in the face of defeat, she was beginning to crumble.

Of course it also pissed him off that she didn't seem to remember him at all and it'd been less than twenty-four hours since he'd licked her until she came then slid his cock deep into her.

"I have no idea what you're talking about. This is my house, not a part of the inn. You said you have a reservation?"

"I do. Or I did. There was a family up there that said they had a reservation but something went wrong. They drove all day to get here only to find out they had nowhere to stay."

Dillon sighed wondering what it had to do with him and his house. And why his one night stand was on his porch.

"We have lots of guests that like to come and see how things are done, taste the new wine, and enjoy the beautiful weather this time of year. I'm not sure how that relates to me."

"The woman at the inn said I could rent this house for the weekend. She said she'd work it out, but I didn't know it was your house. I'll go."

Her lower lip trembled, and he worried she was going to burst into tears. Instead she sucked in a shaky breath and straightened herself up. She lifted the suitcase tucked behind the porch column and started back down the steps.

He stepped toward her as she descended the stairs, close enough that when she reached the bottom he caught a whiff of her sweet scent. It was soft and natural, not hidden behind a heavy stench like so many of the women he slept with. He noticed her face was bare again, only a dot of lipgloss coated her perfect bow shaped lips.

She smiled at him as she walked past, her brown eyes sad, defeated. "I'm sorry I was rude to you."

She turned and started to walk away without another word. Dillon stood watching her for a few moments, frozen in place and trying to figure out what he should do.

Before his brain fully kicked in, he called out to her, "Are you seriously just walking away? You weren't here looking for me?"

She turned, her eyes sliding down him. He wasn't amused

by the disinterested look in her eyes. There wasn't even a glimmer of recognition.

Wow. And he thought their night was pretty fucking fabulous. Nice to see she didn't feel the same.

"I'm sorry," she said, shaking her head and starting to walk away. "I don't think we know each other."

Dillon chuckled to himself. "I might not have told you my name last night, but I think I know you pretty damn well."

Her step faltered, and he wondered if she would turn and come back or simply keep walking. She seemed to be warring the same choices with herself. Finally, she threw back over her shoulder, "Where did we meet?"

Dillon's eyebrows rose and an amused grin curled his lips. "Matty's in Ithaca. Before you even got a drink, we walked out the door. We went to your hotel next door, and just in case you forgot, you came at least ten times in the three times we had sex."

Her gasp was just as throaty as the night before and his cock took notice. He happily would have her naked and screaming his name this time, but he wasn't sure how he felt about his one night stand following him home.

Even if a part of him was impressed.

"How did you find me?" he asked.

Her eyebrows winged up, angling high above eyes that slid over him again. She shook her head. "Are you really him?"

"Who else would be able to tell you all that? Who the hell could I be?"

She shook her head, avoiding his eyes for a minute. Every nerve in his body told him there was something off, something she wasn't telling him, but he couldn't shake the need to protect her. That flash of vulnerability he saw in her eyes told him he couldn't let her walk away.

"You can stay here," Dillon finally said. "I have a guest

bedroom. It's not the luxury of the hotel, but it's clean and it's private."

"I can't put you out like that. There has to be somewhere else."

He shook his head. "Not here. And you'll have to drive a ways to find somewhere else. All the places to stay until you get up to Seneca Falls are small B&B's. This weekend is big for everyone. You said a week?"

She nodded.

"It's fine. We have a wine and appetizer night up at The Drunken Grape tonight and tours all day tomorrow if you want to see a little more of the vineyard. Come on in and chill out for a bit. We'll head up together and straighten all this out."

He heard her muttering something to herself before she finally gave in and headed back to him. "I'm not putting out again," she stated when she stood in front of him, her dark eyes blazing with anger and a hint of fear.

Dillon leaned back on his heels and looked down at her. He kept his eyes focused on hers, willing himself not to drift from her face. "I don't remember saying that was part of the deal."

She looked him over, taking her time. He stood there and took it, knowing she wouldn't find him lacking. He kept himself in very good shape, especially for his thirty-seven years. She'd definitely found him more than adequate the night before. Sharing a house instead of a bed was much less of an intrusion. And hell, he was the one letting her into his home.

"Thank you," she finally said, meeting his eyes.

"You're welcome. Can we go in now? I'll show you around then I need to shower before we go back to The Drunken Grape. By the way, I'm Dillon Young."

"I'm...Katherine Price," she said, almost as though she

couldn't remember her name. He narrowed his eyes wondering why she hesitated before giving her name, but Dillon realized he didn't care. She was staying with him for the weekend and then would be at the inn and gone from his life forever.

Besides, it wasn't like she could hurt him.

3

---

Dillon opened his door and stepped back to allow Katherine in first. She smiled at him and stepped inside. She didn't really know what to think of him. He was gorgeous, that was obvious, but it was also obvious he was one of the workers on the vineyard.

When Katherine booked her trip to Amavita Estates, she wasn't sure she'd actually keep the reservation. It was on a whim. She'd been considering buying a place in the area so she could have a home when she was touring the northeast. Small towns were usually good at keeping secrets and didn't care who you were as long as you didn't cause trouble. She figured her week off would give her time to look around the town and decide if she wanted to live there. She woke up that morning ready to abandon all her plans and go straight to her parents' house, but then she got Quynn's text. Christian was back and wouldn't hesitate to go to her parents' house to find her. Which meant she had to hide and figure out her next move.

Starting with finding a place to stay. Her room was being moved into by a family of four so she couldn't go back to the inn. Staying with her one night stand wasn't a great idea either, but she was stuck.

Katherine glanced around his place and eyed him at the same time. He looked different than the night before. More rugged and a bit dirtier, but sexy as all hell. She stared at his hands, blushing when she thought about the things he did to her with them.

Too bad she wasn't positive it was actually him.

It wouldn't have been the first time someone pretended to know her when they didn't.

The only thing she was grateful for so far was Dillon clearly didn't know who she really was. If he did, he likely would have been falling all over himself to do everything for her, or trying to get her back into bed. Katherine wasn't prepared for any of that, not when she was so fragile.

Dillon's home was well appointed with wide plank wood floors, an open floor plan that allowed her to see the spacious kitchen, cozy dining room, and large living room in one sweeping view. The kitchen looked high end, with handmade cabinets and natural stone counters. A farmhouse sink sat front and center with an array of stainless steel appliances surrounding it.

The living room was just as nice with an insanely comfortable looking black microfiber couch, an ottoman to rest your feet on, and a TV that would put any movie theater to shame.

"It's not much but it's home. This way to your room," Dillon said as he turned into an opening between the kitchen and living room. Katherine glanced around and realized there weren't any other doors which meant she and Dillon would be sleeping close to each other.

Unless he left.

She really hoped he had somewhere else to stay for the weekend.

She took a deep breath and followed him, pulling her suitcase behind her. Dillon went right in the small hallway into a brightly lit guest room that would be more than comfortable for her. The queen sized bed was covered in fluffy white bedding and looked inviting. Katherine stashed her suitcase in the corner of the room, aware of Dillon's eyes following her.

"You have a private bathroom right through here and you are welcome to use the closet and dresser. Make yourself at home. My room is on the other end of the hall. Oh, and your door locks in case you're worried about me taking advantage of you."

He walked out with that running through her head. A few minutes later she heard the water turn on in the bathroom she assumed was in his bedroom. Visions swamped her, images she couldn't erase. Fantasies about Dillon's body beneath those clothes, about what he would do to her if she went to join him. She closed her eyes and could envision the water running streaks through his dirt stained skin, washing every inch of him clean.

It took everything she had in her not to let her gaze travel over him while they were talking on the porch. Under normal circumstances she wouldn't have been shy about appraising a man, but she was scared. She had to be careful until she figured out what she was going to do, what her next move needed to be. Who she could trust.

And she needed to stay hidden.

Katherine was fairly certain the longer she stayed under the same roof with Dillon the harder it would be to avoid jumping him. He was just a vineyard worker, but if he was who he said he was, he had magical hands. And tongue. And that cock of his. She shivered at the memory of him.

Her people would have a fit if she spent more than a night with him, but she knew the only way she'd ever find the love she sung about in her songs would be to find someone that didn't know who she was, someone who would love her for *her* before he knew her as Kate Maddox, country superstar.

She imagined going to Dillon, finding out if his door was locked, and stripping off her clothes before she stepped into the shower with him. She could picture her hands sliding over his heated skin, the water pooling around her fingers and running over her body from his.

Kate had her share of lovers in her life, but none who stuck for long. The guy in the bar was the only one she'd been with at all in far too long. She was in a dry spell if there ever was one, and she knew her reaction to Dillon was partly because of how little action she'd gotten lately. He was insanely attractive. That rough look was something she'd always gone for. She could almost feel his calloused hands on her skin, teasing her into a frenzy all over again.

Her skin heated with her memories of him, and her panties dampened. She stood up and shook her head, catching sight of herself in the mirror hanging over the dresser. "Come on, Katherine, get your head together. You're here for no time at all, and he'd be all over your money instead of you if he knew who you were."

With her resolve in tact, Katherine lifted her suitcase onto the bed and unzipped it. She pulled out a few pairs of jeans, underwear, a couple of t-shirts, some nicer tops, and a couple of dresses. The dresses had been a weakness, not quite stage clothes, but the types of clothes she usually wore when going out. She wanted to be prepared for anything.

With a sigh Katherine unpacked her suitcase, stashing clothes in the closet and her underwear in the drawers. Even if she was only there a night or two, she felt better when her suitcase was unpacked. She might as well make herself comfortable.

She used the bathroom, washing her hands and face, then

went back to the living room to explore. The kitchen was well stocked and so was the movie collection. Katherine knew she wouldn't be bored sitting around there all day. She almost regretted not bringing her guitar but she never would have escaped if she had. Something that big would be hard to hide when you're running away.

She wandered through the living room, picking up pictures of his family as she went. He had a big family, lots of brothers and sisters, or maybe cousins judging by the pictures of older couples she saw. They looked happy.

Katherine wondered again at the home. His employers had to be pretty awesome to build him such a nice house on their property. Of course, she assumed he didn't own it, but it was pretty great of them to house their employees.

Katherine had found Amavita Estates wines when she was growing up. Her parents had always drunk the local brand, being from Syracuse, New York, and wanting to support the vineyard on the Finger Lakes. When Katherine was younger, her family took a trip there. The area was so beautiful Katherine swore she'd come back if she ever got a chance.

After her music career took off, Katherine barely had time for anything fun. It was only part of the reason she wanted a home in the area. She was sick of living out of a suitcase and eating room service three meals a day. If she was lucky, maybe Dillon would let her use the kitchen while she was there.

The water turned off in the shower and Katherine breathed a little deeper. She wanted to appear relaxed and at ease in his home even though she was anything but. Dillon's door opened and he turned the corner, pulling his shirt over his head, giving her a glimpse of firm muscles, tanned skin, and a path of hair that highlighted exactly where she wanted to be going.

It was going to be a long few days.

---

"Thanks for waiting. Sorry about that. Uh, are you ready to go?" Dillon asked, avoiding looking at Katherine.

He thought about her while he was in the shower. She was stunning, sophisticated in an understated way. The way she moved and the way she talked back to him turned him on more than he cared to admit. Even if he hadn't been covered in dirt he would have needed a shower so he could separate himself from her.

Not that the shower helped him. He left the door unlocked as much from habit as from hope that she would join him. Dillon wasn't stupid enough to invite her, not after she'd declared there would be no more sex, but a man could dream. After the cold water failed to calm his desire for her, he turned it to hot and took the edge off his need.

And then he saw her again. She was standing near the window overlooking the vineyard. It was one of the places he always stood when he was trying to figure something out. He loved looking out over the land his grandparents had turned into a thriving winery. Tina and Carmelo Richliano moved to New York from Italy when they were just married. They wanted to escape from her angry family who thought they shouldn't be together and decided to start their life together in the States.

Carmelo worked on a vineyard in Italy so it only made sense to find one when they moved to the United States. He worked at a small vineyard for a family that took them in and treated them as their own. When the family retired, Tina and Carmelo decided to take it over. They started with the one, then slowly acquired more and more land and surrounding vineyards as the business grew. All in all they bought up seventy-three acres in eight different purchases, each including a home or two, plenty of space for Dillon, his three siblings, their five cousins, and the aunts.

When Carmelo died in a car accident, Tina brought their four daughters in to help run the vineyard. Dillon was the only one of the cousins who was born at that time, but he was too young to remember his grandfather. His parents and the other aunts stepped up. Aunt Christina was seeing Uncle David, one of the workers on the vineyard, when Carmelo died. Aunt Jo was dating Uncle Victor, but they were both in college at the time. The six of them, along with the oldest sister, Dillon's Aunt Marie, stepped up their efforts to maintain the family vineyard.

Almost a year ago, the aunts agreed they were ready to step down from the business and turned Amavita Estates over to their nine children. In the last year Dillon had watched three of his cousins and his sister find love, but Dillon was too focused on work to consider love would be in his future any time soon.

As the oldest of the grandchildren, Dillon took on the biggest burden himself. He wanted to protect his siblings and cousins from any hardships. He spent too many hours of his first year as CEO in the office, but he was feeling restless and wanted to get out more.

Sometimes Dillon wanted to back off a little, but he knew he wouldn't. It wasn't like he had anything else in his life worthwhile. He kept women in his bed because he was lonely at times, but not lonely enough to want to keep any of them around. He'd worked too hard to risk losing everything over a woman.

Katherine turned and smiled at him, her eyes quickly drifting over his body. His heart rate kicked up under her appraisal, but her face stayed neutral, leaving Dillon to wonder what she thought of him. It didn't matter, he told himself. She would be gone soon just like they all were.

"I'm ready," Katherine finally said. "Is this a fancy kind of thing or am I dressed okay?"

He looked down at her fitted jeans with the gray v-neck top and black jacket. She looked comfortable but sexy as all hell. She'd make all the men in the room hard in an instant.

"Maybe you should change," he blurted.

"Really?" she said. "I only have two dresses. Should I wear one of those?"

The image of her long legs wrapped around his waist as he pounded into her flashed into his head. *No. Fuck no.* She could not wear a dress or she'd really have every man hard.

"No. It's fine. You're perfect," he growled, heading for the door.

"Would you rather I stay here? That's it. You have a girl-friend, don't you? And you don't want her to see me there with you. Shit. I knew staying here was a bad idea."

"I don't have a girlfriend. Or a potential one. Or anything."

"Why did you tell me to change?"

He sighed. "Just forget it, okay? Let's go."

She didn't appear to be thrilled with his dismissal of her question, but he didn't care. He couldn't tell her he was jealous because every guy there was likely to hit on her.

Dillon stalked outside and slid onto the golf cart he planned to return to his parents at the event. Katherine followed him a few seconds later, arms crossed over her chest and a scowl on her beautiful face.

Dillon drove to the inn and parked out front. He stewed the whole drive and knew he had to say something to her when he saw the pinched look on her face, arms crossed over her chest. He waited for her to get out and reached for her hand. "I'm sorry. I was jealous and pissed thinking of all the guys who would be flirting with you. I have no right, but it's hard knowing you were all mine just last night."

Katherine's eyes lit up and her lips parted just enough that Dillon knew she was more than a bit turned on at the thought.

"I'm not here to meet other men."

"But you're not here for me."

She shook her head. "No. I didn't know you'd be here. But you have to trust me when I say I'm happy you're the one whose doorstep I ended up on."

Dillon huffed a laugh and offered her his arm. "Shall we?"

She nodded.

---

KATHERINE DIDN'T REMEMBER THERE BEING A RESTAURANT when she stayed there before. It was a while ago, but she was pretty sure it didn't exist. The building they were walking into was completely new to her.

Dillon had a wide stride, something she remembered from the night before. He walked quickly in an effortless way that had her rushing to keep up. When they were headed to her hotel room, she was in a hurry, but walking into the inn and the restaurant, she was a bit more apprehensive.

Especially because it meant any number of people could recognize her.

She was thankful she went to extreme measures to protect her true identity. From the peekaboo highlights she wore when she was on stage to the sex-kitten outfits her manager insisted on, few people had ever even questioned if they knew her. And no one had ever asked her if she was really Kate Maddox.

But there was a first time for everything, and she was so nervous she thought she might throw up.

Dillon pulled up short when they reached the porch. He glanced at her and took a deep breath, then let go of her arm.

"Listen. When we walk in there, you're going to be swamped. I'm sorry, but it's just the truth."

Panic settled in, making it hard for her to breathe. So he did know who she was.

"I've never walked in with a woman before. My sister works at the front desk, and I'm guessing she's the one who sent you to my house. Everyone who works here is either a relative or someone who knows me well. My cousin, Zach, brought a woman around for the first time two months ago and you'd think we'd never seen a female before."

"Excuse me?" Katherine said. She was really confused.

"I know we're not together and you're not really here with me, but they're going to go crazy when they see us. We can tell them whatever you want, but they're going to ask questions."

"You're serious?"

Dillon nodded. "I wish I wasn't."

"How about we tell them the truth?"

"That we met in Ithaca last night and you followed me home?" Dillon teased.

Katherine laughed despite herself. "I didn't follow you, so let's go with your sister offered up your house for me to stay in for a few days and since we met before, you offered to let me stay in your guest room."

Dillon shrugged. "Up to you. They're not gonna buy it, though."

"Why not?"

"If Andie's the one who sent you to me, she already had a plan. She's scheming."

"Really?"

Dillon huffed a laugh. "Absolutely. When she finds out we met before tonight, she's going to jump all over this."

Katherine grinned. "Do you really think your sister was trying to set us up?"

Dillon nodded. "Yes. She fell for my best friend last fall and has been trying to find me someone since. That's part of why I go to Ithaca to pick up women. I don't want my sister getting wind of me being involved with anyone."

"I won't say anything to her. But for the record, I don't think that was her intention. She didn't tell me it was your house."

"And she didn't tell me she was sending a beautiful woman to sleep in my guest room for a long weekend either."

Katherine had to admit Dillon had a point. Andie seemed perfectly nice, but she didn't mention anything about the house belonging to someone else when she suggested staying at one of the houses on the property.

Katherine nodded and led the way inside. She wasn't afraid of his family. She'd charmed every interviewer on the red carpet, every talk show host, and more than enough radio hosts. She knew how to manage people.

But she was always Kate Maddox when she did that. Katherine Price was a different story.

The noise inside the inn was more than a little intimidating. It wasn't one sound, more the murmur of an endless number of sounds all blending together that had her frozen just inside the door. Dillon walked in behind her, stepping to the side when Katherine didn't move.

"It's fine," he whispered in her ear, his gravely voice sending shivers down her spine. "Just stick with me."

He grabbed her hand and tugged her toward the buzzing noise as though it wasn't a big deal. It got louder as they walked, the buzzing centering in her ears as distinct sounds of conversation, clinking glasses, and clanging silverware separated from the background murmur.

Dillon kept dragging her toward the back of the inn. He

waved to someone and moved steadily into the crowd, her hand clasped tightly in his. When he stopped and kissed the cheek of the beautiful woman in front of him, Katherine felt seriously under-dressed and frumpy.

"Andie, I believe you've already met Katherine. Katherine, you know my sister, Andie."

"Nice to see you again," Katherine said, extending her hand to Andie.

"You, too," she said with a look that wasn't anything but curious. "You two seem cozy." Andie looked between the two of them, her gaze focusing on their joined hands. Dillon slid his thumb over her wrist then released her.

"We met yesterday in Ithaca, making it a bit easier for her to move in with me for the weekend. Our family can be over-whelming," Dillon said pointedly. "I figured it was for the best to bring her in here. Think you could show Katherine where the food is while I go find Kristen? I told her I'd help tonight."

"Of course," Andie said, a look in her eyes that told Katherine she had more than a few questions.

Shit.

Dillon disappeared into the crowd without a second glance, leaving her with his sister and a very interested look on her face.

"Ithaca, huh? Do you live there?"

Katherine shook her head. "No, just visiting."

"Friends?"

"Hmm?"

"Were you visiting friends?" Andie asked.

"Oh, um, no. Just passing through the area really. I'm from Syracuse. Heading home."

"From where?"

"Excuse me?"

"Where are you heading home from?"

Andie's blue eyes watched Katherine carefully, not letting her escape for even a second. Katherine didn't know how to answer all the questions. She wasn't used to anyone talking to her who wasn't either an employee or an interviewer. Her public appearances were limited to things her agent and manager could control.

And a party with a bunch of strangers was definitely out of everyone's control.

Which meant she was in trouble.

## 4

"WHAT CAN I DO TO HELP?" Dillon asked Kristen when he found her walking out of the kitchen.

"Oh, Dillon, thank God. I thought you weren't coming," she breathed. Her dark hair was tied up in a knot-type thing, but her brown eyes scanned the room. She smiled at people, working the room as she talked to him.

"Sorry. I had something to take care of. Where do you need me?"

"Everything is going fast. Too fast. I think Zach and Michele can use some help in the kitchen."

Dillon nodded and pushed through the doors. Zach and Michele were both scrambling to get things done.

"Where can I help?"

"Plating. We can cook if you can make it all look pretty."

"Got it," Dillon said, moving to their finishing station. He enjoyed the fast pace of a restaurant kitchen. He wasn't nearly the chef Zach was, but Dillon liked to cook.

Kristen was back in within minutes, grabbing the trays Dillon finished as soon as he put the last item on them. They made Italian sausage stuffed mushrooms, ravioli and meatball skewers, caprese sliders, prosciutto and ricotta topped crackers, bruschetta, cheesy garlic bread, and mini lasagna cups. It was a madhouse in the kitchen with everything going on at once.

"What do you need made?" Dillon asked Zach.

"Michele is trying to keep up with the lasagna. I've got the ravioli, meatballs, bruschetta, and garlic bread in the oven. If you can make the sliders, skewer the meatballs and ravioli, and handle the prosciutto crackers, we can get back on track."

"Got it."

Dillon focused on his task, aware of Kristen and the other servers coming back in for new trays every few minutes. When he finally got to where he was ahead of the game, he took a second to breathe.

"You sister brought in a hell of a crowd."

"You know Kris. She'll work her ass off if you give her the room to do it."

Dillon nodded. He didn't know that, but he was learning. Kristen was nine years younger than Dillon so he didn't know her well. It was definitely time he changed that.

"If tonight is like this, tomorrow is going to be even worse."

Zach nodded. "Yeah. We have reservations for every time slot tomorrow. We can't even accept walk-ins. Henry said you were helping set up for tomorrow, but he's going out early because he doesn't think what you guys did is going to be enough."

Dillon sighed. "It's a good problem to have, but I think he's right. Shit."

Zach smiled. "It'll be okay."

Dillon laughed and shook his head. Zach had become the voice of reason over the last few weeks since his own life got blown sky high. He was definitely a much happier guy than he used to be, but he was different. Dillon was a little envious of his cousin.

"Are you guys okay in here? I can go check out there?" Dillon asked.

Zach and Michele both nodded. "We're good. If we need you back, we know where to find you."

Dillon pushed out of the kitchen carrying a tray of food. He circulated the room, saying hi to people he knew. He'd lived in Bereton his entire life, with the sole exception of the four years he spent at college in Ithaca, so he knew pretty much everyone in town.

"Dillon, how are you?" a voice said, stopping him.

He smiled and leaned down to hug one of his grandmother's oldest friends, Violet Gilmore. "Hi Mrs. Gilmore. How are you?"

"I'm a little disappointed, actually."

"Why is that?"

"If I'd known you liked younger women, I'd have set you up with one of my granddaughters a long time ago. All three of them are home now."

Dillon laughed and shook his head. "I'm happy they're home, but I'm not looking for any kind of a relationship right now."

"Then why is that beautiful woman you're dating cozying up to your family? Your grandmother told me she's your new girlfriend."

Dillon groaned. He'd almost forgotten about Katherine and leaving her with Andie. He needed to rescue her before everyone in town thought they were getting married.

"Nonna is mistaken. Katherine is just staying with me for a night or two."

"That's what your cousin, Zach, said about that Gianna woman he's getting married to."

Dillon stifled the urge to roll his eyes. "It's different, Mrs.

Gilmore. I should go check with Katherine. I'll talk to you soon."

Dillon handed off the tray he was carrying to a waiter and made a beeline for Katherine. She was sitting at a table with his sister, Andie's boyfriend, who was also Dillon's best friend, Cody, and Dillon's youngest brother, Leo.

Son of a bitch.

KATHERINE LAUGHED AT SOMETHING LEO SAID, ENJOYING HIS company. She caught the looks Andie and Cody were sharing, amused with a touch of concerned, but Katherine didn't care. She and Dillon weren't a thing. She could flirt with whoever she wanted to.

And she wouldn't be too disappointed if he happened to notice and got a bit jealous.

"Can I borrow this?" Katherine heard behind her seconds before a chair was flipped around and slid between her and Leo.

"Whoa! What the hell, Dillon?" Leo exclaimed, glaring at his brother.

Katherine thought Leo was cute with his short, dark hair and goofy smile, but she much preferred the kiss-the-fuck-out-of-her-outside-the-bar kind of guy to the one who made her laugh.

"Just thought I'd join you. What's going on?"

"I was talking to Andie's friend, Katherine. You're kind of getting in the way."

Dillon slid a hand on Katherine's thigh, not high enough to be indecent, but not low enough to be innocent. "Did Andie mention Katherine is staying at my place for the weekend?"

Leo glanced at their sister then shook his head.

"Oh, okay. Just wondering."

Katherine felt bad for Leo. He really was a nice guy. If she was smart, she'd go for him. Stay at his house instead of with Dillon. But that was kind of her problem, she never did the smart thing. She was impulsive and wore her heart on her sleeve. She always went for the guy who would crush her one day instead of the guy who would worship her.

And she was paying for it yet again.

"How're you doing?" Dillon asked, locking his eyes on hers.

Katherine forced a grin. "Good. I'm having fun. And the food is amazing."

"You should stop in the tasting room. I'll let you try whatever wine you want," Leo said.

Dillon's fingers tightened on her thigh. Not painfully, but enough that she knew for sure he wasn't happy Leo was still trying to hit on her.

"Thanks," Katherine said. "I'm a fan of Pinot Noir. Do you guys make that?"

"I have a few bottles at my place," Dillon said, sliding his hand down to cup more of her thigh. "We can open one tonight."

Katherine grinned up at him, unable to resist his allure. Those dark eyes and his broad shoulders. She'd had dates with some of the most attractive men in Nashville, but none of them were anything compared to Dillon.

Leo huffed. Katherine looked up and saw him glaring at his older brother. She felt bad, but she'd only hurt Leo if she made it seem like she liked him. He wasn't her type, even if he was cute.

"What do you do, Katherine?" Andie asked, dragging the conversation from her warring brothers.

Dillon leaned in closer, his thumb rubbing delectable circles on her inner thigh.

"I sing," she stammered, forgetting her usual cover as a freelance editor. "I mean, I want to. I've always thought it would be cool to sing. I actually work as an editor, freelance, so I can be wherever I want to be."

"But you're from Syracuse?"

Katherine nodded. "I grew up there. My parents and brother still live south of the city."

"Are you going up to see them?"

"Eventually. That was the plan, but I knew I needed a break. I have a couple weeks off so I wanted to have a week to myself. No one knows I'm here."

"Really?" Andie said. "I'm a little jealous of that. I think a trip completely alone would be kind of fabulous."

"Excuse me?" Cody said. "You want to go on vacation without me?"

Andie shook her head. "I didn't mean you. Just that after living here my whole life, I've never been on my own. It's nice to imagine not having anyone to answer to."

"After July you can get away for a little while," Dillon said.

Andie shook her head. "The summer is Cody's busy time."

"Then next winter. Take a long weekend. Don't wait until you're so stressed you hate this place."

"I'd never hate this place," Andie said happily. "I love being here."

"Good," Dillon said with a grin. He leaned back and toward Katherine, draping his arm over the back of her chair. She resisted the urge to lean into him. Christian was always touching her and putting his arm around her, but it was so everyone knew he was with Kate Maddox. When they were alone, he was hands-off. Only that memory had Katherine pausing instead of burying herself in Dillon's warmth.

"Are you going to join us for a tour tomorrow? And the party tomorrow night?" Leo asked.

Katherine nodded. "I think so. I planned to be here so I could enjoy the weekend. It's definitely not going as I planned, but I can't complain about the changes."

"Where are you sleeping, Dillon? Going to Mom and Dad's for the weekend?"

For the first time, Dillon looked unsure of himself. He met Katherine's eyes, silently asking her what she wanted him to do.

And in that moment, she knew for sure he was definitely the man from the night before. The man who'd driven her so crazy she couldn't remember her own name. The man who'd made her come so many times her throat hurt when she woke up. The man who made her thighs tingle with that heated look she remembered all too well from the last time they had sex. When he was on top of her, slow, deep strokes filling her. His eyes locked on hers, searing the memory so deep she couldn't have forgotten him if she tried.

Staring into those dark eyes, she finally saw him.

And she knew their weekend was not going to be spent in separate houses. Hell, if she had it her way, it wouldn't be spent in separate beds either.

"We'll be fine together," Katherine said, holding his eyes. "I know I can trust Dillon."

———

Dillon knew he was being an ass to his little brother, but *fuck*. He was not about to watch him hit on the woman he wanted to possess over and over again. It just wasn't going to happen for Leo, and if he couldn't get over that…

Well, he just had to get over that.

When Dillon stared at Katherine, he saw when she finally recognized him. Like a light switch in the dark, her eyes went from warm brown to liquid heat in a breath.

Oh, yeah, she remembered him.

Finally.

He couldn't stop the slow smile that turned his lips up at the breathy sound of her voice. Nor could he stop his cock from rising at that same sound.

It was going to be nearly impossible to keep his hands off her all weekend, but she was a guest. His guest thanks to his sister, and he didn't mess around at work.

But Leo didn't need to know there wouldn't be any fun going on in Dillon's house over the weekend.

"Hear that, Leo? She trusts me."

Leo finally stood up, slammed his chair into the table, and left. Dillon kept his face carefully neutral so no one knew the chair smashed into his knee. After all, he was the reason Leo was pissed off.

He would make it up to him one day. When Katherine was long gone and Dillon forgot about his brother trying to steal her from him.

"What kind of music do you like, Katherine?" Andie asked.

"Country mostly," she said, dragging her eyes from Dillon's. "The songs have always meant a lot to me. They're not just about sex and drugs, but about relationships and real things that people go through."

Andie groaned. "Oh, I so agree. We have tickets to see Kate Maddox next weekend. We got them months ago. Do you like her?"

Katherine pulled her lower lip between her teeth as tension settled into her frame. Dillon knew how to get her to relax, but he wasn't going to kiss the fuck out of her in front of the entire place.

"I do. Some of it is a little light, but she's had a few songs that really hit me."

Andie nodded. "I know. Most of her stuff is light and fun,

like music you'd put on when you're driving down the coast or something, but she's crazy talented."

Katherine nodded, that line between her eyebrows deepening. "I've always wondered if she'd ever write her own music. I feel like it's so much more personal when artists write their own. Or collaborate. Instead of just singing whatever someone puts in front of you. I mean, she's not a puppet, you know?"

Dillon was as shocked by Katherine's outburst as she appeared to be. He slid his hand down her spine then back up, cupping one of her shoulders and giving it a rub. "You okay?"

Katherine took a deep breath and nodded. "Yeah. I think I just need to have a little while to myself. I'm pretty worn out."

"Okay," Dillon said, immediately getting to his feet. "I'll take you home."

Katherine shook her head. "No, I'm good. I'll find my way on my own. You stay and help. I doubt your bosses would be happy if you left."

He eyed her carefully. How did she not know that he ran the place? He *was* the boss.

"Um, yeah. I'm the CEO of this place. I think it'll be okay if I head out."

She gasped. No games at all with her. She really had no clue who he was.

"Um, no. It's fine. I need the fresh air and the time to myself. You know, clear my head. I'll see you back at your place."

Dillon watched as she rushed through the crowd and disappeared out the front door. Instead of feeling relieved that she was gone, he missed her.

Which was the scariest thing he'd felt…ever.

KATHERINE WANDERED THE FIELDS OF AMAVITA ESTATES, marveling at how quiet it was once she was away from the inn. For a minute, she wondered if Dillon or Leo would follow her, but no one did.

She wasn't sure if she was happy about that or not.

No, she told herself. She could not get wrapped up in another guy. She had to get her head on straight. Falling back into bed with Dillon wouldn't clear up anything that happened in the last twenty-four hours, and it definitely wouldn't take care of Christian Blake.

Nothing would take care of Christian Blake.

Katherine checked her phone for the hundredth time that day, confirming yet again that she had her location disabled. She told herself that Christian couldn't find her anymore, but she couldn't take any chances.

Of course, that also meant Quynn couldn't find her either. She knew it wouldn't be much longer before her best friend freaked out that Katherine wasn't at her parents' house like she said she would be. She had every intention of telling Quynn her plans before she left, but she never had a chance when she knew no one would be listening.

So much for her relaxing vacation. A week on the lake, drinking wine, eating good food, and flirting with sexy men. Instead she was worrying about her ex finding her.

Katherine found her way to the water and walked along the shore. She knew Dillon's house wasn't down by the water, but she didn't care in that moment.

Pulling out her phone again, Katherine stared at the text from Quynn that morning. Katherine was sleeping soundly after a full night with the man who drove her crazy. The things Dillon did made her blush, and ache for more.

But her desire was shattered when she read the text from

Quynn. The text that convinced her not to cancel her reservation and go to her parents' house. The text that made her sick.

She pulled in a deep breath, filling her lungs with the damp lake water filled air. The grapes smelled delicious, but she knew better than to eat one. She didn't like when people downloaded her songs for free online, and she wasn't going to eat one of the grapes Amavita used to build their livelihood.

Katherine still had the sick feeling in her gut. Part of her wasn't surprised Christian was back. Part of her was simply pissed off. When she finally worked up the courage to end things with him, she told him it was because she was going on tour and didn't want him to go with her.

Their relationship was toxic for her. Unfortunately, she realized it way too late, long after she'd told him her real name and a lot more personal stuff that she regretted sharing.

Her phone beeped with an incoming text message. She looked at it, freezing when she read…

Where are you? I came here to see you.

She gulped air, telling herself there was no reason to think he knew where she was. He was fishing. He was good at dragging things out of her that she didn't want him to know. Chances were good he'd gone to her parents' house and realized she wasn't there and was trying to find her.

I don't want to see you.

She hated that she was afraid of him. That she didn't want to face him. He wasn't dangerous, at least, he hadn't been last time she saw him. Not physically.

But he was dangerous to her in other ways. Christian had a way about him. He could fool just about anyone. Katherine had never been able to hide anything from him. She told him her real name on their second date. She fell into bed with him on their third date. And she confessed her desire to write her own music on their fifth.

That was her biggest mistake.

Once she told him she wanted to write her own music, he had something to hold over her. Something to control her with.

She didn't realize it at first. She thought they were falling in love. She started singing so young that she didn't have many relationships as a teenager. The first guy she slept with was a boy she liked when she was in high school. It was a break from school and he invited her over when his parents were visiting his older brother at college. By the time his parents got home, he'd moved on to another girl.

It hurt, but she learned not to jump into bed with a guy unless it was on her terms.

When Christian came around, he was smart. He developed a friendship with her. He played bass in the band that opened for her. They got to know each other, then he asked her out. She never thought he was using her. He already had a music career.

But it wasn't enough for him. He wanted a bigger career, and she was his ticket.

I have something important to tell you.

She sighed. She didn't want to talk to him. Or see him. Or have anything to do with him.

It's about the song we wrote. The one we
worked on during tour.

The one you stole from me and said was
yours?

Her blood boiled as she waited for him to respond. Why she was giving him the time of day she didn't know, but it was her song. She poured herself into that song.

I played it. They want to buy it.

Who?

Why don't you come see me and I'll tell you.

She sucked in a breath and debated. If she could get one of her songs recorded, her label would take her seriously. It would be a game-changer for her.

You know you want this recorded. Maybe
you can even record it. I'll be waiting for you.

Her heart raced. Record her own song? She'd been dreaming of that, but nothing was that simple with Christian. He always had a trick up his sleeve.

Still, she turned toward Dillon's house. It wouldn't be the first time he found her when she didn't think he could. She'd talk to him, then call her lawyer.

And protect everything.

5

DILLON WORKED the room like the professional he was. He knew it wasn't his usual level of involvement, but Zach and Michele were overrun in the kitchen, and Kristen needed the extra hands.

He shook hands with another couple he remembered meeting before when he saw a face in the crowd that shouldn't have been there.

Dillon worked his way through the crowd until he was right behind Albert Perry and cleared his throat loudly.

Perry spun and grinned at Dillon. Dillon had a few inches on the older man, and a hell of a lot more muscles, but he wasn't going to posture in a crowded room where everyone knew who he was, and no one knew who Perry was.

"Can I help you with something? Like finding the exit?" Dillon asked, his voice low but firm.

Perry grinned. "I'm quite enjoying myself here, actually. It's a beautiful vineyard. I'd be willing to say it's the second best vineyard on Cayuga."

Dillon pressed his lips together. "What are you doing here?"

Perry looked around and grinned. His hair was a bit more gray than Dillon remembered it being, and slightly thinner also. He knew the man was pushing sixty, but he could have passed for seventy without much trouble. He'd also put on some weight, his shirt stretched tight over his abdomen.

"I thought this was a party," Perry said. "Isn't it open to the public?"

"You know that doesn't include you," Dillon hissed.

"It doesn't, Dillon? Really?" Perry's voice rose as he spoke, drawing the attention of people nearby.

Dillon grabbed his arm and dragged him away from the crowd. When they were in the privacy of the front hallway, Dillon finally let go of Perry.

"What do you want? Why are you sneaking around here?"

"Sneaking? I'm not sneaking. I'm in the crowd, meeting your amazing customers and making sure they know about the best vineyard on Cayuga."

The shit-eating grin Perry flashed had Dillon clenching his fists. He knew the sonofabitch wanted to get hit. Or wanted something so he had grounds to call the police.

It wouldn't matter that he provoked Dillon.

"You do know that's not legal, right?"

"Legal? What's not legal?"

"Poaching *our* customers from *our* event."

"Oh, see you can't prove anything. I didn't tell any of them my real name. And I didn't give out any literature. I just said they would love Perry Mount Vineyards if they enjoyed Amavita Estates. Once I hire your pretty new chef, I'll be able to open my restaurant and you won't be able to hold parties like this because everyone will be at Perry Mount instead."

Dillon growled, stepping closer to Perry. He wanted to punch the old man, just lay him out, but he knew it wasn't worth it to risk losing Amavita.

"Get out," Dillon said. "Get out of here now, and don't

come back. If I find out you were on this property again, we will be going to the police."

Perry just grinned as if that was his plan all along. Then he turned and headed for the door, leaving Dillon to stare after him and wonder what the hell just happened.

---

QUYNN STOMPED ONTO THE FRONT PORCH, PISSED OFF AND worried. Aside from one text message that morning, she hadn't heard anything from Katherine.

They were supposed to meet at Katherine's parents' house outside Syracuse, New York, but Quynn has serious doubts that her friend was actually there.

She pounded on the door, straining to hear something through the silence that greeted her. She pounded again, dragging her phone from her purse and sending Katherine another text demanding she call her back, adding that she was on the front porch and didn't have a key.

Why they didn't stay in a hotel was beyond her.

Quynn pounded again, ringing the doorbell and pounding on the door. She knew Katherine's parents weren't home, which left Katherine. And dammit, she had to be there.

"Katherine! Where are you! Open up!"

The door flew open, Quynn's fist landing on a very delicious male chest that was definitely not Katherine's.

"Jesus Christ! Will you stop!"

Quynn stepped back and gawked at the stunning man in shorts glaring at her. His dark hair was sticking up in all sorts of directions, like someone had been running their hands through it for hours. He smelled like a warm and delicious man, fresh from bed if she had to guess. Dark hair circled his pecs and headed south with her eyes, taking in each and every sculpted ab until her line of vision was interrupted by his red shorts.

"Who are you?" he demanded, his voice more than a little annoyed.

"I'm Quynn. Katherine told me to meet her here. Is she inside?"

"Quynn? Katherine? Are you fucking kidding me?"

When the sexy guy turned and walked away, leaving the door open, Quynn grabbed her suitcase and dragged it inside, closing the door behind herself. The house was just like she imagined it would be. Cute, homey, with that smell like fresh baked cookies that came with all good homes.

Quynn missed that smell.

She left her suitcase in the front foyer and followed the half-naked guy deeper into the house. She passed a staircase and an office before she was in a large, bright kitchen with white cabinets, black granite countertops, and stainless steel appliances. One that had the sexy guy framed by the open door and a carton of orange juice tipped to his lips.

Quynn licked hers and admitted she needed to get laid. It had been so long she couldn't remember the last time she'd had someone else take the edge off for her. Which was even more depressing.

"Uh, is Katherine here?" Quynn asked, drawing the attention of the guy again.

He glared at her as he finished his orange juice, rinsed the container, and shoved it in a bin under the sink.

"No. She's not here. Which you would know if you talked to her."

"I did talk to her. Well, texted her. She said she'd meet me here. Who are you?"

He smirked then rolled his eyes. "I guess I'm not surprised she didn't tell you about me."

Quynn threw her arms out to the sides, still not getting an answer from the guy.

"I'm her brother. Frank."

"Brother?"

He nodded. "Why else would I be here?"

"How old are you?"

He snorted. "Are you going to judge me because I live with my parents? Meanwhile you live off my sister. Yeah, you have grounds."

"I don't live off Katherine," Quynn insisted. She didn't, did she?

"Yeah, okay."

He turned to walk away, leaving her in the kitchen alone.

"Wait, where is she? She was supposed to be here."

Frank shrugged. "No idea. Not my day to watch her."

"Are you always this big of an asshole?"

"When someone wakes me up three hours before I need to be up so I can go into work for the night? Um, yeah. I am."

"Work? You work nights?"

He huffed a laugh. "You didn't even know I existed until you woke me up and now you're questioning my work schedule. Should we sit and braid each other's hair while I share my life story with you? What would you like first? The part about being a cop with shitty hours or the part about my ex-wife cleaning me out when she ran off with my former best friend? Because I'm sure either of those juicy stories will give you plenty to think about as you try to figure out why my sister never mentioned me." He moved closer and dropped his voice to a whisper. "I'll give you a hint. She doesn't trust anyone."

With that tidbit, Frank turned on his heel and walked away, slamming a door somewhere in the distance and leaving Quynn completely alone in a house she'd never been to before.

She glanced around the kitchen, trying to figure out what she was going to do. Katherine wasn't returning her calls or texts, and she wasn't at her parents' house like she said she would be.

Quynn pulled her phone out again and pressed to call Katherine. It rang twice, then she actually answered.

"Hello?"

"Shit, Katherine. Where are you?"

"I'm fine. I'm sorry Quynn."

"Sorry. What are you sorry for? Are you okay?"

She heard the quick intake of Katherine's breath and grew even more concerned.

"I'm fine. I freaked out. I had reservations and was going to cancel them, but I can't go there."

"What's going on?"

"Christian's back."

"I know. I told you that."

"He's been texting me. Someone wants to record our song, but he wants me to meet with him to talk about it."

"No," Quynn said immediately. She couldn't have Katherine going back to Christian. He was the worst kind of bad for her at the end. He talked down to her and took advantage of her. She became someone else when Christian was in her life. Someone neither of them wanted her to be ever again.

"I know. I don't want to see him. I thought he was here."

"Where is here?"

"I can't tell you that. I have no idea how he finds things out, but he always does. You know that. I can't risk that he has your phone bugged or something."

Quynn snorted. "He's not that smart."

Katherine chuckled softly. "No, I don't think he is, but I can't take the chance that maybe he is. I can't see him right now."

"You're stronger than you used to be."

Katherine sighed. "I want to be, but I know I'm not. I won't ever take him back, I know that, but he gets inside my head. I can't risk that."

"So come here. I'll keep him away from you. Me and *your brother.*"

"Ah, so you met Frank?" Katherine said, sounding appropriately chagrined.

"Yeah. Um, thanks for not telling me you have a brother. I thought we were friends."

"We are."

"Best friends."

"We are."

"Then why the hell did I not know you have a brother?"

Katherine sighed. "I don't know, Quynn. I'm still trying to figure out everything. I was with Christian for so long and he still has me so messed up."

"But I've known you longer than Christian. And I've never done the things he did to you."

"I know," Katherine said, her voice soft. "I'm sorry, Quynn."

Quynn shook her head and forced the anger away. It wouldn't do Katherine any good to think Quynn wasn't completely in her corner.

"It's fine. I'm sorry. You're right. You have to protect yourself, I get that. So what's going on right now?"

"I met a guy Thursday night. In Ithaca. He was amazing. And…I'm staying with him for the week."

"Wait, what? You met a guy and you're staying with him for a week? Who are you and what have you done with my friend?"

Katherine laughed huskily. Well, damn. It had been a while since Quynn heard that.

"It's not that big of a deal. Staying with him was sort of an accident. I didn't know who he was when I came here. But I like being with him. And he doesn't know who I am, so I can relax."

Quynn wanted to tell her friend to be careful. That she didn't know this guy, but it had been far too long since Katherine was even interested in a guy, let alone spent a night, or a week, with anyone.

Quynn took a breath and forced a smile onto her face, hoping it would come through in her voice. "You deserve some happiness, Katherine. Go get it."

"Thanks, Quynn. And I'm sorry about my brother. You can stay in my old room."

"No," Quynn said, shaking her head. Her blonde hair spilled over her shoulder and she pushed it back impatiently. "I'll go to a hotel."

"Actually, I think you'd be good for my brother. He needs someone to give him a kick in the ass."

Quynn snorted thinking of the sexy, pissed off man. She did not think he wanted anyone to push him. Especially not her.

"Um, sure. I'll see," she said, knowing she'd be out of there as soon as she hung up the phone.

"Thanks, Quynn. I'll be in touch soon."

Quynn hung up and sighed. She turned to go, but instead found Frank watching her.

"That my sister?"

Quynn nodded.

"She tell you to watch out for me?"

Quynn shrugged.

"I don't need anyone watching out for me," he growled, going to the fridge again.

Quynn huffed. "Clearly." She started toward the door, intent on leaving.

"Katherine's room is the first one on the right at the top

of the stairs. Make yourself at home. And let me know if you need anything."

"Excuse me?"

"Her room. I'm assuming you're staying here."

Quynn looked around. "I planned to, but…"

"I'm sorry. I don't understand Katherine's world and I probably never will, but you planned to stay here, so stay."

"Wait, why are you being nice to me?"

Frank shrugged. "If Katherine trusts you, I trust you. I love my sister. And if she's close to you, then you belong here. I'll let you get settled."

Then he disappeared, leaving her to stare after him and wonder what the hell just happened.

---

DILLON LEFT THE APPETIZERS AND WINE PARTY WHEN THE LAST dish was washed and the last bottle of wine was stored in the cooler. He was exhausted and had no idea how his cousins dealt with guest all day every day. They were a pain in the ass.

Never mind dealing with Perry and his empty threats about stealing Michele and leaving them without a crowd.

Dillon was exhausted by the time he finally made it back to his place. All he wanted was a hot shower, a cold drink, and a warm woman.

Unfortunately, he wasn't likely to get any of them.

Katherine wasn't in the kitchen or living room when Dillon walked in. He kicked off his shoes and headed straight for the fridge. He was fresh out of cold beer so he turned and went for the wine rack. He grabbed a bottle of pinot, thinking back to Katherine's comment that it was her favorite, and poured two glasses.

Dillon sipped his and let the alcohol soothe him for just a

minute. He could have easily finished his glass and poured himself a second before he went to get Katherine, but he didn't. His parents taught him to be a good host, and he needed to be a damn good host. Katherine wasn't some random woman, not really. She was supposed to be a guest at the inn, and instead she was a guest in his home. One who agreed to let him stay there with her. One he hoped was still okay with it after spending the evening flirting with his brother.

He knocked on Katherine's door and waited for her to open it. He heard her moving around in the room and wondered what she was doing. When she opened the door, he saw the telltale signs of crying.

Puffy eyes? Check.

Red cheeks? Check.

Trembling lips? Check.

"What's wrong?" he demanded, reaching for her without hesitation.

She shook her head and refused to step into his arms. She turned from him and went to sit on her bed.

"Did something happen at the party?"

She shook her head again.

"What is it? You have to talk to me."

"Why?" she blurted. "We don't know each other. We never would have seen each other again if I hadn't ended up here. Us meeting has been a fluke from the first moment."

Dillon shook his head. "It was random, sure. But who cares. You're here. I'm not going to let you sit in here and cry when there's a perfectly good glass of wine with your name on it."

That got her attention.

"I thought you could join me for a glass. But if you'd rather sit in here by yourself, I'll just drink them both."

Katherine rolled her eyes and grinned, following him

back into the kitchen. He handed her the glass he hadn't already sipped from and grinned when she breathed the fruity bite of the pinot. When her lips pressed to the edge of the glass, his cock twitched and he decided to stop watching her.

The silence between them rang in Dillon's ears, telling him the TV wasn't on like usual. He needed something to distract him from wanting to carry her to his bed and remind her how good they were together.

"I guess I never showed you how to turn on the TV. Sorry about that."

"I don't watch much TV actually. You have a great movie collection though. I'll keep busy while you're working. If you don't mind that is."

Dillon shook his head. "No, I don't mind at all. I'm a little surprised, though. Most women don't approve of my movie selection. They always tell me I like violence too much."

Katherine shrugged. "I like action movies. I grew up watching them. My dad was a big Steven Seagal fan and, of course, James Bond. When I was little I wanted to be a Bond Girl, but I'm not shaped right for that. Way too much junk in my trunk, plus, I'm too curvy. I'd have to drop about forty pounds to be anywhere close to that."

Katherine commented about her weight matter-of-factly. She didn't look at him as she said it, as though she was bothered by her weight but had come to accept it. He didn't know how to tell her she was the most perfect woman he'd ever seen.

"You don't need to lose any weight. You're stunning," Dillon said softly. He didn't say it to manipulate her, to get her into bed again. He just wanted her to know how beautiful she was.

"Thanks," she mumbled off-hand.

He could tell she didn't mean it, that she didn't trust his

words. She needed to know he meant it, but how far do you push a stranger, who's already shared a bed with you and said it wouldn't happen again, to convince her she's gorgeous.

"You can brush it off if you want, but it's the truth. You're the most beautiful woman I've ever seen, and trust me, I've seen my fair share. You would be the sexiest Bond Girl ever if you were cast in that role. Your curves would have every man in the theater wishing for a private place to go jerk-"

"STOP!" she shouted, covering her ears. "Don't finish that sentence. Please."

Dillon laughed at her pink cheeks and frantic behavior. He'd embarrassed her, but it'd worked. She forgot about thinking she wasn't perfect and listened to his words.

"I'll stop if you admit that you're beautiful."

"Why do you care?"

He shook his head and stepped closer to her. He let his voice drop, knowing she liked it when he did that. 'I don't understand how women that look like you can ever think they're less than perfect. I bet you want to be one of those models, like a size zero or something, right? What you don't realize is men don't like women like that. I would be afraid I'd crush a women that small. That and I'd feel like a pedophile since they usually look prepubescent. But you, you're the sort of woman every guy keeps in his spa—"

"STOP! Jesus, what's wrong with you," she said, laughing. "You don't even know me and you're talking about guys masterbating at every turn."

"I told you how to get me to stop. I'll quit talking about how gorgeous you are if you'll just admit it. Hell, I came home this morning and had your face in my mind when I—"

"Fine. I'm beautiful. Are you satisfied?"

Dillon grinned at her, and she finally smiled back. "I'm nowhere near satisfied with that answer, but I'll take it for now. Okay, beautiful, are you hungry? What do you want for dinner? And tell me you're not one of those women who only eats salad because I'm fresh out."

Katherine laughed huskily. "No, I'm not one of those women. I like all kinds of food. Whatever you want to fix will be fine. Do you mind if I turn on the radio? I like music."

Dillon picked up a remote on the island in the kitchen and pressed a button. Country music blared from hidden speakers and Katherine laughed while Dillon fumbled with the remote to turn the volume down.

"Sorry," he mumbled when the music returned to a normal level. "I like it loud. It gets quiet out here by myself."

"Its fine. I'm used to loud music."

Dillon opened the fridge and looked around for something to fix for dinner. After being on his feet for hours, he wasn't in the mood to stand for too long to fix dinner but he'd offered. Normally on days like that he would drink some wine and heat up a pizza from his freezer, but something told him the woman in his house wouldn't go for frozen pizza.

## 6

DILLON SIGHED ALOUD as he faced the open fridge. Katherine couldn't help but wonder if he was regretting taking her in. He looked like he was in a stand-off with the fridge. Maybe he wasn't sure what to make for dinner, or he had a plan and she ruined it. Then again, it was late and he was just getting home, he could have just been dead on his feet.

One of Kate's songs came on the radio and her body flushed. She was pretty sure if Dillon didn't recognize her when they met, he wouldn't all of a sudden figure out who she was. He didn't say she looked familiar or reminded him of someone which meant she was likely safe.

But she couldn't take any chances.

Talking over the song she said, "We can order something in if you don't have anything for tonight."

"Uh, no," Dillon mumbled. He ran a hand through his hair and continued staring at the fridge. "I usually throw in a pizza when I get home this late."

"Pizza's fine with me."

He looked at her, confused and questioning, and asked, "Really? You don't seem like a frozen pizza kind of girl."

Katherine laughed out loud, finding his appraisal of her hilarious. If he only knew how often she ate frozen dinners, take-out, or leftovers. She gave off an air of high class, but her life was the furthest thing from it, especially when she was on tour. Katherine could cook, but she wasn't allowed when the bus was moving and after a show she was usually so dead on her feet she had no desire to do anything but crash.

"Frozen pizza is fine, seriously. Anything. I'm just grateful you're willing to take me in."

"So you wouldn't normally eat pizza."

She laughed again, wondering why he was so convinced she didn't like pizza. "I eat pizza all the time. Didn't we just have a conversation about my overly curvy figure? I didn't get it from salad."

It was Dillon's turn to laugh. The sound of his deep laugh echoed off the walls and vibrated through Katherine's soul. She closed her eyes and let the sound bounce through her, like the drums during one of her shows. It anchored her, gave her the strength to believe she was safe with him, that she could be herself, the person no one knew anymore. She could drop the Kate Maddox act and just be Katherine.

"I eat a lot of frozen meals so seriously, frozen pizza is fine."

"You're not really a guy, are you?" Dillon teased.

Katherine grinned at him, enjoying having him tease her, having anyone tease her. "I'm fairly certain you know the answer to that question. But yeah, I have the eating habits of a truck driver."

He laughed again and she watched as his eyes squinted and his mouth fell open wide. He clutched his stomach, pulling his shirt tighter against his chest and abs, the white nearly transparent against his tanned skin. His muscles rippled with his laughter and Katherine felt her mouth going dry as all the moisture in her body puddled between her legs.

Grateful that Dillon didn't notice her momentary ogling of his body, she pulled herself together and tried to calm her breathing again. God, she needed to get her head on straight. He flirts with her and she's ready to jump him again? No.

"Okay, pizza it is then."

Dillon pulled a pizza out of the freezer and unwrapped it. Katherine glanced at what he was doing and wondered what brand it was. Quynn never picked up pizza that good looking. If it tasted half as good as it looked, she would ask Dillon what kind it was.

He got the pizza in the oven and lifted the open bottle of wine. "Need a refill?"

"Sure. Is there anything I can do to help you?"

Dillon shook his head and filled her glass up again. Katherine took a sip and savored the small bite before the boldness of the wine hit her tongue. It was perfect. Katherine had been drinking Amavita Estates wines for years, but pinot noir was always her favorite wine, of any brand.

"This is really good. Do you get free wine as a perk of employment?"

Dillon studied her, pausing long enough for Katherine to wonder what he was thinking. "Yeah, all of us are able to take as much as we want."

"That's nice. I'm pretty sure if I worked here there wouldn't be enough pinot to sell because I'd drink it all."

Dillon laughed, studying her again, almost as though he wanted to say something else. He kept his own confidence and checked on the pizza. "It's almost done. Tell me a little about you, Katherine. You said you're from Syracuse, right?"

Now it was Katherine's turn to hesitate. "Uh, yeah. A little over an hour from here."

"Have you been here before?"

"When I was in high school, yeah. My parents always bought the wine from here and wanted to visit one summer. My dad's a teacher and my mom works in the office at the elementary school where I went so we would always take summer trips."

"It's beautiful this time of year, that's for sure. It's hard to have to work every day, but the winters are nice too, not too cold compared to some of the rest of the state."

Katherine nodded and sipped her wine, realizing her glass was already empty. Dillon leaned over and filled it back up for her before she could think about it. She wasn't driving anywhere so she figured why not.

"You're the CEO?"

Dillon nodded.

"What do you do on the vineyard? You certainly didn't look like a CEO when you got home today."

He paused, considering her again, then said, "I guess I do a little of everything."

Katherine didn't press for further details, sensing he didn't want to let her know. They were essentially strangers after all. "Do you enjoy it? Besides the long summer days?"

"Yeah, I do. It's a great place to work and I couldn't imagine being anywhere else."

"I know what you mean. It's nice when you find something to do that feels like it's as much a part of you as a limb. Like your life would never be the same if you couldn't do it anymore."

"You sound like you love your job. I'm guessing you're talking about singing and not editing, though, right?"

Katherine fumbled her glass and nearly dropped it, a drop of wine splashing over the edge and running down the side of the glass. She held it up and licked the drop off the glass, not willing to waste any of her favorite wine. It wasn't nearly often enough that she got to indulge. Being on tour meant she had to keep from drinking because the effects of alcohol were ten times worse when she had to get up on stage and sing.

She set the glass down and looked back at Dillon. He was gawking at her, his eyes dilated and lust-filled, his muscles bunched under his shirt, and his pulse raced in his neck.

Seeing Dillon so turned on by something as simple as her licking wine off a glass heated her body. Her nipples stood on end, pressing painfully into her bra, and the moisture between her legs became thicker. Her head spun, although she was pretty sure it wasn't from the wine, but from the hunk of muscle in front of her.

"If you're sticking by your original promise, you can't do shit like that in front of me," he gritted out, not looking her in the eyes.

It took Katherine a minute to remember her promise that she wouldn't sleep with him again and couldn't stop the smile that crossed her lips. She pulled her lip between her teeth and ducked her chin to her shoulder. Being able to effect him that badly made her feel as beautiful as he tried to convince her she was earlier. She wasn't toying with him, at least not on purpose, but she liked seeing how much he desired her.

"Is the pizza almost ready?" Katherine asked, desperate to change the subject.

Dillon checked it again and nodded. "Yeah. I feel bad that I don't have anything else. It's been a busy week getting everything ready. I should send Andie to the grocery store since she sent you to stay here."

Katherine laughed. "That would be a good punishment, don't you think?"

Dillon grinned. "Maybe. I imagine she didn't intend for me to stay here with you. She probably figured you'd be calling for food from The Drunken Grape all weekend or ordering in."

Katherine tilted her head, wondering if he was right. From the moment Dillon showed up, Katherine knew she wanted him to stay with her. Especially knowing Christian was looking for her.

"I'm sorry I'm invading your space. I probably should have gone somewhere else."

Dillon shook his head. "I'm glad you're here. Even if you aren't going to sleep with me again."

Katherine smiled, wondering how long she'd manage to keep that promise.

---

DILLON WOKE UP EARLY THE NEXT MORNING WITH A GROAN. He rolled out of bed and headed straight for the shower. Katherine kept him up all night, and he was in need of some relief.

Of course, it was the Katherine in his dreams, not the one in his spare bedroom who kept him up. He'd have happily traded fantasy for reality, especially since he knew how good the reality was with her.

He took care of his throbbing cock in the shower then washed quickly. He dried and dressed and was out the door before he even thought about waking her up.

It wouldn't end well for him because there was nothing better than a warm, sleepy woman, but Dillon remembered all too well how dangerous they were.

He walked from his house to the inn, letting the fresh air wake him up. He loved the smell of the vineyard, fresh dirt with the lake filtering in when the wind blew. Once in a while he'd grab a grape, but he always heard Uncle Victor's voice chastising him when he did.

Dillon smiled at the memory, his eyes scanning the horizon for his cousins. He knew Henry and Ryan were out there somewhere, getting their morning work done before the tours interrupted their day.

Dillon went in the back door of the inn, straight into The Drunken Grape. A few guests were enjoying breakfast, but the dining room was mostly empty. Dillon poured himself a cup of coffee and grabbed a muffin from the buffet, then stuck his head in the kitchen.

"You guys ready for tonight?"

Zach and Michele both turned and nodded.

"Absolutely," Zach said. "We've got everything set up. What are you doing here already?"

"I thought the meeting about the tours was at nine?" Dillon said, setting down his coffee so he could dig out his phone.

"It is. I just didn't realize you were joining the crew."

Dillon nodded. It killed him that none of his cousins ever went to him for help, or thought he would pitch in a little extra. Especially Zach. When he found out he had a daughter and was working different hours, Dillon filled in for him in the kitchen. But Zach was questioning Dillon's commitment to Amavita, and that stung.

"Good. Kristen will be happy for the help. I don't know who's running each station, but she was hoping to have one person for each."

"That's my plan. I'm all in this, too."

Zach gave Dillon a strange look, one Dillon didn't stick around to understand. He'd revealed a lot more than he ever intended to Zach not long ago. He couldn't tell his younger cousin how disconnected he felt most days.

Dillon ate his muffin as he headed for the tasting room. Kristen was behind the bar, as usual, with Andie, Henry, Ryan, Leo, Jake, and Sean on the other side.

"Morning," Dillon said, joining the group.

"Hey, Dillon. We're going to head out there soon. The first group shouldn't be here for about an hour, so we're just getting ready."

"Sounds good," Dillon said. "Where do you need me?"

"You? You're helping with the tours?" Kristen asked.

Dillon nodded. "That was the plan. Unless you don't need me."

Kristen shook her head. "No, we do. Absolutely. This works out so much better. Thank you. Okay," she said, addressing everyone. "We'll have five stations in the field. One person will take the group out there and get them from one stop to the next, answering questions along the way. That way we can keep all the groups moving along. Andie is going to be at the Riesling. Dillon, will you take the Pinot?"

"Definitely," he said.

"Okay, and I've got Leo at the Syrah so he can answer any last questions and walk the groups back to the inn, giving the guide the chance to greet the next group. Sean is at the Chardonnay, and that leaves Henry, Ryan, and Jake. One of you needs to take the Sangiovese and the other two can run groups with me."

"I'll take the Sangiovese," Jake said. "You guys know more about the grapes than I do."

Henry shook his head. "Not likely."

"You do it every day. I just have to talk about the one wine. You two will know the answers to all the questions that people will ask."

"I like it," Kristen said, cutting off further discussion.

Dillon had never seen her work like she was. She had things down pat, and she wasn't taking shit from any of them. She was damn impressive.

"I'm giving each group about forty-five minutes to get through the whole thing. Tours are going to start every twenty minutes, which gives us a fifteen minute gap between each group we'll lead. It should be more than enough time for each group to walk out, taste five wines, and be back in the gift shop. And Alyssa is covering in here?"

Jake nodded. "She is. And so are Marie, Tina, and Jo. They didn't want Alyssa on her own."

"Good. I think this is going to go really well. Thanks for the help everyone."

They all nodded and started to disperse. Dillon took the opportunity to talk to Kristen.

"You really have a handle on all this, don't you?"

She blanched. "I'm sorry. Did you want to run it?"

"No, no," Dillon said quickly. "I wasn't trying to take over. I've never given you enough credit for how organized you are. I think it's going to be great."

"Thanks. I couldn't do all this without everyone's help. Thank you for that."

"Any time, Kristen."

She smiled, but he could tell she didn't think he meant it.

Just like the rest of them.

Dillon grabbed his crate of wine and headed out to the pinot. A table was already in place when he got there, with a crate of glasses on a smaller table nearby. Dillon opened two bottles of wine to get started and waited for the crowd to arrive.

QUYNN SAT IN KATHERINE'S CHILDHOOD BEDROOM wondering what in the hell she was still doing there. Katherine paid her well enough to get a hotel room. At a place with room service and a spa and a car service that would take her anywhere she needed to go.

Yet she sat on Katherine's old bed, unwilling to leave.

Quynn spent her evening answering media requests and putting off all the events Kate was supposed to have over the next week. She had an interview scheduled on a national morning show, but if she was in hiding, there was no way she could make it.

And if Quynn couldn't get in touch with Katherine, she couldn't confirm anything.

Quynn read another request for an interview with Kate since the media heard she was in town, and sighed. She needed to find Kate.

Commotion downstairs brought her attention away from her computer. Quynn jumped off the bed and rushed to the stairs, hurrying down to see Katherine.

Multiple voices were in the hallway as Quynn approached, one she recognized as Frank's. The others she couldn't distinguish, but Katherine had to be there.

Quynn turned the corner and saw an older couple, the woman with dark hair with a red tint and the man with gray thinning hair. They were hugging Frank, and the woman kissed his cheek.

Frank noticed her standing a few feet away and pulled back. "Mom. Dad. This is Katherine's assistant, Quynn."

"Oh, Quynn! It's so nice to finally meet you. Katie talks about you all the time. We're so happy you could come here with her."

"Thank you, Mrs. Price," Quynn said.

Mrs. Price tugged her in for a tight hug, something Quynn wasn't used to. Her family was never very demonstrative with affection, preferring instead to hand over money to say they cared.

Quynn liked the Price's way better.

"Where's Katie? Is she upstairs?"

Quynn and Frank exchanged a glance that told Quynn Frank wasn't any happier about the situation than she was.

"She's not here, Mom," Frank said.

Mrs. Price turned and looked at her son. "What do you mean? Where is she?"

It was Quynn's turn. "I don't actually know. She turned off her phone's locator. She's hiding."

Mrs. Price's blue eyes narrowed, her light brown brows tugging together. Mr. Price stepped forward, putting his arm around her shoulders.

"What is she hiding from?"

"Her ex-boyfriend. Christian Blake."

"Is he dangerous?" Mr. Price asked.

Quynn shook her head. "Not that I know of. Katherine never said he was, but he took advantage of her. Tried to use her to boost his own career."

"Why did she let him?"

Quynn smiled. "He was tricky about it. I think Katherine should tell you the rest, but she doesn't think she can read him. He wants to get back together, and she just ran."

"And you have no idea where she is?"

Quynn shook her head, tossing her short hair. It stuck in her lipgloss before she swiped it away, her eyes going to Frank's. He was staring at her lips, raw lust in his gaze. Katherine's parents kept talking, worry lifting their voices, giving Quynn a chance to study Frank.

He was definitely attractive, his dark hair tousled in a sexy way that made her want to run her fingers through it. His broad shoulders led to heavily muscled arms that she suddenly wanted to wrap herself in.

It had been way too long since she'd had a guy warm her bed. She killed herself to take care of everything for Kate. She loved her job, but it got more than a little lonely at times.

Which led to ogling her friend's brother that she didn't know existed twenty-four hours earlier.

Quynn dragged her eyes back to Katherine's parents, who were still talking to each other.

"Katherine is smart. She said she had a reservation somewhere before all this but was going to cancel it. Christian was texting her yesterday so she got scared and decided to stay wherever she is."

"But you don't know where that is?"

Quynn shook her head again. "I'm sorry. I don't. She has her concert next week. She'll be here for that. I know she was going to do some appearances this week, but I don't think she's going to show up. I'm trying to reschedule things for after the concert."

"What are you telling people?"

Quynn forced a grin. "That she's spending time with her family."

Mr. and Mrs. Price exchanged a look that said they approved of that answer.

"I know this is hard for you, but this is normal for us. Katherine sometimes needs time to herself. She doesn't like being Kate Maddox all the time. She wants to be Katherine Price once in a while. And right now is one of those times."

They both nodded, their shoulders sagging with relief that Katherine disappearing wasn't that far off normal. Quynn wasn't going to tell them that she'd never gone off and refused to come back, but it made her more than a little anxious.

Mr. and Mrs. Price talked for a few more minutes, then made their way up the stairs with their luggage, leaving Quynn alone with Frank.

"That wasn't the whole truth, was it?" Frank asked.

"Hmm?" Quynn asked, playing dumb. She made her way to the kitchen, hoping she could find fresh coffee.

"The truth. Katherine doesn't usually do this, does she?"

"Sure she does," Quynn said, searching cabinets for a mug.

"But not like this."

Quynn didn't answer.

"Talk to me. If I need to worry about my sister, tell me."

Quynn still didn't respond, pouring a cup of coffee and going to the fridge for milk. She splashed a bit in, then put the milk back, turning to escape.

Frank stepped in front of her, blocking her path. She looked up at him, shocked when she saw the fear in his eyes.

"Tell me the truth, Quynn. Please."

Quynn dragged in a deep breath. "Fine. No. It's not normal. She'll take off for a night, go to a bar and meet a guy, but she's never vanished like this. I talked to her last night though, you were here, and she's fine."

"But you don't know where she is."

"No. I have no idea."

Frank ran a hand through his hair, standing the ends up even more. "I don't like this, Quynn."

Quynn huffed a laugh. "Trust me, neither do I."

7

KATHERINE STRETCHED and arched her back, rolling her neck. She didn't usually sleep so well in a bed she wasn't used to, but she passed out hard.

It was probably more thanks to the four glasses of wine she had than the bed.

She pulled in a deep breath and sat up. The navy comforter fell to her waist, exposing the thin white tank top she slept in and her peaked nipples.

Which immediately brought her mind to Dillon.

She half expected him to try something the night before. Especially when she had so much to drink and was clearly feeling like shit. Most men would have, but Dillon Young was definitely a different type of guy than most. She was grateful for that, but it still surprised her. Katherine expected everyone to want something from her.

She swung her feet from the bed and listened to the silent house. Dillon mentioned something about tours in the vineyard and suggested she go on one. He was supposed to be working. She should be, too, exploring the town at least, but it was hard to pass up the chance to be outside and enjoy a place like Amavita Estates.

Katherine padded to the kitchen and found the house completely empty. She knew made herself a cup of coffee and cooked an omelet, then took a shower and dressed in an outfit she hoped was okay for a day in a vineyard.

She slid her phone in her pocket and was halfway out the door before she shook her head. She went back to her room and left her phone on the nightstand then headed out into the sunshine.

The vineyard had a buzz that was different from the night before. A steady hum that usually only came with lots of people. Fear welled up inside her knowing she'd been found out. Laughter rang out from nearby. Too near.

Katherine needed to get away.

"Katherine!" a voice said in the distance.

She turned and saw someone waving to her. Andie. Dillon's sister. The woman who told her she could stay at his house.

And she called her Katherine.

Katherine walked closer, knowing she could get information out of Andie and be gone before anyone knew she was there.

"Are you joining a tour?" Andie asked.

*Shit.*

"Tour?"

"Yeah. I figured Dillon would have mentioned it. We're offering tours through the vineyard today. We've never done it before. Kristen thought it would be different to show visitors what the grapes look like on the vine and be able to taste them right out here in the field. It's going well so far."

"Oh, tour! Yeah, he mentioned it. I completely forgot, though. It's really noisy out here today."

Andie chuckled. "Yeah, people are having fun. We didn't

expect the crowds we're getting, but it's been great for us. Kristen estimated each tour would be about fifteen people, but they're closer to thirty. It's been a busy morning."

"That makes sense," Katherine said, almost to herself.

"Why don't you wait here with me and join the next tour. It should be here soon."

Katherine nodded. "I think I will. Thanks. I was heading that way anyway. Thought I might catch Dillon."

Andie grinned. "I knew you two would get along. Sorry for kind of tricking you, though. He was pretty pissed off at me about that."

Katherine shook her head. "It's fine. I certainly didn't expect to find someone else there, but Dillon is a very considerate host."

"My big brother definitely has his good points. Has he cooked for you yet? He's a really good cook."

"Andie, are you trying to hook us up?"

She shook her head. "You two already did that."

"But you didn't know that when I got here."

Andie sighed. "No, I didn't. Dillon needs to chill out some. He's wound pretty tight and we all worry about him. He needs to get laid."

Katherine choked out a laugh. If Andie only knew just how much Dillon got laid a few nights ago, she wouldn't worry so much about her brother. Plus, he was clearly very skilled, which meant he wasn't a novice when it came to women.

Katherine started to respond, but voices grew louder, approaching them. She turned and saw a very attractive guy leading the way straight toward her.

Andie laughed and leaned in. "That's my brother, Sean. This will be the perfect tour for you to join."

Katherine wasn't sure what she meant by that and wasn't sure she wanted to know.

———

Dillon smiled as his latest group walked away, chatting happily about the pinot. Kristen was doing a damn good job engaging with the crowd. He knew she was good with people, but knowing it and seeing it were two very different things.

The tours were going remarkably well. He was impressed with the size crowds they were bringing through. He'd already run out of glasses twice, but Kristen had whatever tour guide wasn't with a group running back to the inn and loading up glasses and getting them out. Dillon was happy to see his dad and Uncle David were helping also. Kristen really did have the buy-in from the whole family.

With the few minutes he had for a break, Dillon checked his phone and scanned through some emails. He hadn't heard from any of the others about Perry being on site, but they might not have seen him. He was keeping his eyes peeled in each group, but he didn't think Perry had balls that big. He wanted to take over Amavita, or sink them at least, but he wasn't stupid.

That was the hardest part for Dillon. Stupid he could outthink. Devious was harder to figure out.

He tucked his phone away as he heard the next group approach. His brother, Sean, was leading the group. Their mom had Sean's daughter, Emily, and Zach's daughter, Summer, for the day, but all the cousins were helping out, which made Dillon smile.

What didn't make him smile was the look on Sean's face when his eyes dipped to Katherine's cleavage. She was walking next to him, talking animatedly about something. Her jeans hugged her curves again, but the top she wore was casual, a white t-shirt with a glittery green guitar. Her brown hair was loose around her shoulders, her brown eyes hidden by large sunglasses.

Katherine laughed at something Sean said, putting her hand on his arm. He laughed with her, then said something that had her clutching her side.

Dillon was going to kill his second brother in as many days.

When they finally made it to his station, he was fuming. Fuming in a way that made it hard for him to unclench his jaw and say something. When Sean gave him a wide-eyed glare, he finally forced the words out.

"Welcome to the pinot noir. This pine cone looking cluster of dark grapes produces a light colored red wine. It's medium bodied, with low tannins so fans of red wine who don't like headaches tend to lean toward pinot noir."

The group laughed as all the others did. Dillon kept his eyes from Katherine, although he could feel her watching him from where she stood next to Sean.

"Some pinot tends to be a little sweeter, but most varieties are neither overly sweet nor overly dry. It's a wine that goes well with many foods and can be enjoyed by almost all wine drinkers. We have a bunch of grapes if you'd like to try those first, then you're welcome to enjoy a taste of our pinot noir."

Dillon poured glasses of wine as the guests reached for the grapes. He heard them talking, but he couldn't focus on any of them. It took all his control to pour the wine and not smash the bottle over his brother's head for touching what was his.

"Hey," Katherine said softly when she approached.

Dillon nodded but didn't speak. She grabbed a glass and moved away from the table to let others get their wine.

"What's your favorite wine?" a middle-aged woman asked

him, sipping her glass. Her husband stood next to her, his hand low on her hip.

"Pinot is my favorite. I like that the flavor changes so drastically depending not only on the year, but on what I cook that night."

"What's you favorite thing to eat with this wine?" her husband asked.

"I'm a big fan of steak, so I'll eat steak with just about any wine. I also do an Italian chicken where I roast a cornish hen in Italian seasonings and put it over rice pilaf with a side of vegetables like mushrooms, asparagus, and squash. It goes just as well with that."

"We had it with pizza last night also," Katherine butted in. "That was delicious, too."

Dillon met her eyes for a second, long enough to see the challenge she had in hers. She wanted to know what he was going to say.

"That's what I mean," Dillon said. "The wine is very versatile. It can go with a number of things and be as good with all of them."

Katherine finished her wine and set the glass on the table. Instead of moving back to where Sean was, she leaned against the edge and lifted her chin to meet his eyes again.

And smirked at him.

"I wasn't sure I'd see you out here today."

She nodded. "You made the tours sound really interesting. I ran into Andie on my way here from your place. I thought I'd join the tour."

He heard whispered chatter behind her and glanced at the women. They looked like they were in their twenties, and they were vaguely familiar. He couldn't place them, but they giggled when they caught him watching them.

He looked back at Katherine and saw her watching him. Another smirk on her face.

He laughed and shook his head.

"Are you going to continue with the tour, or do you want to stay here and help me?"

"I'd love to stay with you," Katherine said, moving to his side of the table. She stacked the dirty glasses in the rack he had half full and stood back so Dillon could answer questions.

When Sean started to move on, he searched for her and called out when he saw her with Dillon. "Katherine, we're moving again. You coming?"

She shook her head. "I'm going to stay here with Dillon. I'll catch the rest of the tour later. Thanks Sean!"

Sean was clearly unhappy with that answer, but he was smart enough to move on.

Dillon couldn't hide his shit-eating grin.

---

KATHERINE KNEW IT MADE HER A BAD PERSON, BUT SHE KIND of loved seeing Dillon jealous when she talked to his cute brothers. First Leo, then Sean. Jeez, his parents made some beautiful kids.

But Dillon was definitely the one she was most attracted to. He also had the advantage of being the one she met first, but she knew it wouldn't matter. Sean was cute, but he had a look in his eyes she knew meant getting involved with him wouldn't be easy. And Leo was too young for her.

But Dillon…

In another world maybe.

The crowd moved on without her, and those girls, women really, left, too. She couldn't explain why she felt possessive of him when she heard them talking about the hot guy at the pinot station. They obviously went on the tour already and made a second trip so they could see him.

Katherine made sure they overheard her comment about being at his house the night before for dinner.

Yeah, she had her own jealous side.

"I thought you'd want to hang around my brother. He's probably closer to your age."

Katherine grinned at Dillon and shrugged. "I'd guess, but I've always had a thing for older men. Especially older men who know how to make a woman feel good."

Dillon stepped closer to her, turning his body so they were in perfect alignment. "How do you know my brother can't take care of a woman?"

She cocked an eyebrow at him. "Are you trying to get me to go with him? Because I don't tend to stay where I'm not wanted."

She moved to go around him and was rewarded by a large hand low on her belly. His bicep rested against her breast, his side pressed against hers. He shifted, barely enough to make a difference, but it put his lips in contact with the shell of her ear.

"He wasn't in that hotel room when you screamed loud enough to wake the neighbors. That was all me, honey."

Katherine looked up and held his eyes for a long moment. Long enough that she saw the flare in his nostrils and the darkening of his already dark eyes. "Then there's no reason for me to chase after your brother."

Dillon turned her slowly, his large hand sliding from her belly to her hip and around to cup her ass. She moaned softly when she felt him hard between them.

"So you were teasing me with him? Flirting with my brother to piss me off?"

She shrugged. "Not really, but I can't say I mind the results."

He growled and captured her lips in a rough kiss that had her clutching at him. To say he shocked her would be an understatement. After she told him she wasn't going to sleep with him again, Dillon had been very considerate of her. He only touched her in a purely innocent way.

But there wasn't anything innocent about the way the man kissed.

His tongue swept through her mouth, telling her he knew exactly how to kiss her. He thrust his slick tongue alongside hers, pulsing in her mouth and tugging her closer to his body. He pulled back just enough to nip her lower lip, then dove right in again and devoured her.

She just hung on for dear life.

No man had ever turned her to mush with just a kiss. But Dillon Young was a man of many, many talents.

Her knees weakened, but he caught her, wrapping his other arm around her to support her. He lifted her onto the table they used to serve the wine and pressed between her spread thighs. She gasped, breaking their kiss.

"Dillon," she moaned, a little too loudly.

"Fuck," he whispered, dragging his lips from the trail they were on down her neck. "I'm sorry, Katherine. I'm working. And we're in public. I shouldn't be doing this with you. Not now."

He pulled back and walked the few steps to the row of vines behind them. He ran a hand through his hair and down his neck before hanging his head.

Katherine jumped off the table and went to him. She wrapped her arms around him from behind, threading them up his chest until she reached his racing heart.

"I was just as gone, Dillon. You're addicting for a woman who hasn't had much attention from a man lately."

He spun and gave her a look of disbelief. "How is it possible men haven't been all over you? You're built for sex."

She laughed softly. "I don't know about that, but I've been busy. I haven't really had time to date, and the last relationship I was in ended kind of rough. I guess I've been a little gun-shy."

"Really?"

She nodded. "I know. Hard to believe with how we met, but yeah. It had been well over a year before I met you."

He closed his eyes and reached for her, tugging her against his chest. "I wish you hadn't told me that. Now I'm going to be even worse when my brothers and cousins and every other male who comes through here look at you."

Katherine laughed against his hard chest, loving the way her head fit perfectly under his chin. "I think you're overestimating men."

"And I think you're underestimating yourself. Or do we need to talk about how hard I came this morning thinking about you?"

"You did?" she asked, gasping.

Dillon held her gaze and nodded. "Absolutely."

Her body heated all over, the image of Dillon stroking his long, thick cock turning her on more than she had any right to. She barely knew him, and after her week was over, she'd never see him again. He was just a guy, and she was going to go back to being Kate Maddox.

Damn, if that wasn't a depressing thought.

Voices found them before Katherine could think any more about Dillon or what her life was going to be like when she left Amavita. It was a good distraction for her because neither were trains of thought she needed to be on.

---

DILLON STOOD BACK AND WATCHED KATHERINE WORK. THE woman impressed him over and over again. From the way she gushed over Amavita Estates wine to the friendly way she addressed all the customers, men and women. She made everyone feel comfortable, jumping right in after he did his spiel.

"How long have you been working here?" one of the men asked her before their group left.

She shook her head. "I don't, actually. I'm just a huge fan of the wine. I'm visiting this guy for a few days and figured I'd hang out here and get the inside scoop."

"Are you coming to the fundraiser tonight?" he asked.

Katherine looked back at Dillon, a question in her eyes. "We'll be there," Dillon answered for her, resting his hand low on her back. Katherine smiled at the man and waved as he caught up to the rest of the group.

"Fundraiser?"

"We're having a fundraiser for the local firefighters. They're a volunteer company, and my cousin, Ryan, is one of the volunteers. The community is pretty tight around here, but we wanted to do something a little more than we usually do."

"What's involved in this?"

"Kristen set the whole thing up. There's a silent auction and a big party. We have a DJ coming in, and Zach and Michele are cooking an amazing dinner beforehand. It's the fancy event for the weekend."

"Fancy?"

Dillon shrugged. "I'm wearing a suit. Kristen and Andie are talking about dresses."

"And you didn't think to mention it to me?"

Dillon smirked at her. "Honestly, no. I'm a guy. We shower and throw some clothes on and we're good. I don't think about the whole woman thing. Want me to call Andie?"

Katherine rolled her eyes at him. "No. I'm good. I have a couple dresses I can wear, I just didn't think I'd need them. You'll have to tell me if they're too much."

He wrapped an arm around her waist. "If it is, I don't think I'll have to tell you."

Katherine laughed and tickled his neck with her fingertips. "Are you saying you still don't want any other men looking at me? I thought we were just having fun."

"So you're okay with me dancing with other women tonight?"

"Hell no," Katherine blurted.

Dillon smirked.

"Fine. We're both admitting this is between us and only us."

"Exactly."

They finished up with their last group, letting out a sigh of relief when Kristen came by and told them they were done. She said she hoped to see them at the party, making Dillon feel like shit that she didn't expect him to be there.

When they got back to his house, Katherine rushed off to her room, saying she needed a shower and more time than she had to get ready. Dillon went to his room, torn between wanting to knock Katherine's door down and get to her and distracted by what Kristen said.

He took a quick shower and dug his suit out of the back of his closet. He had a few, but he was thankful he didn't have to wear them often. The last time he had one on was Uncle Victor's funeral.

Thankfully, he had a good reason to wear his suit this time.

Dillon ran his fingers through his wet hair and debated shaving but decided he didn't feel like it. He went to the kitchen and poured himself a glass of water while he waited for Katherine.

Dillon's stomach rumbled, reminding him he didn't have much for lunch that day. Kristen said they would get a lunch break, but since the tours were more popular than she expected, they didn't get a chance to take a break. Kristen had Michele run food out to all of them, but Michele didn't realize Katherine was there and only had one lunch, which he happily shared.

He grabbed a slice of cold pizza from the night before and ate it leaning against the counter. His mind wandered to the last few days. He never thought he'd meet a woman like Katherine. He had fun with her all day. Even the night he met her, things were different. Like she was someone who could fit into his life. Someone he wanted to be a part of his life.

It had been a long time since Dillon considered keeping a woman around longer than a night or two. He could still remember the last time he did. Daphne Morris was the woman he thought he'd spend his life with. The woman Dillon fell for when he was in college.

Right up until he learned who she really was.

"Are you ready to go?" Katherine's voice interrupted his thought.

Dillon turned away from the window to look at her and nearly swallowed his tongue.

"Holy shit," he breathed. He couldn't stop looking at her. From her endless legs on display through the slit in her dress that he swore went to her waist, to the bare back that showed everyone she wasn't wearing a bra, to the fuck me heels that made Dillon hard at the thought of having them digging into his spine later.

"Do I look okay?" she asked.

Dillon shook his head. "No. Absolutely not. Go change."

## 8

KATHERINE STIFLED her laugh when she saw the serious look on Dillon's face. She thought he was joking about her changing, like he was the night before, but she caught the look in his eyes and knew he was dead serious.

"I can't take you in there looking like this. Every man in the county will be trying to take you home."

"I'm coming back here with you, Dillon. No one else."

"Hell, it doesn't even have to do with that. Are you wearing underwear?"

She rolled her eyes at him.

"This isn't that fancy of a party. I think you'll be uncomfortable."

Katherine took a deep breath and had to admit he was a little right. Just walking out of the bedroom had her slightly on edge. If it was just her and Dillon, maybe. But knowing how many other people would be there… She needed to dial back the Kate Maddox and be more Katherine Price.

"You're right," she confessed. "I always feel uncomfortable in this dress."

"Don't get me wrong. It's a hell of a dress. But I can't walk in there with you looking like that."

Katherine grinned at the heated look in his eyes then went to change into the other dress she packed.

In ten minutes, she was back in the living room in a handkerchief dress that hugged her top half and flared out on the bottom. The greens, blues, and purples swirled artistically and hid all the parts of her figure she didn't like. The high neck and capped sleeves helped add to the modesty of the dress, until you looked closely and realized the top layer of the dress was sheer.

"Do you own anything that doesn't make me want to strip you naked and skip the party?"

Katherine grinned. "I'm not sure. I was wearing jeans when we met."

Dillon snorted. "Point proven. You ready to go?"

Katherine nodded and took Dillon's offered arm. He looked down at her heels and shook his head.

"We need to drive, don't we?"

She shrugged. "I'm okay. I'm used to wearing heels around. I don't mind the walk."

"It'll take us a little while to get there, and longer by the time we're leaving and it's dark. I'll just drive."

The drive was quick and the parking was horrible, but Katherine knew that was a good sign. Dillon parked on the far side of the inn and walked her around to the back where the doors into The Drunken Grape were open, music spilling out. He held her hand as she walked across the uneven paver patio in her heels. If he knew how regularly she wore heels, he wouldn't think twice about her walking on an uneven surface in them.

"We have a table held for us, but it's with the rest of my family. I hope you're okay with this."

Katherine nodded. "I don't mind at all. It sounds great."

Dillon gave her a rueful smile. "I hope you're still saying that at the end of the night."

Katherine laughed and let him lead her to the table in the corner with two open chairs, one next to Leo and one next to Andie.

Dillon stepped behind the chair next to Andie and pulled it back for Katherine to sit in. She grinned up at him, knowing he put her there so she was away from his brother. He pursed his lips, giving her a look she thought was supposed to be stern.

She just wanted to laugh.

Dillon lowered himself into the seat next to her, his knees brushing hers before his warm thigh settled alongside hers.

"Are you going to introduce us?" an elegant woman across the table asked.

"Sorry, Ma," Dillon said. "This is Katherine Price. Katherine, my parents, Pauline and Michael."

"It's nice to meet you both."

"You also," Pauline said with a grin. "Dillon doesn't normally bring dates to any events."

"Oh, well, I was supposed to be a guest of the inn. I gave up my room so a family could stay and Andie suggested I stay with Dillon. Since we already knew each other, it worked out well."

"You already knew each other?"

Dillon sucked in a quick breath, telling Katherine she said something wrong.

"Ma. Don't."

"Don't what?"

"Don't start. Katherine isn't staying here. She was supposed to be a guest. Meaning she doesn't live in the area. She's here for a week and then she's leaving again."

"It's a great place to live, Katherine. What do you do?"

"I'm a singer actually."

"Really?" Dillon asked. "I thought you said you were an editor."

"How do you two know each other if you didn't even know what she did for a living?"

"Mom," Andie blurted, her eyes widening with obvious intention.

"What? Oh!" Pauline said. She gasped and ducked her head.

Katherine's cheeks burned as everyone at the table realized exactly how she and Dillon met.

"Well, all of you act like sex is such a big deal. I had four children. Obviously, your father and I had sex," Pauline said.

"Ma!" Sean exclaimed, nodding his head to the young girl next to him.

"Sorry, Emily," Pauline said, looking chagrined. "Anyway, we're happy you're here, Katherine. What kind of music do you sing?"

Katherine floundered, unsure why she admitted the truth to Dillon's family.

"I've always wanted to be a country singer. But it doesn't always pay that well so I also work as a freelance editor. I can take on tasks when I'm free and travel to sing in different places all over the country."

"That sounds like a busy life," Pauline said. "I imagine it would be kind of lonely traveling by yourself so much."

"Ma," Dillon said forcefully.

"It's fine," Katherine said. "It can be pretty lonely. I love seeing different parts of the country, but it's hard not having a real home base. At least, not one I spend any real amount of time in."

Dillon's hand rested on her thigh, rubbing circles with his thumb. She knew it was meant to be comforting, but all she felt was even more alone. She didn't have anyone in her life, in her real life, who knew when she needed a warm hand on her knee. Or a glass of wine when she was upset. Or a compliment when she was feeling unattractive.

Yet she'd known Dillon for two days and he'd known when she needed all those things.

How was she going to go back to a life without him in it?

---

"Are you hungry?" Frank asked when he heard Quynn walk down the stairs.

"Are you talking to me?" she asked, stopping just outside the kitchen.

He turned and tried his hardest to keep his eyes on her face instead of letting them trail down her curvy figure. If he'd known his sister's personal assistant was so gorgeous, he would have taken Katherine up on some of the tickets she'd offered over the years.

"Yeah. I was going to cook something. If you're hungry, you're welcome to join me."

"Um, where are your parents?"

"They went out. Friends of theirs are having a small party tonight. Since Katherine didn't show up, they figured they'd go."

"They aren't worried?"

Frank nearly laughed. "You convinced them there's nothing to worry about."

"Oh, um, yeah. There's not. I'm sure everything is fine."

Frank snorted. "Yeah, okay."

Quynn sighed, the sound dragging Frank's attention back from the fridge to the beautiful woman sinking into a chair at the kitchen table Frank had eaten every meal at for most of his life. The only time he didn't think of that table as his was the four endless years he was married and eating at someone else's dinner table.

Until he caught her screwing his best friend on that same table.

"I'm not sure what you like, but we have some steaks and chicken. I think there's some pork in there. Or if you're a vegetarian, we can do a salad and I can grill some chicken for myself. You tell me what sounds good."

Quynn sighed heavily and closed her eyes. Frank wished he could find his sister and get her to come home, but he'd tried all day to reach her and she never answered her phone. He was getting worried. Even if Quynn said Katherine disappeared at times, he knew his sister rarely went anywhere without telling someone where she was going and what she was doing.

Being gone and afraid to tell anyone worried him.

And he could see the toll it was taking on Quynn.

"I want a steak. Medium. Juicy. Something delicious and extravagant and expensive. How about we go out somewhere? I'll pay."

Frank shook his head. "Nah. I'm good. If you want to go out, feel free, but I'm kind of a homebody."

He wasn't willing to tell her that he couldn't afford a nice dinner out, and he sure as hell wasn't going to have her pay for him. If his cheating bitch of an ex-wife hadn't taken him to the cleaners in the divorce, he could afford to take a beautiful woman out to dinner, but his ex was still in school and the courts decided he had to support her until she was finished. So he was left broke, and she was living it up with her new boyfriend and milking Frank dry as she dragged out her last few years of school.

Bitch was too nice of a word for her.

Quynn thought for a second then nodded. "I can't tell you the last time I had a home cooked meal. Can I help you?"

Frank was a little shocked by the request, but more than happy to have the company while he cooked. It was one of the only things he enjoyed about being married, and one of the many things he felt Whitney stole from him when she cheated on him. They cooked together frequently, but he hadn't shared the kitchen with anyone since their divorce.

"Of course. What do you want to go with the steaks?"

"Let's see what you have."

Quynn dug through the pantry as Frank grabbed the steaks and sprinkled them with salt and pepper. He went out to start the grill and came back in to see her looking a little less stressed.

"How about some garlic, Parmesan mashed potatoes and a veggie blend?"

"Perfect. Do you like a sauce on your steak? I usually do either a gorgonzola or béarnaise sauce."

"Both sound amazing. Jeez, who needs a fancy dinner out when you're around."

He could tell her tone was teasing, but it rubbed Frank wrong. Whitney said the same thing about his skills in the bedroom once, then she cheated on him.

Frank silently put the steaks on the grill and stayed outside with them as Quynn worked on the veggies. When he was finished, he walked back in, relieved to see she was done with her part so they could eat and he could retreat to his dungeon in the basement again.

Frank sat down across from Quynn with a full plate and found himself starving. He wanted to figure out something to say to her, but he was still stewing over her innocent comment.

Even though it was completely unfair to her.

"You gonna tell me what I said, or do I have to guess?"

"About what?" Frank asked.

"Whatever I said that pissed you off."

Frank grunted but didn't answer.

"So that's how it is. Good to know."

They ate dinner in silence. Frank knew it was delicious, but he could barely taste it. When Quynn finished her meal, she carried her plate to the sink, rinsed it, and put it in the dishwasher. She was almost out of the kitchen when Frank spoke.

"I live here because I can't afford to live on my own."

Quynn paused.

"I got divorced a little over a year ago. My ex cheated on me. But since she was in school, finishing her graduate degree, I have to pay her alimony."

"That's some screwed up logic," Quynn said, settling at the table again.

Frank huffed a laugh. "Yeah, tell me about it. She told me that I was so good in the bedroom she'd never have a reason to cheat with me around. Then she did."

"And I said there'd never be a reason for a nice dinner with you around…shit. I'm sorry."

"I never told anyone about her saying that. Hell, I never really thought about it."

Quynn reached over and rested her hand on his. He met her eyes and held them for a moment too long, both of them pulling back quickly.

"Sorry," Quynn said standing up. "Um, thanks for dinner."

She went to the sink and started washing dishes. He sat at the table for another minute, then joined her, silently working together to wash and dry the dishes from dinner. When they were finished, Quynn made a move to leave the kitchen again.

Frank reached out to stop her. "Thank you."

"For what?"

"For having dinner with me."

Quynn smiled at him. "Any time."

D illon watched Katherine work the room, amazed yet again at how easily she talked to complete strangers. It wasn't a surprise to him that she had all the firefighters eating out of her hands, but she had their wives and girlfriends just as smitten as they all were.

"She's pretty amazing," Kristen said, offering him a glass of wine.

"Thanks for this. She is. She has a way with people.'

"We've never had a fundraiser that brought in this much money. People are dumping their checkbooks out to help because of her."

"Good. Then we can help the firefighters. We needed this to be a success."

Kristen nodded. "Ryan said they've been hoping to get money for a new truck. I think this will go a long way."

"Absolutely." Dillon only wished it were that easy to raise the cash they needed to buy bottling equipment. Not that he'd take money from the community but still. It would be nice to be able to throw a party and bring in their own income.

"I think the tours today went well. What did you think?"

"It was excellent, Kristen. You've done a hell of a job this weekend. We need to talk about more ideas you have. Have you given more thought to local groups we can work with to bring more to our guests?"

Kristen nodded. "There are a few I've been in touch with. Now that summer is unofficially here, I was going to talk about a few of my ideas next week."

"Good. If your other ideas are anything like this weekend, I have no doubt it'll all be a hit."

"Thanks, Dillon. I really hope so. Oh, let me check on something. Do you need anything from me?"

Dillon shook his head. "Let me know if you need my help though, okay?"

Kristen looked surprised for a second but nodded. "Thanks."

Kristen said hi to Katherine as she walked away. Dillon grinned at Katherine, pulling her close to his side when she stopped next to him.

"You're making a lot of new friends tonight. Are you having fun?"

Katherine nodded. "Your family is great. I love being here."

"Kristen said we've never raised this much for the firefighters before."

"That's amazing."

"Yeah, and it's all because of you."

She shook her head, that sexy brown hair bouncing over her shoulders. "I didn't do anything."

He laughed. "Yeah, you did. You're charming the pants off everyone here, getting them to open their checkbooks in ways we've never managed to do before."

"Well, I'm happy to help. My brother is a police officer. I've always believed in supporting the local public safety officials. Even before he was on the police force, my parents were big supporters. They always taught us that those people put their lives on the line for us and we owe them our respect and as much as we can give in the way of support."

"Your parents sound like great people."

She smiled, a genuine smile that touched her eyes and told him how much she loved her family. "They are. Just like your family."

"Speaking of which, I think my brothers are hoping to steal you away from me later."

Katherine laughed and snuggled closer to him. Her arm slid around his waist and she rested her head on his chest. Her scent teased him, forcing him to dip his nose into her hair for a sniff.

"I'm not going anywhere," she said.

"How about outside? Want to see if we can find some stars?"

Katherine nodded and headed for the door without waiting for him. He followed her outside, smiling at the way she twirled in the moonlight. Her hips swayed, teasing him, then she glanced over her shoulder and smirked at him.

Then took off into the vines.

<hr>

Katherine didn't know where she was going, but that was part of the fun. She knew Dillon would follow her. That was a damn good feeling.

She took a right to get away from the party, then ducked under one of the rows of vines just to tease Dillon. She could hear him moving close behind her, giving her just enough space to lead the way, but not so much that he couldn't see her. She knew he was playing the same game she was.

Katherine laughed as she rushed down the next row. She looked up at the sky and gasped when she saw how many stars were out. She paused, just long enough that Dillon caught up to her.

"Dance with me," he whispered against her ear.

She smiled and spun in his arms. He held her close, not giving her a chance to move away from him in the slightest. She loved how he seemed to touch her all over at once. One hand low on her waist, the other scanning her spine in slow strokes that put every nerve ending on high alert.

Dillon hummed a tune in his throat, giving them a beat to sway to. Katherine tried to place the tune, but she couldn't. She gave in to the feelings and rested her head on Dillon's shoulder, giving herself over to him even more than she did the night they spent together.

They swayed in the darkness, the stars their only back-drop, alone in the world as far as they were concerned.

"So the editor thing is just for now. You're a singer?" he asked, breaking the tentative silence between them.

Katherine smiled, nodding. Her heart rate kicked up, hoping he didn't ask her to sing. She knew her voice was fairly easy to recognize with the husky quality that had made her a star. A phone sex operator's voice her first agent said.

That was only part of why Katherine fired him.

"Yeah. I've always loved to sing. Joined my church choir when I could read, sang in summer theater, and even did a few school musicals."

"And you're still chasing the dream?"

Katherine nodded. "I think when there's something in your blood, you chase it no matter how out of reach it seems."

Dillon shook his head and laughed lightly. "That's not a dream I'd ever want. I can't fathom being in the spotlight like that. Fame has never been a dream of mine."

Katherine understood. She hadn't put much thought into fame when she started her career. She auditioned for every studio who would hear her, and ended up with her pick when the time came.

"Fame has never been a goal of mine. I always thought artists who hid their true identity were doing it right. Making sure they could have a private life."

Dillon shrugged, spinning her around again. "I can see that, but I still wouldn't want any part of it. It all feels so impersonal. Assistants and staff and people trying to dig up as much dirt on you as they can find. It doesn't seem like a good life."

Katherine wasn't sure how to respond. "I think famous people need all that, though. They need the staff. They need the support. It's not like they can handle everything on their own."

"Yeah, but I think that's what bothers me. Fame takes away your humanity. It turns you into someone who doesn't have time to dance under the stars or go to a benefit for a volunteer fire company. It means benefits where you spend thousands to eat just so you can be seen wearing a designer dress and starving yourself to fit into the right clothes."

"How do you know anything about it?" Katherine blurted. She was sick of people judging her from the outside. Turning her life into something it wasn't. Telling her who she was without bothering to get to know her.

"Whoa," Dillon said, throwing his hands up as Katherine jerked out of his grasp. "I didn't mean anything by it. I can't see you being that way."

"But if I'm famous then I would be. Because fame turns you into a shallow idiot and steals your decency. Isn't that what you said?"

Dillon sighed. "I wasn't trying to upset you Katherine. I'm sorry. I hope you make it. I hope you become the next Kate Maddox. I hope you find all the success in the world. And I hope you remember where you came from."

"I'd never forget that," Katherine said softly.

His words sunk in deep. Talons digging into her and refusing to let her walk away from the truth. She did all those things he said. She hid who she was. She dated the wrong men because they were men who got her seen. She went to the benefits that her agent sent her to. Same for parties and tours and even her friends. Quynn was the only person who wasn't family that she could count on.

And even that was limited.

She didn't tell Quynn the whole truth about who she was. She kept secrets from her. All the time.

She wasn't who anyone thought she was.

"I wasn't trying to hurt you," Dillon said, reaching for her again.

"I know," Katherine said, skirting his reach. "I know. But it's not easy to hear."

"Why? Why would it bother you? You're not like that."

Katherine laughed softly. If he only knew. "Maybe not. But I could be one day. If I become famous, and I have an assistant and a staff and people who help me be who I am when I'm on stage, then how would I be different?"

Dillon sighed and ran a hand through his hair. "What happened here, Katherine? How did we get so far off track?"

Katherine closed her eyes and took a deep breath. She tried to calm herself. "I'm sorry, Dillon. I shouldn't have gotten so upset."

He shook his head. "It's fine. Let's just head back to the party."

Katherine agreed, walking ahead of Dillon toward the light of the party. She walked inside, pasted on a grin, and lost herself in the crowd, forgetting about the divide between herself and Dillon.

9

---

DILLON WATCHED as Katherine walked away from him into the crowd and knew his hopes for sharing his bed were shot to hell. She flirted even more with the firefighters and all the single men in the crowd. He didn't know if she was intentionally pissing him off or not, but it was working.

"Son of a bitch," he muttered under his breath, grabbing a glass of wine from the bar.

"You okay?" Sean asked.

Dillon nodded sharply, but Sean followed his gaze and grinned when he saw Katherine smiling up at the big, tattooed firefighter.

"Lost to a firefighter, huh?"

"Fuck you."

Sean's grin widened. "Feels good to have someone else play in your sandbox."

"What do you want, Sean?"

His brother shook his head. "Not a thing, big brother. Not a thing."

Sean walked off, leaving Dillon to stew.

He was still stewing when Katherine joined him at the

end of the night. She had a smile on her face as she stuffed a slip of paper in her back pocket.

Phone number.

"Did you have fun?" he asked, trying to keep his voice light and even. He failed miserably.

"I did," she said with a grin. "Tons of fun."

They drove back to his house and silently went to their bedrooms. Dillon had no idea how he'd fucked up the night so badly, but he knew there wasn't any way to salvage it.

Dillon went to bed frustrated and horny after spending the day with Katherine and only having her in his arms for a short time.

Too short.

Dillon was more of a night owl than a morning person, but he woke up with the sun Sunday morning. He went for a quick run through the vineyard, then started the coffee pot while he took a shower.

Their Sunday picnic was the big thing on the schedule for the day. With the Memorial Day holiday the next day, Dillon knew the picnic would be one of their biggest of the year. It always was.

He dressed in jeans and an Amavita Estates t-shirt since he planned to work the picnic. He wondered if Katherine would show up, but he wasn't about to ask her. If she was there, he'd talk to her.

Dillon poured a cup of coffee when he heard the door to Katherine's room open. She padded out into the kitchen looking way too sexy in her rumpled clothes and sleep tangled hair.

"Morning," she said, walking straight into his arms.

He set his coffee down and wrapped his arms around her, his cock stirring. He pressed his nose into her neck and breathed her in. She clutched at him, sighing against his chest.

"I'm sorry," she whispered. "I shouldn't have gotten so upset yesterday."

He shook his head. "It's my fault. I don't want you to stop trying for your dreams. I shouldn't have said anything."

"You're right though. A lot of people lose who they are. They forget why they got into the business and lose themselves in the fame."

Dillon nodded. "Yeah, but not everyone lets money go to their heads. I know you won't."

She pulled back and smiled, but it didn't reach her eyes. The argument was still bothering her, so Dillon decided to change the subject.

"We have a picnic today. Do you want to come?"

She nodded. "I'd love to."

"Good. Coffee?"

She groaned. "Yes, please."

Dillon laughed and handed her a mug. She accepted it, adding a splash of cream and a spoonful of sugar, then took a greedy sip.

"So good," she moaned.

"You're going to kill me today, aren't you?"

She looked up at him from under her lashes full of innocence. "What are you talking about?"

Dillon laughed. "Nothing, sweetheart. Drink your coffee. Want me to wait for you?"

She nodded. "Can I take a quick shower? How fancy is this picnic?"

"Not fancy at all. You can see what I'm wearing."

She wrinkled her adorable nose. "I wish I had one of those shirts."

"You can have one of mine, but it'll be way too big on you."

She shook her head. "Not with these boobs. I'll be lucky if it fits."

"Yep," Dillon growled. "Definitely going to kill me today."

Katherine laughed, her cheeks turning a cute pink color. She shook her head and finished her coffee. Dillon grabbed an extra t-shirt for her to wear and left her to her shower.

They were at The Drunken Grape thirty minutes later, Dillon very impressed that Katherine could be ready so quickly. Her damp hair was tied back in a ponytail he couldn't wait to get his hands on later.

As long as he didn't screw things up again.

His first stop was the kitchen to see if Zach needed any help. He was good so Dillon directed Katherine to a table with some breakfast while he went to find Kristen.

"What do you need?"

"Dillon! Hi. What are you doing here already?"

"I thought you said you needed help this morning?"

Kristen nodded. "Thanks. Yeah. Ian was supposed to come but he's still hung over. I need a few cases brought in here if you don't mind."

"Of course."

Dillon helped Kristen get everything set up then checked back with Katherine. She was carrying food out of the kitchen, setting up the buffet for Zach.

"He put you to work?"

Katherine nodded. "I offered. Figured he could use the help."

Zach walked out of the kitchen. "Hey. You ready to help too?"

Dillon nodded. "Is Gianna coming?"

"Yeah. She and Summer are getting ready now. They don't really like mornings."

Dillon grinned and grabbed a tray. The first guests would be arriving any minute, and they didn't like to keep people waiting for food.

The picnic got crowded in a hurry with people coming in

and carrying food to the patio outside. Music played from speakers Kristen set up and guests started dancing.

Dillon looked around for Katherine, hoping to pull her onto the dance floor, and saw she was already out there. Dancing with his brother.

---

KATHERINE THREW HER HEAD BACK AND LAUGHED. LEO WAS A lot of fun. He was definitely too young for her, but she was enjoying his company. He had a goofy side, a carefree side, that drew her in. She'd never had the opportunity to be so loose.

Ever.

"I'd be drunk all day if I worked in the tasting room."

Leo chuckled again and spun her. "Yeah, it was a hard lesson to learn when I started out. I wanted to be cool and impress all the ladies so I'd drink with them. It ended up with a few too many days of me fall down drunk before my shift was over. Kristen bailed my ass out more times than I can count."

Katherine laughed again as Leo stumbled in their dance, pretending. "You'd think after growing up here you would know how to hold your liquor, or at least how to know when you've had enough."

Leo nodded. "You'd think so, wouldn't you? But I'm the baby of the family, and Ryan is the only cousin younger than me. When you're not just the youngest of four, but one of the youngest of nine, it's a whole different world when you're finally old enough to drink."

"I have an older brother. I know exactly what it's like. My brother more or less has his shit together, but I feel like I'm a mess all the time."

Leo chuckled softly. "Yeah. I know that feeling. Speaking

of brothers, mine looks pretty pissed that I'm out here dancing with you."

Katherine shook her head. "He'll be fine."

"Yeah, maybe when he gets you in his bed and makes you forget I exist."

Katherine grinned, keeping it to herself that Dillon already had her there and would any time he wanted again.

Dammit.

"Leo," Dillon practically growled.

He was so close Katherine could feel the heat spilling from him and warming her back. She wanted to lean into him, but the opportunity to tease him just a little more was too appealing.

"Dillon," Leo said calmly.

"You know she's with me."

Leo nodded, his hands loosening on her. Katherine held tighter to him, not giving Dillon the chance to interrupt them.

"I don't remember you asking me if I'd like to dance with you. I'm having a wonderful time with Leo."

Leo smirked and winked at her. Thankfully, he was in on her ruse and didn't seem to mind in the least that she was toying with him to make Dillon jealous.

"You'd rather be with my little brother than me?"

Katherine shrugged. "He's only a couple years younger than me. I've heard younger men have really good stamina."

Dillon really did growl that time. And he yanked her away from Leo, dragging her into his arms. He pressed her tight against his body, letting her feel how much he wanted her.

Katherine was aware of Leo backing away, and chuckling, but her focus was on Dillon.

"Don't toy with me, Katherine. I don't lose women to my little brothers."

"I was just dancing," she protested. "Besides, the whole jealous thing kind of turns me on."

"And it kind of pisses me off."

She leaned her body against his and lifted onto her toes so she could whisper in his ear. "None of the men here have seen me naked. Or been inside me. I'm not staying with any of them tonight. All that is all you, Dillon."

"Let's keep it that way," he growled back before he claimed her lips.

Right there on the dance floor with half the town watching them.

Katherine usually tried to avoid being the center of attention just in case anyone realized who she was. She didn't want to risk something triggering a thought for some stranger and her secret being brought into public.

But when Dillon's lips pressed against hers, his tongue probing her mouth, his hard body plastered to hers, she didn't fucking care.

"Let's get out of here," he said in her ear.

She nodded, ready to jump back into his bed. She knew it was stupid, to hide from one man in the arms of another, but she liked Dillon. Maybe it was a bad decision to get involved with him when she knew it wouldn't go anywhere beyond the week she was there, but she wanted to have fun for once. She wanted a little of that carefree feeling that radiated off Leo. Maybe she soaked a bit of it up.

They were almost to the hallway when an older man with thinning gray hair and a creepy smile stepped in front of Dillon. His body immediately tensed as he met the guy's beady eyes, and Katherine knew whatever he had to say was not going to be good.

"Perry," Dillon growled.

"Good afternoon, Dillon. Who's your friend?"

Dillon tucked Katherine behind him, protecting her from Perry. The asshole didn't deserve to be in her presence, let alone meet her.

"What are you doing here?"

"I came for the picnic. Didn't your cousin tell you? Or is it your brother? I can't keep all of you straight."

"I thought I told you to stay off my property."

"Oh, but see I heard it's not yours yet. You still have, what is it? Six weeks until the contract is up."

"So?" Dillon didn't know how Perry knew about that. It wasn't exactly a secret, but it wasn't something they advertised either.

"You can't exactly kick me out when you don't own the place. Even when you kids all take over, it's not like you're the only one with a say."

"None of us want you here. All you've done is try to copy us. I guess I should be flattered that you come here for ideas. Never mind the fact that stealing from us is illegal."

Perry grinned. "Still on that kick, huh? You all really need to let go of those petty accusations."

"It's the truth, Perry. We know you stole from us."

He tapped his chin. "That's funny because the cops never found anything at my house. I think it was just the worried ramblings of a man who knew he wasn't the best in the area any longer."

Dillon stepped into Perry's face and glared down at the evil little man. "Don't you dare speak about my Uncle Victor like that. You have no right to say anything about him."

Perry immediately put his hands up and backed away. "You're right. I apologize. Victor was a good man. He taught me everything he knew. I'd never have been able to buy Perry

Mount and turn that miserable old vineyard into the success it is today without his guidance and advice."

"You need to leave, Perry. Now."

Perry shrugged. "I was heading out anyway. I just wanted to say hello since I saw you leaving with… What was your name again?" he asked Katherine.

Dillon kept a hand on Katherine's side, ensuring she was behind him. "She's none of your business."

Perry slid his eyes back to Dillon and grinned. He knew he had him. Katherine was off limits, which meant she was the next scab Perry would pick.

Dillon took a step toward him, and Perry backed away. Dillon kept walking until Perry was out the front door and driving down the road away from The Drunken Grape.

"Who was that?" Katherine asked when his dust trail was no longer visible.

"Albert Perry. He owns Perry Mount Vineyards across 89."

"He's kind of a dickwad, isn't he?"

Dillon chuckled at her accurate assessment and nodded. "One hundred percent."

"You ready to go? Or do you need to tell someone that he was here?"

Dillon thought about it for a minute. A part of him wanted his siblings and cousins in on the news that Perry was snooping around still. After Jake, their handyman and his cousin's husband, spotted Perry in the vines a few months ago, everyone had been on high alert. But they hadn't found any signs of him. Seventy-three acres was a lot of property to watch constantly, but Dillon had a feeling Perry showing up now was personal.

And was all about him.

"No," he finally said. "I don't need to bother any of them with this. I'll take care of him."

Katherine waited a beat, then nodded.

When they were back at his place, he was still strung tight and needed to chill out for a few minutes. Otherwise taking Katherine to his bed wouldn't be for the right reasons. And he had a lot of right reasons for sinking into her.

"Do you mind if I play for a few minutes?" he asked, nodding to his old guitar in the corner. It had been his grandfather's. Nonna gave it to him when he was a teenager. He always loved music and took to it quickly. He'd never thought to make a career out of playing, but it calmed him when nothing else seemed to.

"You play the guitar?" she asked, sounding more surprised than he thought she would.

"I do. I have for more than twenty years."

"You must be pretty good."

Dillon shook his head. "Nah. I just enjoy it. Took lessons when I was young so I knew how to actually play, but I'm nowhere near good."

"Were you ever in a band?"

He shook his head. "Not good enough for even that."

Katherine sighed. "That's too bad. I've always had a thing for guitar players."

Dillon chuckled. "Well, maybe I can play for you when you're rich and famous."

Her brown eyes dimmed just a bit, and Dillon wanted to kick himself for bringing up their argument from the night before. He didn't want to fight with her. He wanted to play, then he wanted to spend the rest of his night worshipping every inch of her body.

He picked up his guitar and sat on the edge of his coffee table. He strummed a G, then shifted into a C. He kept play-ing, toying with a melody that had been poking him for a while. He'd never written a song, and never had a desire to do so, but he heard music and played it. He never bought sheet music for songs he liked, just picked up the guitar and played what felt right at the time.

"What are you playing?" Katherine asked, moving closer to see him play.

"Nothing really. There's a tune in my head and I just play."

"It sounds good," she said, smiling at him. "Do you sing or write music?"

Dillon shook his head. "Nope. Just play a little here and there. When I'm stressed."

Katherine laughed. "This isn't a stressed out guitar. This is a guitar that is well loved and well used."

"Maybe I'm stressed a lot."

Her eyebrows winged up. "Are you?"

Dillon shook his head. "I enjoy playing. If I was any good, I'd write a song for you to sing. Maybe it could be your breakout hit."

Katherine smiled at him, but it felt stiff. Again, he said the wrong thing bringing up her career.

Dillon ducked his head and went back to playing. The chords came easily and a tune tacked on, giving the music a rhythm that soothed the anger in Dillon. Perry floated away. His fight with Katherine went with it. All that was left was Dillon and Katherine, staring at each other.

With the same needy look.

"Katherine," he groaned.

She didn't reply, just attacked him. He eased the guitar from between them as he kissed her. With his guitar safely on the floor, he tugged her onto him, spreading her thighs wide so she could straddle him. He surged up into her, chuckling when she gasped at the brush of his erection against her core.

Hell yeah.

Dillon stood and carried her to his bedroom. He kicked

the door closed for good measure and had them both breathless by the time they made it to his bed.

"I love seeing the name of my vineyard plastered across your chest."

"I have a feeling you're going to love seeing your lips there even more."

He grinned. "I love the way you think."

Dillon sealed his lips to hers again, working her shirt up her belly, over her breasts, and between them. He dove back into her, capturing her lips again as he lowered her to his bed. He expertly flicked the clasp on her bra free and released her breasts into his waiting palms. Her nipples were hard and ready for him as he swiped rough thumbs over her sensitive flesh. She moaned and arched her back, pressing herself even more into his palms.

She tugged at his shirt, dragging it up between them. He broke their kiss to yank it off then brought his lips down to her nipple, sucking and teasing her as she writhed on his bed.

"I love seeing you on my bed," he growled as he moved to the other side. "You're not going back to the guest room tonight, Katherine. You're mine all night long."

"What about the fireworks later?" she breathed, clutching his head to her chest.

"We'll make our own damn fireworks," Dillon growled. He wasn't sharing her any more that night. Her room at the inn opened the next day, and if she decided to go back there, he only had one night with her.

It wasn't going to be enough.

## 10

KATHERINE SIGHED HAPPILY as Dillon kissed her nipples. She knew she wouldn't come like that, but he could get her damn close. The man had a magical tongue.

He unbuttoned her jeans and worked one of his large hands inside, shoving her panties and jeans down just far enough to slide a finger into her. Katherine called out, her hips lifting as he filled her.

She tugged at her jeans, kicking them free once she managed to work them past her knees.

"Much better," Dillon said, kissing her belly and moving farther down. His finger slid in and out of her, her slick channel coating him with each pass.

He eased her thighs wider with his free hand and nipped at her inner thighs. She arched into him, desperate to have him put his lips on her.

She didn't have to wait long to get her wish. Dillon swiped his tongue over her, starting where his fingers entered her all the way up to her throbbing clit. He circled her, then flicked her with his tongue, and she almost came just that quickly.

"Don't hold back, Katherine. Let me have all of you."

He groaned and slid a second finger into her. Katherine's eyes crossed and her body tensed. She was close, so close. He swirled his tongue again and thrust his fingers in hard, and she went flying.

"Oh, God, Dillon. Yes! Oh, fuck yes! Yes, yes, yes!"

Katherine came hard. So hard that she couldn't breathe for a few seconds. Her limbs were delightfully heavy and her chest burned with the need to fill her lungs with fresh air. She hadn't felt that good since the last time she shared a bed with Dillon.

Before her breathing returned to normal, Dillon stripped out of his clothes and rolled on a condom. He was poised at her entrance, watching her.

"That was amazing," she murmured.

"We're not done yet."

She shook her head. "I hope not."

"What was that you were saying about younger men and stamina?" he asked as he slammed into her.

Katherine moaned at the intrusion, her body welcoming him like an old friend who'd finally returned home. The thought made her toes curl, and the next thrust made her core throb.

"Yes, Dillon," she sighed. She dragged her nails down his chest, loving the way he thrust deeper when she did.

"You feel so good," he groaned, tilting his hips. He hit her in a new spot, her eyes fluttering closed with the riot of sensations zipping through her.

"Dillon. So good. Dillon. Yes."

He cupped her ass and lifted her, changing the angle yet again. She gasped at the impact, then panted with each repeated collision of their bodies, hers drawing closer and closer to another orgasm.

"Oh, shit. Dillon. I'm close. So close. Oh, God. Please.

Fuck. Please," she begged. She didn't care. If he stopped, she'd die. If he didn't get her off soon, she'd have to do something about it.

But she loved him pushing her there.

He gritted his teeth and slammed their bodies together, manipulating her how he wanted her with each stroke inside her. She went limp, unable to control herself, and on the next thrust, she snapped.

"Yes! Dillon, yes! Oh, shit. Harder. Fuck me. Harder. Yes!"

Dillon kept going, getting not one, but two orgasms out of Katherine in rapid succession. She swore she was going to break. She was damn happy she had a few days before her concert because her throat was sore as hell.

When she came down from her two amazing orgasms, she realized he never came. He was sliding in and out of her in slow, even strokes, like he was in no hurry and they had all the time in the world.

"Mmm, that feels good," she murmured. She clenched her channel around him, smiling when his stroke picked up just a bit.

"Stop doing that."

"Why? It feels good. I like having you inside me." She did it again.

"I might not be able to hold out much longer if you keep doing that."

"I want to feel you come. Why are you holding out?"

"You said you want a younger man with better stamina," he growled.

She stared at him for about two seconds before she burst out laughing. She laughed so hard, she couldn't breathe. He got mad and tried to get up, but Katherine wrapped her legs around his waist and refused to let him go. They both knew he could get away if he wanted to, but he let her hold him there.

"Last I checked, it was your name I was screaming a minute ago. And I didn't know your name a few days ago, but it was definitely all you that made me come that hard."

"You seem to have an issue with my age, Katherine. I don't want there to be any issues between us."

"I was teasing you. I guess it wasn't very nice, but I kind of like making you jealous. Your brothers are harmless and more than willing to flirt with me for the same reason. It was a win-win. We make you jealous and I get another night of amazing sex."

"Just one?" he asked with a lifted eyebrow.

She shrugged. "I didn't want to be presumptuous. It's clear you don't make a habit of sharing your bed."

He shook his head and leaned forward so she had no choice but to look him in the eye. "I've never shared my bed, Katherine. Ever. I'm not saying I was a virgin when I met you, but no woman has ever been in this bed until today."

Katherine swallowed hard at what he was telling her. She tried to dismiss it as the situation they were in, but she wanted it to be more. As impossible as that was.

"Then hopefully we can make good use of the fact that I'm in your bed, and more than ready for you. And you can prove your stamina to me a few more times before morning."

"Abso-fucking-lutely."

---

Quynn punched the End button on her phone and sighed. She was getting really sick of Katherine ignoring her calls. She'd already put off two of Kate's interviews that were supposed to record Monday, and she was going to have to cancel more if she didn't hear from her.

"Still not answering?" Frank asked, walking into the kitchen where Quynn set up a mini-office for the day.

Quynn shook her head. "I don't get it. She's never gone completely off the grid like this before. Not this long. If I didn't know better, I'd wonder if she still wants to be Kate Maddox."

"Maybe she doesn't," Frank said calmly.

The thought did not sit well with Quynn. "Why wouldn't she? Did she say something to you? Have you talked to her?"

"Whoa! No. I haven't spoken to her. She's never mentioned anything. You know my sister a lot better than I do these days. I just imagine this kind of life would be exhausting. I know that's why she went with a stage name to start with. Maybe it's catching up to her."

Quynn pulled in a deep breath, thankful Frank didn't know something she didn't know. "It isn't easy. I know she's worn out a lot, but I think this is all because of Christian. They wrote a song together, and he's trying to sell it."

"If she doesn't want to be with him, why would she want to write a song with him? And since when does Katherine write her own songs?"

Quynn shrugged. "I don't know. But your existence proves that there's a lot about Katherine that I don't know."

"Yeah, but you know Kate Maddox."

Quynn sighed. "I thought I knew Katherine Price, too."

Frank clapped his hands, startling Quynn. "Let's go out. You need to get out of the house, and I'm hungry."

"I'm not hungry," Quynn protested.

"You need food. Let's go get something to eat. We can go anywhere you want. My treat."

She shook her head. "No. You don't have to do that."

Frank shook his head. "I want to. Come on, Quynn. Don't make me beg."

Quynn raised an eyebrow and grinned in spite of herself. She had to admit, Frank was growing on her. A lot.

"Okay, fine."

He smiled, transforming his whole face. She wondered why in the world his ex-wife would ever choose anyone over him when he smiled like that.

"Let me change into something else and we can go."

Frank nodded as Quynn rushed off to Katherine's room with her computer and her planner with Kate's schedule.

In five minutes, Quynn was back downstairs with her hair freshly brushed, and a clean outfit of jeans and a flowing red top that she knew drew attention.

She wouldn't be disappointed if she drew a little of Frank's attention.

Not that she'd do anything about it. He was her friend's brother, and her life was *not* in Syracuse. It was wherever Kate was.

Frank drove to a neighborhood bar near the house and led Quynn inside. They sat at a table near the front window and flipped through the small menu.

"Sorry," Frank said. "This probably isn't up to your normal standards. We can go somewhere else."

Frank got up as the waitress came over.

"Can I get you guys something to drink?"

"We were going to head out actually. Sorry about that."

"No, we weren't," Quynn insisted. "I'd like a glass of wine. White. Whatever you have."

"Quynn?"

She leveled him with a look and Frank slid back into his seat.

"For you?"

"A beer."

"Draft or bottle."

"Bottle."

"Okay. I'll be right back."

She walked away, leaving Quynn and Frank alone again.

"What makes you think I wouldn't want to stay here?"

He shrugged and avoided her gaze.

"You think I'm a snob, don't you? That I wouldn't want to eat somewhere that doesn't have an expensive menu and white tablecloths."

"I know how my sister lives. I've seen enough pictures to see that this isn't the normal scene for you guys."

"For Kate, maybe. But not for me. I don't get recognized when I go out. And eating at expensive restaurants would not only get pricey but would get boring. I like places like this the best. Places where you know the food is good because locals keep coming. They have good prices and good people and you don't feel like you have to impress anyone. I bet Katherine loves it here, too."

Frank gave her a small smile and nodded. "She does. She always comes here when she's in town."

"I'm not that different from Katherine. I'm really just an ordinary woman who happens to have a pretty cool job."

"Ordinary? I'm not so sure about that."

Quynn laughed. "I grew up in a small town in Virginia. My mom was a teacher, and my dad was a librarian. I went to college and had no idea what I actually wanted to do with my life until I moved to Nashville with an ex-boyfriend. I met Kate at a bar, and we became friends. It was a few months before she hired me. I haven't looked back since."

Frank bobbed his head from side to side. "Okay, yeah. I guess you are pretty ordinary. Or your upbringing was. Now isn't the same, though."

Quynn shrugged. "Maybe. I still feel like I'm the same person. I'm sure my old friends would disagree. Who's the same as when they were growing up, though? We all change, don't we?"

"Hopefully," Frank said. "I think there are some people who don't. People who peaked in high school and want to relive those glory days forever."

"Yeah," Quynn agreed. "I'm definitely in the thank-god-high-school-is-over camp."

Frank laughed. "Definitely."

The waitress returned with their drinks and took their orders then left again.

"So what do you do for Kate?"

Quynn sighed. She'd been asked the question countless times, but it was different coming from someone who knew the whole truth. She knew she could be honest with Frank about her job.

"I make sure Katherine doesn't become Kate."

Frank chuckled for a second then asked, "How do you do that?"

Quynn sipped her wine and twisted her hair into a knot that fell as soon as she let it go. "I arrange her transportation before and after shows so no one actually sees her. I keep her schedule. I make sure she knows who she really is. I give her breaks. I try to keep her sane. Although I'm seriously doubting my skills right now."

Frank smiled, that debilitating grin that made Quynn all warm and fuzzy inside. "I think the fact that Katherine has gone off grid says that you're doing a great job. She wouldn't trust just anyone to handle her entire world while she hid out. What do you think she's doing?"

Quynn shook her head. "I have no idea. If I knew, I'd go get her."

"I think she's shacked up with some guy."

"No," Quynn said immediately. "Not Katherine. I mean, she said she's staying with this guy she met, but I don't think it's like that. Christian really messed her up. She doesn't trust herself with men anymore. The other night was the first time she went out since things imploded with Christian."

"Wasn't that more than a year ago?"

Quynn nodded. "Exactly. I kept telling her to get back out

there, but she refused. When she went out Thursday after the show in Binghamton, I was shocked, but I didn't say anything because I was afraid she wouldn't go."

"And she's still with that guy?"

Quynn nodded. "That's what she said, but there's more to it. There has to be. The guys she picks up are ordinary guys. In a bar. No one famous. No one who understands what she's going through. That way there's no pressure to stay in touch. She doesn't even get their names most of the time."

"Tell me you're joking," Frank groaned.

"Nope."

"I really thought my sister was smarter than that. She can still get so many things. And what if she ended up pregnant. She's crazy."

Quynn laughed. "She's really careful. She carries condoms with her and is anal about her birth control. She knows there's always a risk, but she does her best to minimize it."

Frank sighed, and they were interrupted by their dinners arriving. After assuring the waitress they didn't need anything, they dove into their meals.

"Is your food okay?" Frank asked after a few minutes.

"Delicious. I love food like this. Good comfort food."

Frank nodded. "Exactly."

They ate in companionable silence for a few minutes before Frank asked, "Any idea where she actually is?"

Quynn laughed softly. "This is making you crazy, isn't it?"

He nodded. "It's the cop in me. I don't like leaving mysteries unsolved."

"It'll be solved if I can ever get in touch with her. She's supposed to be doing interviews all week. It's just not like her. Even with Christian, it's not like her to do this."

"Do you think she's okay?" Frank asked, a worried note slipping into his voice.

Quynn nodded, knowing she needed to reassure him.

"Yeah. She said she's fine. She won't tell me where she is, but I think she's okay."

"How do you know someone else isn't texting you?"

Quynn sucked in a deep breath. "I don't, but you were there when I spoke to her. Besides, if something happened to her, we'd have heard about it. People would target Kate, not Katherine. And they'd make it public."

Frank pushed his empty plate away and ran a hand through his short hair. "Shit. I like this less and less. I wish I could do something, but I can't even use my resources because no one knows who she is."

"We've talked about that. I mean, not about you, but about her being Kate still. I told her to come out and tell everyone who she really is. Then Christian wouldn't have anything to hold over her."

"This guy's a real piece of work, isn't he?"

Quynn snorted and rolled her eyes. "That's too kind for him."

Frank laughed. "It sounds like it." He took a breath and looked around. "I think we need some dessert."

Quynn smiled. "I'm always up for dessert."

Frank smiled warmly at her. His voice dropped, heating her from the inside out when he said, "Me, too."

11

---

KATHERINE STRETCHED, still half-asleep, and found herself unable to move far. A warm arm had her pressed to a hard body with a very hard appendage.

Dillon.

She grinned and snuggled against him, rubbing her bare bottom against him. He groaned and slid his hand from her belly up to her breast.

"Cruel woman."

"Only if I don't make good on it."

Dillon nipped her shoulder and plucked her nipple. Her core tingled, getting her ready for him. His hand left her breast and tickled its way down her body to probe her center. They both moaned when he slid two thick fingers into her.

"I don't have any complaints about your stamina," he teased, circling her clit with his thumb as he eased his fingers in and out of her. "Then again, you are still young."

"I've never had sex this many times in one night," she confessed.

"Does it count now? It's technically morning."

"It counts," she gasped, her body hummed with pleasure as he worked her into a frenzy.

"Maybe it doesn't. Maybe I should stop."

"No! Don't stop. Please, Dillon."

He chuckled and kept going until she was begging him to make her come. Then he brought her over the cliff and back down.

He slid into her as her mind cleared. "Condom?"

"On," he said with a groan, sliding deep and hitting a new spot with the different angle.

"That feels good."

He kissed her shoulder and teased her clit again. Katherine reached down, resting her hand over his, then moving her fingers further to feel him sliding in and out of her. Dillon groaned.

"I like having you touch me. Feeling your fingers on my cock when I'm inside you is going to make me come harder."

"Yes, Dillon. Please," she moaned.

He eased in and out of her, neither in a rush to end their time together. Katherine couldn't stop thinking about leaving him and going back to the inn. Hell, she couldn't stop thinking about leaving him forever when her time there was over. Dillon was definitely going to be the guy she compared all others to in the future.

If she could ever try with another guy.

Katherine kept her fingertips on Dillon as he stroked in and out lazily. She could tell when he was close by the way he breathed, but he kept up the slow pace, gently teasing her clit the entire time.

"I'm close, Katherine. Are you gonna come with me?"

Katherine shook her head. "No. I'm not there yet."

He pressed into her clit and her hips bucked against him. "Let's get you there, sweetheart."

He swirled his fingers around her clit, pinching and

flicking as he continued his slow assault on her channel. The fast pace of his play against her clit combined with the languid strokes inside had her on the edge in record time.

"Oh, shit. Dillon. Yes."

She came with a shudder before she could stop it. Her body tensed around him, her channel clamping down on Dillon and drawing out his orgasm. He buried his face in her neck and trembled against her, holding her tightly from behind.

They laid there together, neither of them letting go. When Dillon softened and slid out of her, he finally let go and went to the bathroom. Katherine heard the shower turn on and thought about joining him. She waited until she thought he was almost done before she got out of his bed. She glanced back at it, hating that she'd never spend another night there.

Katherine pushed the thought away and joined Dillon in the shower. She had time to feel bad later.

***

DILLON FINALLY MADE IT UP TO THE INN LATER THAN HE planned, but it was worth it to spend some extra time with Katherine.

She packed her stuff before they left his house, but she didn't bring it with her. They didn't talk about it. About her leaving. He wasn't ready for her to go.

He thought about going back to his place and hiding her stuff, but that wouldn't keep her with him. Not for long enough.

"Hey, Katherine. Hey, bro," Andie said when they walked in the door.

"Hey. How's everything so far?"

"Good. It's been a relatively quiet morning since a lot of

guests are checking out. Oh, speaking of which. Katherine, your room should be ready in the next couple hours. We'll get it cleaned first so you can get in there as early as possible."

"Thanks," Katherine said with a grin.

"You don't have to rush off," Dillon said. "You're welcome to stay at my place as long as you want."

Katherine smiled up at him. "I appreciate it, but I'm sure you want me to get out of your way."

Dillon pressed his lips together in a grin but didn't say anything. He wasn't going to force her to stay with him. He wanted her to decide to.

"I'm going to check with Kristen. I'll catch up with you in a little while."

Dillon walked away and found Kristen laughing with customers in the tasting room. She was always smiling.

Dillon moved behind the bar with her, pouring a glass of wine for a waiting customer.

"Thanks," Kristen said with a surprised grin. She tossed her hair behind her shoulder and winked at the guy across the bar who slipped her a tip.

"Andie said it's been quiet, but it doesn't look like it in here."

Kristen shook her head. "Nope. I've been busy. I think a lot of people thought it was a good day to drink since they're all off work." Kristen filled another glass of wine. "What are you doing here?"

"I'm helping."

"Where's Katherine?"

"She's talking to Andie about her room."

"Ah," Kristen said with a smirk.

"What?"

"Nothing, cuz."

Dillon rested his hip against the edge of the bar top. "Spit it out, Kris."

"You don't want her to leave. It's obvious."

Dillon shook his head. "No. We're just having fun."

Kristen snorted. "You're never brought anyone home before. At least not that I've known. She's different for you."

Dillon shrugged. "She's just a woman."

Kristen grinned. "My brother said the same thing about Gianna. I think you're in trouble, cuz."

Dillon started to shake his head but stopped. Dillon really thought about it and had to admit to himself that Katherine was different for him. She wasn't like the other women he slept with, women he was happy to get rid of as soon as possible. It was the opposite with Katherine.

"Just realized it, huh?" Kristen asked with a smirk.

"Shut up, Kris."

Kristen just laughed.

***

"I hope you don't think I was trying to trick you when I told you to go to Dillon's house. I had no idea you two had met."

Katherine shook her head and smiled at Andie. "It's fine. I think he assumed it was a trick of some sort, but I didn't think that at all."

"Good. I really thought he'd just give up his house and let you have it. He's the only one of us that has a house to himself which was why I suggested you go there. That was really the only reason. Less people to shuffle."

Katherine grinned. She had wondered, but it made perfect sense. "I imagine it can be kind of lonely by himself."

Andie chuckled. "Sometimes I think he would prefer it to be quieter. My brothers and I go over there every so often, and my boyfriend is Dillon's best friend. There are usually a lot of people at his place."

"That's how I'd want it to be. I like being around people."

"You said you travel a lot. Is that for singing?"

Katherine stammered over her answer. Her lies were getting tangled with the truth the longer she spent with the family. She didn't like lying to them. It wasn't as easy as it was with most people. She felt guilty for it.

"Um, yeah. Mostly."

"That's really cool. Have you met any famous artists? I would love to meet Kate Maddox. I wish you could come with us to the concert."

"Oh, I'll be gone by then," Katherine said, feeling the need to run. "Um, I should go find Dillon."

"We were hoping to see you again," a voice said from behind as Katherine tried to escape.

She spun and found the family she'd given up her room to. Four smiles told her she'd made the right choice letting them stay.

"Hi. How are you?"

"We're so great. Thank you again for letting us have your room. It was really not necessary."

Katherine waved her hand. "Not a problem at all. It worked out well for me."

"Good. We're happy to hear that. Are you staying the rest of the week like you planned?"

Katherine glanced at Andie and nodded. "I am."

"We got you this. I hope it's okay. We just wanted to repay your kindness in some way."

Katherine accepted the bag from the woman. She felt bad that she didn't even know her name. Andie cleared a spot for Katherine to set the bag down as she dug through it.

Wine, plastic wine goblets, bottle stoppers, wine charms, a wine bag, and a gift certificate for The Drunken Grape filled the bag. Katherine was so touched she could barely speak.

"Thank you," she whispered. "You didn't have to do this."

"And you didn't have to give us your room. You made this weekend possible for us. We had such a great time with all the activities, and it was all thanks to you."

Katherine was more than a little choked up. She couldn't believe they were so kind. Most people she knew did something nice for someone as a statement. To make sure they got an invite for the next party, or an extra ticket to a show. They didn't do something like that just because they were good people.

"That's so sweet of you. Thank you. I'm Katherine, by the way."

"Nice to meet you, Katherine. I'm Nancy. And that's Mike, and the kids are Anne and Brendan."

"It's nice to meet all of you."

"Well, we're headed back home. The kids are in school for a few more weeks. But thanks again, Katherine. Enjoy the rest of your stay."

Katherine grabbed her bag of goodies and nodded. "I will. Thanks."

Katherine went to find Dillon while Andie checked the family out of their room. Katherine's room. She took a deep breath. She didn't want to stay there. She knew she should, but she didn't want to. She wanted to stay with Dillon.

"Hey, Katherine," Kristen said from behind the bar. "You look lost. Everything okay?"

Katherine nodded and went into the tasting room. There were a bunch of people in the gift shop, but the tasting room was relatively quiet.

"I'm good. Thanks. Just thinking about moving into here later."

"You know you don't have to, right?"

"I'm sure Dillon's sick of me by now."

Kristen laughed. "Not even a little. He wants you to stay, but he thinks you want to get away from him."

"Did he tell you that?"

Kristen shook her head and poured a glass of wine. She passed it to Katherine with a wink. "He didn't have to. You're here until Friday?"

Katherine nodded.

"Stay with him. We'll fill the room. Dillon doesn't take enough time for himself. He's always so busy running this place. He needs to enjoy himself more."

"I can see that about him."

"Then stay. If it's what you want, and it's what he wants, just stay with him."

"Are you sure it's what he wants?"

Kristen smirked, then whispered, "Why don't you ask him yourself?"

Katherine turned and saw Dillon watching her. His eyes traveled from her ass up the ample curves of her figure until they met her eyes. She recognized the desire in his gaze, but there was something else there, too. Something that told her Kristen was right.

Katherine moved toward Dillon as he stepped toward her. She smiled up at him when they were close enough to talk, but neither of them reached out. She hated the divide between them. The subtle way they were both pulling away.

"Hey."

"Hey."

"Um, so I was talking to Andie about my room."

His eyes shuttered.

"I was wondering what you think about me giving up the rest of my reservation."

She nibbled on her bottom lip while the words sunk in.

He took a step closer, his eyes lighting up. "You want to stay with me?"

Katherine hesitated for a second then nodded. "You can tell me to come here. I didn't give up my reservation yet. I won't be mad if you want to get rid of me."

He hauled her against his chest and inhaled her neck. "Not a chance."

Katherine sighed into Dillon, wrapping her arms around his neck. He kissed his way up to her lips and captured them in a kiss that told her exactly how much he wanted her to stay with him.

It was a lot.

DILLON SPENT THE REST OF THE DAY WITH A SMILE ON HIS FACE knowing Katherine wouldn't be taking her suitcases out of his house just yet. Yeah, she had to leave, but he had a few more days with her.

They wandered around the inn, handing out American flags to everyone who came in for a drink and those who were there for lunch. By the time they closed The Drunken Grape, Dillon was ready to get Katherine back to his bed.

Nothing killed that desire like running into his parents in the tasting room.

"What are you guys doing here?" he asked them after shaking his dad's hand and kissing his mom's cheek.

"We wanted to see Leo and Kristen at work. We don't get here often, and definitely not when they're having fun and working."

"We all stay pretty busy around here," Dillon said.

"Especially you. Got a minute?" his dad asked.

Dillon nodded and followed his dad to his office. Michael, Dillon's father, was the former CEO of Amavita Estates.

When Dillon was a kid, he imagined the day he would take over for his father, but as he grew up he realized he didn't have a choice in the matter. He never thought he'd feel so unsettled sitting in the same chair, looking across the desk at the man who taught him what to do in that office.

"What's going on, Dad?"

"I saw Perry here yesterday."

Dillon sighed. "I know. I spoke to him."

"What did he want?"

Dillon shook his head. "He seems to just want to taunt me. Friday night he said he's trying to poach Michele. Sunday he was on his way out and tried to talk to Katherine. I don't know what his end game is."

Michael ran a hand over his clean-shaven face. He was always the picture of the corporation, clean-cut with short, neat hair. It had grayed with age, but Dillon knew his father took pride in his appearance. He always said people responded better when they knew you cared about how you looked.

Dillon rubbed his own scruffy cheeks and wondered if Perry thought he was an easy target.

"Have you told the others about it?"

Dillon shook his head. "I was thinking about talking to them tomorrow. Without knowing what he's trying to do, it's hard to warn everyone. I don't want to cause a panic."

"Which is why you shouldn't tell them. Dillon, you're the CEO. You're in charge of this place. This vineyard lives and breathes on your back. If it fails, it'll be on you. And when it grows, that'll be on you also."

"We all work together, Dad."

Michael shrugged. "You might want to think that, but they all follow you. They look up to you. I made a lot of decisions when I was CEO that the rest of them never knew about."

"Like what?" Dillon asked. He was more than a little skeptical. His father had always managed by committee, and he definitely took the advice of Nonna and Aunt Marie, the oldest of the sisters.

"The restaurant was never going to be called The Drunken Grape. I told everyone that was the name that won, but it wasn't."

"You're lying."

Michael shook his head. "Nope. I think some of your younger cousins were afraid the name would piss off the aunts, but I knew it would fit with the area and with the direction Amavita was going."

"How did you keep that from everyone?"

"The same way you're going to keep the fact that Perry was here from everyone. For the good of Amavita. You work hard here. You all do. But your job is drastically different from Leo's or even Andie's. We could still exist without either of them. The fact that you agreed that everyone would get the same salary tells me you're a good man, and I hope that never changes, but you have to know that running this place is drastically different than taking reservations or pouring drinks."

Dillon didn't like the way his dad talked down about his siblings. They all worked their asses off, and had been for years. He wasn't special just because he had the business degree and sat in the office. Dillon felt that made his impact harder to see. At least, it made it harder for him to see it.

"We're all doing our best, Dad."

"I know, son. But you need to protect them from things they don't need to know. This is one of those times when you need to shove the truth down deep for the good of the vineyard. We're at the start of the season, and we can't have everyone on edge because they think Perry's going to show up again."

"What if he does?"

"Then you handle it, Dillon. Don't let him take anything else from this family."

Dillon nodded, feeling sick. He didn't want to tell his cousins about Perry's visit because he didn't want them to worry when he wasn't sure there was something to worry about, but keeping things from them because they didn't need to know seemed like he was trying to sneak things past them.

It wasn't his style. And he was kind of pissed that it was his father's style. But Dillon had only been in charge for a little over ten months. His dad was in charge for years. Maybe he was right.

## 12

Frank was in the lunch room Monday evening, heating up his dinner, when he heard it.

"Hey Tucker, you going to the Kate Maddox concert this weekend?"

Frank kept his eyes forward, focused on the microwave spinning so he didn't get involved in the conversation. He could grab his dinner and go somewhere else to eat. Anywhere else. He did not want to sit and listen to a bunch of guys talk about how hot his sister was.

"Hell, yeah. But I'm bringing the old lady. Says she likes her music. I just like her ass."

"She's got a few more assets, too. What do you think, Price?"

Fuck.

"About what?" Frank asked, hoping his food would be done soon so he could get the hell out of there.

"Kate Maddox. She's hot, right?"

"Yeah, sure. I guess."

"You guess? What's not to like about her?"

Frank shook his head. "Nothing. She's just not my type is all."

"What is your type then?"

An image of Quynn popped into his head, giving him more than enough inspiration.

"Blonde. Short hair. Curvy. Loyal, friendly, likes to laugh."

"I can get behind that," Tucker said. "In fact, I'd like to get behind that."

Hayes laughed and nodded. "Absolutely. But I like them with a bit longer hair. You know, so you have something to hold on to."

Frank grabbed his food from the microwave and slammed the door.

"Whoa, what's wrong with you?"

Frank pulled in a deep breath and reminded himself Kate would be gone in a few days and they guys would go back to bitching about their wives instead of sharing their fantasies about screwing his sister.

Not that any of them knew she was his sister.

"Nothing. I'd catch you guys later."

Frank didn't wait for an answer, just walked out. He found a quiet spot to eat and set his food down. Since he was on his break, he pulled out his phone and sent a text to Katherine.

You telling where you are yet?

Her reply was almost instant.

Nope.

Are you okay?

Yes.

How do I know this is really Katherine and
not some psycho who took her phone?

His phone rang in his hand, with his sister's face filling the screen.

"Hello?"

"Seriously? You think I've been kidnapped?"

Frank shrugged. "How am I supposed to know? I'm a cop, sis. And you've gone off grid. Quynn is freaking out, and I'm not a whole lot better."

"I'm fine, Frank. I promise."

"Where are you?"

He heard her breath and knew she was debating telling him.

"I met someone."

"Quynn said there was no way you'd be *with* the guy. She said you were too fucked up by that Christian asshole. Speaking of which, you should have told me so I could kill him."

Katherine chuckled. "Yeah, like you could have gotten close enough to him to lay a finger on him. He has a security detail."

"And why don't you?"

Katherine sighed. "Don't need one. That's why Kate leaves when I walk off stage. No one knows who I am when I'm out."

"That's really why you're staying, isn't it?"

"Partly, if I'm honest. But I like Dillon. A lot."

Frank took a bite of his dinner. "Who's Dillon?"

"I met him in Ithaca. Then I ran into him the next day at… Anyway, I'm staying with him."

"So, he's your one night stand, and you decided to stay with him?"

Katherine sucked in another deep breath. "It sounds bad when you say it like that."

"How would you say it?"

"I didn't plan to see him again, Frank."

"Do you think that makes it sound better?"

"I don't know. All I know is I like being here. I like being with him. And after the disaster that was my last relationship, I'm not ready to come out of hiding."

"You know you're killing your career right now."

"No, I'm not."

Frank swiped his sleeve across his lips. "You are. Quynn has been killing herself to get all your interviews rescheduled. And she has no idea what to tell these people. People who set their whole week around you. These are small town papers and stations. They don't have a back-up when their lead story for the week flakes on them. I'm not sure this is you, anymore."

He heard a hitch in her breath, like his words hit a little too close to home. "You don't know what it's like for me, Frank."

He shook his head. "You're right. I don't. And you don't know what it's like for everyone else anymore, Katherine. You've forgotten where you came from. For a guy you never intended to see again."

"It's not like that."

An alarm sounded, telling Frank he needed to get back to work. "I gotta go."

"Frank, wait."

He sighed. "What?"

"I'm sorry."

"Don't apologize to me, sis. I think Quynn deserves a call. And maybe a gift basket for all those interviews you canceled. Rumor has it you earn enough to cover something like that."

Frank didn't wait for Katherine to respond before he hung up. He knew he was partly pissed at his coworkers and was taking it out on her, but he didn't think she was being fair to Quynn. And Katherine clearly didn't care about it.

She was different. Even if she didn't want to admit it.

---

KATHERINE FELT LIKE SHIT WHEN SHE HUNG UP WITH HER brother. After deciding to stay with Dillon, she was flying high, but talking to her brother brought her right back down to earth.

Kate Maddox was not free from faults.

Neither was Katherine Price.

She went into Dillon's room to answer the phone, and she heard him getting dinner ready for them. She was grateful he liked to cook. She intended to help him, but she knew Frank was right. She really needed to call Quynn.

Quynn answered on the first ring. "Katherine? Is that you?"

"Hey, Quynn. I'm so sorry I haven't returned any of your calls."

"You better be. What the hell is going on?"

"I'm still here. I'm fine."

"Are you going to tell me where here is?"

"No. But I'm safe. Dillon is taking good care of me."

"What kind of care?"

Katherine sighed happily. "The best kind."

"Damn," Quynn said. "I almost came from that sigh. If he can make you feel that good when he's not even there, I can only imagine how good he is in person. Wait, he's not there is he? You're not having sex right now?"

"Ew, gross. Why would I do that?"

Quynn exhaled loudly. "Just had to check. I'm not sure I

know you anymore. First, you have a brother I've never heard of. Now, you're shacking up with a guy you met in a bar. Who are you?"

Katherine laughed. "I'm having fun, Quynn. I know it's not fair to you, though, and I'm sorry."

Quynn sighed. "It's fine. I feel like a schmuck crashing with your parents, but it's fine."

"No, it's really not. I should have told you what I was thinking."

"Were you ever planning to do these interviews?"

Katherine pulled in a breath and nodded. "Yes. I was. I wanted to. I still want to. But I don't know what to tell Dillon about where I'm going every day. I didn't know how to pull it off."

"I could have helped you with that."

"I know. I really was going to cancel my reservation and go home, but after Christian…"

"He hasn't been here. I'm assuming he's been here before, but I haven't seen him."

"Good. Hopefully he doesn't show up."

"I think Frank will kill him if he does."

Katherine laughed. "Probably. I just talked to him. He sounded like he might try to even if Christian doesn't show up."

"He'd never get close to him."

Katherine nodded. "I know. I told him that."

"He loves you. He wants to be there for you."

"He doesn't want my life. He's happy with everyone not knowing he's related to Kate Maddox."

"He wants you to be happy, Katherine. He doesn't care about anything else."

"You've certainly gotten to know him well over the last few days."

"Yeah, well, there's no one else to talk to," Quynn said, sounding defensive. "And he's a good guy."

"Quynn O'Hara. Do you have a thing for my brother?"

"No," she sputtered. "Of course not."

"You know I wouldn't care, right?"

"His life is here, and mine isn't. It wouldn't work so it doesn't really matter what I think of him."

"What if there was a way for him to be with you?" Katherine asked, her mind running with options.

"He's not, so it's irrelevant. Anyway, I'm glad you finally called me. Are you going to be here Saturday?"

Katherine accepted the change and nodded. "I'll be there Friday. I don't want to be rushing to get up there. I should be in by dinner time."

"Will you tell me where you went once you're here?"

Katherine grinned. "Maybe."

Quynn laughed. "It's the best I expected. Stop ignoring my calls."

"I will. I'm sorry, Quynn."

"We're good. See you Friday."

"Yep."

Katherine hung up feeling marginally better. What her brother said still bothered her, and reminded her of the fight she had with Dillon. She wasn't that shallow, insensitive star that couldn't be bothered, was she?

Katherine wandered back into the living room with the thought playing in her head. She didn't want to be like that. She wanted to be someone that others could count on.

Except she'd skipped out on a week's worth of interviews without a second thought. That didn't scream reliable.

"Everything okay?" Dillon asked when he saw her in the room.

Katherine nodded. "Yeah, it's fine."

Dillon grinned. "You don't really look fine right now. What's going on?"

Katherine shook her head. "Just some stuff going on that I should have taken care of."

"One of your freelance things?"

Katherine nodded. "Yeah. I was supposed to do a few things this week, and I'm feeling guilty for not being available."

"Do you need to go?"

"No. It'll be okay. I'll catch up next week. And then I'll be off for a little while."

"You will?"

Katherine nodded. She had a few phone interviews scheduled over the next month after the concert was over, but they were far enough between that she may as well have been off. Since she had to push all the local interviews out, she would only have closer to three weeks before she had to go to the studio, but it was a much needed break. Time to stop being Kate for a little while and just enjoy being Katherine. She still hadn't decided what she was going to do on her vacation, but she hoped she could disappear.

Again.

"Where are you going to be?"

Katherine shrugged. "I don't know yet. Maybe someplace with a beach."

Dillon smiled but there was tension in it. Katherine wondered how she could read him so easily when it always felt like she was flying blind when talking to people she knew. With Dillon, it was like she knew every nuance of who he was already.

"Want to play?" he asked, holding out his guitar.

"Excuse me?"

"Play. If you're a singer, I'm going on the assumption you play the guitar also. Most do."

Katherine nodded. "I do. But I usually play music that's already written. I don't play my own music."

The lie rolled off her tongue easily. Before the song she wrote with Christian, it had been years since she'd written a song. She loved the process, but between her label and Christian, it was ruined for her.

Until she heard Dillon play the other night.

"Play something you know. Or sit with me and I'll play. I know. Let's go outside. It always sounds different outside. Let's see if something triggers you out there."

"What about dinner?"

"I have a timer set. We'll be able to hear it outside."

Katherine followed Dillon and his guitar out to the picnic table in his backyard. She ached to get her hands on a guitar, but Christian was the one who came up with the music for their song. She could play notes, and was good, but she wasn't a composer. Lyrics came much more easily to her.

Dillon sat on the table and strummed the guitar, letting out a beautiful sound that sunk deep into Katherine. She sat next to him and closed her eyes, listening to the melody Dillon played.

Words danced in her head.

*Falling for you was like breathing*
*Love came easy*
*Your hands on me, your heart in mine*
*Your laugh, your smile, your kiss*
*You loving me, I felt so safe*
*I fell for you so fast*
*Like being on a roller coaster*
*Out of control*

She hummed along with the music, singing the words in

her mind only. She knew if she sang them aloud, he'd recognize her voice.

Dillon played for a while, his song developing and changing as he played. She wondered if he ever wrote songs or if he just strung chords together in random order. Either way, he had a gift.

He stopped playing after a few minutes and passed the guitar to Katherine. She rested the body on her lap and pulled in a deep breath. She closed her eyes and let Dillon's music fill her mind. Without looking, she played the same chord progression he played. She followed his music, singing the song in her mind, hearing the tune and shifting the beat when she wanted it faster or slower.

She could feel it. It was there. It was a part of her. A song that she knew she had to write, that she had to sing. Her label would never let her record it, but she had to do it anyway. She had to try.

For Dillon. And for herself.

---

KATHERINE WAS GORGEOUS SITTING ON THE TABLE PLAYING HIS guitar. Dillon couldn't keep his eyes off her. She tilted her head back, exposing her neck. Her chest rose and fell with each breath she took. A light breeze blew off the water, carrying the damp feel on the air and picking up Katherine's sweet scent with it.

He was so busy staring at her that he didn't realize she was playing the same chords he played until she started over again. He wondered if she was writing a song in her head. Her lips moved as though she was singing to herself, but no sound came out.

"Sing for me," Dillon said softly.

Katherine's eyes popped open as though she'd forgotten he was there. He smiled at her.

"Are you thinking of a song?"

She nodded.

"Will you sing it for me?"

She hesitated then shook her head. "I don't like to sing for other people until the song is written."

"Do you write a lot of your own music?"

She shook her head again. "No. I sing other people's songs."

"I thought most musicians wrote their own, especially starting out."

Something flashed over her eyes before she smiled and glanced away from him. "Yeah, they do. And I probably would do better if I wrote my own stuff. It's not that easy, though. You really have to find something that you're passionate about."

"I know one thing I'm pretty passionate about," Dillon said, sensing she could use a change in subject.

He eased the guitar from between them and pulled her on top of him on the picnic table. He was already hard and ready for her when she straddled his hips and lowered herself onto his lap.

His tongue went straight into her mouth, tasting her for the first time in what felt like entirely too long. How was he so addicted to a woman he'd only known a few days?

His hands guided her hips over him, loving that she was comfortable enough to grind on him in his backyard. They didn't need privacy. They just needed each other.

Katherine moaned, sending a jolt straight to his cock. He ached to be inside her, but he wasn't that big of an asshole.

"Inside Katherine. Now. I need you."

Before they could get off the picnic table, his oven timer beeped. He was more than happy to eat cold, leftover lasagna, but Katherine's stomach growled and he knew he had to feed her.

"We're not done, sweetheart. Next time I have you on top of me, I'm not stopping for anything."

Katherine shivered against him and grinned. "Neither am I."

———

WHEN THEY FINISHED DINNER, KATHERINE WAS FEELING FULL and blissfully happy. She worried when Dillon said he wanted her to sing for him, but he didn't press. She appreciated that, although she knew he didn't understand it.

Dillon poured her another glass of wine and they went to the couch to watch TV. She was more than happy to go straight to his bedroom, but she knew Dillon liked downtime after dinner. He liked to chill out on his couch, and he never liked to rush things when it came to getting in the bedroom.

Katherine sat close to Dillon, her leg against his. She sipped her wine and took a deep breath. She felt good being with him. Like things were the way they should be. She even considered going back to see him after her concert and her week of interviews, but she wasn't sure she could do that. She was supposed to go back to Nashville to record a new album, and she'd have another tour eventually. She couldn't drag Dillon all over the world with her. He had a life. A life she was a little jealous of. Family, friends, all the wine he could drink.

It was nice.

He shifted, his thigh rubbing hers. His hand landed on her leg, high up. His thumb rubbed circles on her jeans covered skin. His scent engulfed her as they sat there, a masculine scent that reminded her of lazy days on the lake and first loves.

Katherine sighed and rested her head on his shoulder. He draped his arm around her, snuggling her on his chest. His thumb did that tantalizing circle thing on her back, low on her back. He brushed bare skin where her top rode up and she swore she was going to have him right there on the couch if he didn't hurry the hell up.

Dillon kissed her forehead, lingering. His lips trailed to her cheek, then her ear. His thumb dipped beneath the edge of her jeans.

She was burning up.

Katherine decided she wasn't going to wait any longer. She slid to the floor and maneuvered between his legs. He looked at her like she was crazy.

"What are you doing?"

"You have me so turned on, I'm dying. I figured I'd return the favor."

"How's that?"

She smirked and unbuttoned his jeans. He lifted his hips for her to tug them down, bringing his briefs with them. His cock stood up, hard and ready for her. She licked her lips as her mouth watered.

She breathed Dillon in as she moved closer, savoring every part of what she was doing. His stomach muscles were pulled tight, waiting for her. When she wrapped her lips around him, his fingers immediately went into her hair.

"Fuck, Katherine. You weren't the only one dying, sweetheart. You're not gonna be able to do this long."

She groaned around him, disappointed. She liked having him in her mouth. His shaft was long and thick. His musky scent surrounded her again, more potent between his legs. She inhaled him, closing her eyes as she bobbed her head up and down his cock.

"Oh, God. Katherine."

Dillon's fingers tightened in her hair seconds before he

lifted his hips and pumped into her mouth. Her eyes teared, but she refused to stop. He'd given her more orgasms than any other guy had in such a short time. She was going to push past her gag reflexes and suck him until he either came or forced her to let go.

About every three strokes he jerked into her mouth. His hands held her in place, and she swore he hit the back of her throat. She sucked a breath in though her nose and did everything she could to relax and take him in again.

And again.

The next time he thrust deeper into her, she moaned.

"Fuck. Katherine, tell me now. I'm close, sweetheart. If you don't want me to come in your mouth, you need to move. Now, honey."

She shook her head and sucked harder on him. She swirled her tongue around his head when she drew him out, then slid her mouth right back over him.

"Oh, shit, Katherine. Oh, God. Fuck. Yes. Yes. Yes, honey, yes!"

She let him guide her head as he came hard in her mouth. A swell, then a burst deep in her throat. She almost choked when he came so hard, but she held it in and loved every second of it. She'd happily do it again and again to have him feel that good.

When he stopped spurting, he dragged her up to his lap and kissed her until his cock throbbed under her.

"Again?"

"Fuck yeah. I'm nowhere near done with you. But now it's your turn."

## 13

DILLON STRIPPED Katherine slowly as he kissed her. He couldn't wait to get her naked, but he knew drawing it out would make it that much better for both of them.

Her shirt stayed on his couch. Her bra hit the floor in front of it. He drew one nipple then the other into his mouth until she was clawing at his back. She pulled his shirt off and tossed it toward his kitchen. He kicked his pants and briefs off the rest of the way in the hallway, then dropped to his knees and kissed her belly.

"I can smell you, sweetheart. I bet you're already ready for me."

"I am," she said with a moan.

Dillon pressed his face to her and nuzzled her with his nose, knowing she'd feel it through her jeans. She gasped, then moaned, then pressed his head against her again.

"It'll be much better if you let me take these off, Katherine."

She released his head after a second and helped him remove her jeans, leaving her in a pair of red lace panties.

"Have you been wearing these all day?"

She nodded.

"How did I miss that this morning?"

She shrugged.

"I love red lace. And on your sexy body it's fucking amazing."

She went to cover up her belly, but he tugged her hands away.

"Don't hide yourself from me, Katherine. You're beautiful. Every inch of you turns me on. I could take you right now, even after the best blow job of my life, but I want to make you come a few times first. Then I'm going to spend all night making you scream."

"Oh, God," she moaned.

Dillon pressed his tongue to her lace covered clit, making her jump. He wanted to make her come right there, in the hallway. He couldn't even wait long enough to get her the twenty feet to his bed.

He slid a finger beneath the edge of her panties and into her channel. She immediately clenched around his finger. He put his other hand on her belly and pressed her backward until her back hit the wall. He toyed with her nipple and pressed his tongue hard onto her clit.

"Oh, shit. Dillon. I don't know if I can stay standing any more."

He hitched one of her legs over his shoulder and groaned at how wide spread her legs were.

"I want you to come like this. Right now. I want these panties so wet that you get come all over your sexy legs as you pull them off. Use the wall. I won't let you fall. But you will come, Katherine. I'm not waiting until we get to my room. You need to come now, sweetheart."

Her hips moved as he talked, then she moaned. He thrust a second finger into her and used the lace of her panties to add friction to her clit. She was getting close. Her breaths shortened. Her fingers tightened on his shoulder. The words she tried to speak became less and less intelligible.

"Oh, fuck, Dillon. I'm going to come. Shit. I'm coming. I'm coming now!"

She screamed her release, soaking her panties just like he wanted her to. He didn't waste any time getting her to his bed as she came, trembling in his arms like she was in shock.

He stretched her across his bed and eased her panties down her legs, making sure she felt how wet they were as he removed them. He rolled a condom down his length and slid into her, groaning when she gripped him tight with another orgasm.

"Dillon! Oh, God!" she screamed, her fingers curling into his bed for purchase.

He couldn't go slow with her clawing his bed, her legs wrapped tightly around his hips. He leaned over her, capturing a nipple between his teeth and he pistoned his hips into her over and over again.

"That feels so good," she groaned, her hands running down his back to his ass. She cupped him, urging him to go faster.

He was happy to obey her request.

He drove deep into her, his balls smacking her with each hard thrust. He clenched his teeth, forcing down the intense need to come. He needed to feel her again. Just one more time. Then he could let himself go.

Dillon changed his angle just enough on his next thrust to make her gasp. Her breath skipped, and her body tensed just enough that he knew she liked that. Hell, he did, too. He did it again. Not letting up on her until she was begging him.

"Dillon. Please. I need to come. Oh, shit. Please, Dillon."

He pressed in harder, once, then again, and she clamped down on him.

"Yes! Oh, God, yes! I'm coming! Oh, shit. I'm coming!"

He lost himself in her, letting her orgasm drag his out of him. He held her eyes, needing to see every twist of her face as she came for him. He groaned, then screamed her name as he flooded her.

When his body stopped pumping, he collapsed onto her, unable to support his own weight. She wrapped her arms around him and held him in place as they both struggled to breathe and make sense of what the fuck just happened.

Or maybe that was just him.

Her heart pounded under his ear, the steady beat making sense to him. After he thought he'd lost her, she was back in his bed. Staying with him again. He knew it was only for a few more days, but he wanted it to be longer. He didn't want her just for the week. He wanted her for as long as he could have her.

And he hated that it was only for the week.

He pushed off her a few minutes later, going to the bathroom to trash the condom. He splashed some cold water on his face and admitted to himself that Kristen was right. Katherine was definitely different. She was everything for him. Letting her go was going to be impossible. Which meant he had to make the most of the time they did have.

---

KATHERINE WOKE WITH A START. SHE WASN'T SURE IF SHE heard something in the house or if it was her imagination running wild on her again. Her heart pounded in her chest, and her body was tense, trying to be still and silent, listening for unusual sounds that would tell her what jolted her awake.

She slid quietly out of bed and grabbed the first article of clothing she could find, a t-shirt of Dillon's. She slipped it over her head and it fell off one shoulder, looking both fashionable and sexy, even though she didn't intend either.

Katherine padded into the bathroom and got herself a glass of water while she decided if she should go out into the living room and see if something was going on.

When Katherine stepped out of the bathroom, she saw Dillon lying in bed. He was stretched out on his stomach, his arms spread wide like he'd done a belly flop and landed there. She smiled to herself and realized he basically had after their last round of love making.

*Love making? Was that really what it was?*

No, she couldn't be in love with Dillon. They were only sleeping together because they were there together and the attraction between them was off the damn charts.

Her face heated as a voice in her head recited *Liar, liar, pants on fire*. She knew it was more than that. The time she'd spent with Dillon was better than any time she'd been with anyone else. Not only was the sex unbelievable, but he was kind and caring and everything she sang about in her songs.

If only she could tell him who she really was.

Katherine hated lying to him, hiding the truth about herself from him. At first it had been easy because he hadn't been anyone of significance, but she knew as she watched him sleep that he was as significant as any man had ever been, maybe even more. He was the man she would think about every time she wrote a new song. He was the one she'd wish was there on tour with her or she'd want to call before she went on stage, even if it was just to hear his voice.

Walking away from Dillon was going to be the hardest thing Katherine had ever done, but she knew she had to do it. Her time at Amavita Estates would come to an end. She had responsibilities, and it was only a matter of time before Christian found her. And he wouldn't come alone, he'd come with as many photographers as he could find to record their 'reunion.'

Katherine knew walking away and keeping Dillon and his

family out of her life was the best thing for them, for all of them, especially Dillon. She just hoped she had the strength to do it.

With nerves jumping around under her skin, Katherine padded out to the living room and looked around the open space. Nothing seemed to be out of the ordinary so she chalked up her being awake to a dream. She headed back to bed, to Dillon's bed.

Still in his shirt, Katherine slid under the covers and curled up on her side. Tears ran silently down her cheeks and she wiped them on his shirt, thankful he was still sleeping through her pity party.

His fingers touched her back and Katherine froze, afraid to move and wake him up if he wasn't truly awake. The mattress shifted under his weight and his arm snaked around her middle. He tugged her toward him, pressing her back to his front. His hand toyed at the edge of the t-shirt until he found her skin then his big hand settled on her stomach. "Sweet Katherine. So perfect," Dillon whispered sleepily. His lips pressed against her shoulder where his shirt had slipped and his other arm slid under the pillow her head was on and wrapped around her in a bear hug.

Katherine's tears fell quicker in the silence. She hugged Dillon's arms around her, not wanting to ever leave the safety and loving comfort of his arms and his bed. She would, though. She'd find a way to walk away from him. To let him go back to his life instead of bringing him into the mess that hers was. He didn't want what she had. He told her he couldn't imagine a life in the spotlight. He wasn't interested in fame, and she couldn't get away from it. She would walk away, go back to her life and forget the man who taught her how to live. And how to love.

QUYNN HEARD FRANK COME HOME EARLY TUESDAY MORNING from his night shift. She wasn't sure how he'd feel about her going to see him, but she wanted to tell him she heard from Katherine finally. He was worried about his sister as much as she was.

She slipped out of bed and stepped into her slippers before going downstairs to see if she could catch Frank. She knew he was working three nights in a row, so he would be going to bed soon.

He was in the kitchen, eating something over the sink when she walked in. He turned when he heard her footsteps and nodded. He looked tired, like he'd had a long night. Quynn figured she should tell him then leave him alone.

"I talked to Katherine last night."

He nodded. "I know."

"How do you know?"

"I called her. She answered. I told her she needed to call you."

"Oh," Quynn said, feeling silly. Katherine mentioned Frank, but Quynn didn't realize they'd spoken. She thought Katherine called her because they were friends and she wanted to tell her what was going on. Instead, she was just doing as she was instructed. "Well, thanks then."

Quynn turned to leave, but Frank stopped her.

"Quynn."

"Hmm?"

"I'm sorry my sister isn't better to you."

"She's fine," Quynn said immediately. She was not going to complain about her boss, especially to her boss's family.

"She's not. Not this week. Did she tell you she's with that guy? Dillon?"

Quynn nodded. "Yeah. She sounds happy."

"She shouldn't have taken advantage of you like she does. It's not fair to you."

Quynn just shrugged.

Frank set his bowl in the sink and ran the water to rinse it out. He turned the water off and turned to face Quynn.

"I had a shitty night. I told Katherine off, then I was out on calls all night. It seems everyone in the city went fucking nuts last night. All I wanted to do when I got home was crash."

"And I'm keeping you up," Quynn said, feeling guilty. "I'm sorry. I thought you'd want to know about Katherine, but since you already know, it's irrelevant. I'll let you go to bed."

"Quynn, wait."

"Yeah?"

"It was all I wanted to do. But now I want to do something else."

Quynn's breath caught in her throat. Frank moved toward her, his gaze dropping to her lips. Her mind raced for a reason he would be walking toward her with that look in his eyes, but she came up blank.

He was going to kiss her.

And she was looking forward to it.

He moved slowly, as though afraid she was going to refuse him. She dragged in a ragged breath, smelling his musky scent, a hint of something that lingered beneath the surface. Not cologne, but something that had to be unique to him. He stopped right in front of her, his hand lifting to cup her cheek. She nuzzled against his palm, realizing it had been longer than she cared to think about since a man had touched her or kissed her.

"Quynn," he groaned, dipping his head.

She tilted hers up to meet him in the middle, her hands going around his neck to pull him closer. His lips brushed hers, still tentative. She needed that. A slow kiss, one that could build naturally. She didn't need him to dive in and try to sleep with her. She needed him to kiss her like he was dying to feel her lips against his.

And he did. He lips moved over hers, dotting closed-mouth kisses on her lips from one end to the other. He moved across her cheek and kissed his way to her ear. He nipped at her, then kissed back to her lips. His tongue traced the seam of her lips, and she eagerly opened for him.

The coolness of whatever he ate was still on his tongue, adding to the complexity of their kiss. His tongue slid alongside hers, tasting her, then tangling with hers before he angled his head another way and slid his tongue against her cheek.

He kissed her like he was trying to learn everything about her from a kiss. And she wanted to tell him all of her secrets.

How she hadn't been with a man in far too long. How she was hurt that Katherine didn't really trust her. How she'd always wanted to be famous so she wouldn't feel so alone. How being Kate's assistant was the loneliest she'd ever been at times.

And how she liked him more than she knew was sane.

He kept kissing her, teasing her with nibbles and kissing his way down her neck before returning to her hungry lips and kissing her again.

She could feel how much their kiss affected him with every press of their bodies together. His uniform scratched her skin as she wound her way around him. He held her close, close enough that she was sure he knew she wasn't wearing anything beneath the thin tank top and shorts she slept in.

Frank finally pulled back, his hands on her hips and burning her up with fingertips dangerously close to where she throbbed for him.

"Shit. Was that okay?"

Quynn nodded. "More than."

"I know you're going back with my sister and this can't be more than a few kisses, but thank you."

"For what?"

He gave her a half-grin. "For erasing all the shit that ruined my night."

Quynn smiled, feeling like the a superhero that she could take away the sadness and pain in his eyes. She couldn't imagine the kinds of things he saw in his job, but she was happy she could erase all that for a minute.

"It was definitely my pleasure," Quynn said with a grin.

Frank leaned in and kissed her once more, then turned and headed for his room in the basement. He stopped at the door to the kitchen. "I wouldn't mind if you happened to be up tomorrow morning when I got home."

Quynn smiled. "I'll be here."

Frank glanced back at her over his shoulder and nodded. "Something to look forward to."

Then he was gone, leaving Quynn to swoon all on her own in her friend's kitchen over her friend's brother.

14

Dillon hated leaving a warm and soft Katherine in his bed Tuesday morning, but he had a business meeting to get to.

Everyone was already waiting for him when he walked into the inn. He thanked Andie for the cup of coffee she handed him and sipped it before he stood in front of his cousins and siblings.

"Kristen. Excellent job this weekend. From my perspective, everything went very well. Can you give us a run down of it and how you think it all went?"

Kristen stood, giving Dillon a chance to settle into a seat and drink his coffee as she talked.

"Everyone I spoke to over the weekend went on and on about our events all weekend. We had a fair number of guests we weren't counting on. The tours exceeded our expectations and were definitely the biggest hit. The firefighters' dance raised a ton of money, enough for them to move forward with their plans. Monday was quiet, like we expected, but the tasting room was packed most of the day. I was asked by a lot of guests if we had other events like that planned, and if we were going to make this an annual event."

"What would you like to do?" Dillon asked, an idea forming in his mind.

Kristen met his gaze evenly. "I'd love to do more. We did well, and everyone had a lot of fun."

"Good," Dillon said. "We'll talk after this." He stood as Kristen returned to her seat. His coffee cup was empty, but the caffeine hadn't sunk in yet, leaving him feeling exhausted with a hint of energy that felt just out of reach. "How are the vines?"

"Good," Henry said. "Everything has started out well so far this year. Ryan and I have kept an eye the area Jake caught Perry looking at a few months ago. So far, everything is normal."

Guilt warred with obligation in Dillon's stomach as he debating telling his cousins he caught Perry on Amavita not once but twice over the weekend. In the end, he stayed silent.

"What else is going on?"

Andie spoke up first. "We filled the one vacancy we had for the inn yesterday afternoon. Obviously, there are no guarantees, but we're still booked through Labor Day. Maybe we could do another event around then. Bookend the summer."

Dillon nodded, but before he could comment, Leo said, "I thought we were booked all weekend. How did we have a vacancy yesterday?"

Andie shot Dillon a look that said it was up to him to answer the question. He nodded and focused on his baby brother.

"Katherine decided not to resume her reservation."

"Damn. She's gone?"

Dillon glanced at Andie again, then shook his head. "No. She's still staying with me."

The room erupted in a combination of disbelief and applause.

"Dillon finally caught one."

"How long is she staying?"

"She should have been mine."

Dillon ignored them all and tried to get their meeting back on track. "Jake. Any projects we have coming up?"

Jake shook his head and grinned. "Nope."

*Damn.* So much for that distraction.

"What's going on with you and Katherine?" Sean asked.

Dillon could tell they weren't going to let it go. He rolled his eyes and looked around the room. If his dad was there, he'd be pissed. He always insisted the business meeting was for business only. Personal matters had no place in business. It never mattered who was fighting with whom, Michael insisted they leave their issues at the door.

Dillon wasn't doing such a good job with that rule.

"Katherine is in town until Friday. Then she's leaving. That's it."

"No way is that it. Why did she stay with you?"

Dillon shrugged. He hated being on display. He was the one in charge. The cousin who protected the others. He didn't put his personal life in the spotlight. Ever. He preferred to keep to himself.

"Isn't it obvious?"

"He's falling for her."

"She's got her hooks in deep."

"She probably wants a cut of Amavita."

And there was the issue. It was always the issue for Dillon. A woman who wanted him for what he could give her. Katherine never struck him as one of the women who would use him, but neither did Daphne. She played him. Right up until she decided there were bigger fish for her to catch and dumped him the day he was going to propose.

"Katherine isn't like that. And why would you think a woman would go after Dillon and not you if she wanted a cut? We all own an equal share," Andie said, disputing Leo's insistence that Katherine was only with him for one reason.

"He's falling all over himself for her. No woman has ever managed that. How did she get him?"

Andie glared at Leo. "It doesn't matter. He likes her, and we're not going to convince him that she's interested for any reason except that he's a good guy. So shut up."

Dillon heard the message beneath Andie's words. Dillon was being stupid when it came to Katherine. She was going to use him and destroy him, and he was going to stand by and let her.

Fuck.

"If there's nothing else going on, we can end the meeting. Thanks everyone. Get to work."

Dillon left the room, retreating to his office almost immediately. There was a knock on his door a few minutes later, but he was not in the mood to talk to whoever it was that thought they could give him good advice.

"What?"

Kristen poked her head inside. "You said you wanted to talk after the meeting."

Dillon swore at himself and nodded, waving Kristen inside. "Sorry I ran off."

Kristen snorted. "Please. I'd have gone, too. Leo's being an ass. He's just jealous because he hasn't gotten laid lately and you clearly are. And by the woman he thought he had a chance with Friday night."

"Did he tell you all this?"

Kristen shrugged. "We talk when the tasting room is empty. He really thought Katherine was into him until you showed up."

"I slept with her the day before she came here. She was mine first."

"There's the caveman I know and love," Kristen said with a roll of her eyes.

"That's not what I meant."

She snorted again. "Yeah, okay. Listen, Dillon. I get that Leo is being a dick right now, but don't worry about it. He'll get over it. Katherine seemed to like talking to him, but she looked at you way differently than she looked at him. Trust me, she's not interested in Leo."

"Does that just make me an asshole then?"

"How so?"

Dillon sighed. "Never mind."

"Uh uh. You don't get to do that. Why do you think you're an asshole?"

"I made sure he knew she was off-limits."

Kristen held his gaze and fought a grin for a few seconds before she burst out laughing.

Dillon sat there and watched her double over, tears streaming down her cheeks. He grew more and more irritated the longer Kristen laughed at his expense.

When she finally calmed down enough to speak, she said, "You're so screwed."

"Excuse me?"

Kristen rolled her eyes. "You're falling for her and don't even realize it. You think this is just sibling rivalry. Leo isn't trying to steal your toy, he wants your woman."

Fury rose up in Dillon so quickly, he saw red. His fists clenched, ready to fight his brother who wasn't even there.

"That's what I'm talking about. You're falling for her. You're pissed at just the thought of Leo talking to her, and let's not forget that Sean was hitting on her, too."

Dillon slammed his palm against the surface of the desk. He closed his eyes and let the pain radiate through his hand. Kristen snickered at his outburst.

"Can you pull together another weekend for Labor Day

like you did for Memorial Day?" Dillon growled, needing to get their meeting back on track.

"Absolutely."

"Similar events?"

"Yep."

"Have you made much progress working with other local places to get a collection of things to do in the area? We were supposed to talk about that at the meeting, weren't we?"

"Yes, but it's okay. I'd like a few more places, but I have a good start. I'll be in touch with them over the next few weeks and start funneling business both ways."

"Good. We'll talk more about that next. I want to transition you into an outreach type of role. Get you out of the tasting room some of the time and into the world of the guests."

"What do you mean?" Kristen asked, sounding more than a little unsure.

"I mean, you need to be more involved. We've never had crowds like we had this weekend. Our guests stayed here instead of going to different vineyards. People saw Amavita as a destination. That's the way things should be."

"We can't throw parties like that every weekend or they'll lose the appeal."

"I agree. And it's going to be part of your job to figure out what we can do to get people here and involved. Start thinking, Kris."

Kristen nodded, her eyes staring off and unfocused. Dillon wasn't sure if that was good or bad, but it was too late to bring it back in. He set her on a path he knew was good for her. She just needed to work it out.

She stopped at the door and turned back to Dillon. "Katherine likes you just as much as you like her, Dillon. I don't know if that makes things better or worse, but she does like you. A lot."

Dillon let her words sink in and grinned. "Thanks, Kris."

"It's the truth. I think she'd stay if you asked her to."

Dillon breathed a laugh. He knew that wasn't true, but it was definitely an idea with merit.

---

"ANOTHER EVENT WITH KATE MADDOX WAS CANCELED TODAY. The interview was supposed to air tonight after the news, but the singer was unavailable," the broadcaster announced.

"That's the third event we've heard about that she's canceled. Has there been any word about how she's doing?" the female co-anchor said.

The guy shook his head, his perfect dark hair not shifting an inch. Frank scoffed.

"No word. The only thing I've heard is that she's unavailable and spending time with her family, but no one is talking about what happened."

"I hope she's okay. If she has to cancel her concert this weekend, there will be a lot of disappointed fans."

"I think Kate Maddox is already disappointing fans. It seems the flighty Nashville star is back to her unreliable ways."

Frank turned off the TV, disgusted at the anchors. Since when was his sister big news?

Oh, yeah, since she became famous.

"She'll bounce back," Quynn said from behind him. "She always does."

Frank glanced at her over his shoulder. She was wearing a pair of jeans that hugged her curvy legs and drove him crazy. Her top was one of those loose ones, hanging off one shoulder to expose her bare skin. He wanted to drag his tongue across her flesh until they both forgot all about his sister.

"Are you that worried?" Quynn asked when Frank didn't answer.

He pulled his head out of his ass and grinned. "Sorry. I got distracted. And yeah, I am that worried. She's destroying her career. Why is she doing this?"

Quynn shrugged. "I wish I knew."

"I never thought she was cut out for this life. I told her when she moved to Nashville that she wouldn't make it."

"Why?"

Frank chuckled to himself. "She's always been private. She hated when people in high school knew what was going on in her life. She has no privacy anymore. She's constantly under a microscope. I don't know how she deals with it. I don't know how either of you deal with it."

Quynn shrugged, her shirt slipping farther down her silky shoulder. "I'm not really famous. No one knows who I am. And Katherine is how Kate survives. She wouldn't be able to do what she does if she was constantly in the spotlight, but she stays hidden. She takes off her extensions and changes her clothes, and no one ever knows who she is."

"Don't you think that's a different form of stress? To worry that someone will figure out who she is every time she changes her clothes and hair and whatever else?"

Quynn sighed. "I guess, but it's her solution."

"She can't tell everyone who she really is. She'll never get a break."

"I think the opposite is true. I think she'll have fewer people chasing her. Every reporter out there, every photographer, every fan, they all want to be the one to catch her. To figure out who she really is and expose her secret. Once she's out, no one is going to care anymore. They'll move on quickly."

Frank sighed. He ran a hand through his hair and down his cheeks. He was still exhausted from working night shift, but he wanted to see Quynn so he got up earlier than normal. He was hoping they could have dinner again.

"Do you have any plans for tonight?"

She shook her head, a smile teasing her lips. "No, why?"

"I was going to cook dinner if you want to join me."

"Oh, yeah?"

Frank stood and walked around the couch, bringing himself face-to-face with Quynn. Her pulse fluttered in her neck, her eyes widened, and her breathing picked up just enough that he could hear the difference.

"I'm hoping to be able to steal a kiss or two before I have to go into work tonight, too."

She smirked. "I think that could be arranged."

The door to the garage opened, alerting them to his parents' presence. Frank groaned, but Quynn laughed.

"I was wondering where they were," Quynn said, cupping his cheek and bringing her lips up closer to his.

"They're ruining my night, that's where they are."

"Then you better steal one of those kisses quickly."

He didn't wait for her to finish speaking before he sealed his lips to hers. They only had a few seconds before his parents would be able to see them, so Frank took advantage of every single one of them, slipping his tongue into her mouth and getting a taste before he stepped back.

The dazed look in her eyes when his parents walked in had him grinning like a fool. He was just as lost as she was, but he hid it better. The last thing he needed was his parents finding out he was getting involved with Katherine's best friend. They worried about him enough. Adding a week-long fling to his list of accomplishments wouldn't give them a great feeling about his ability to get back on his feet.

"Hey guys," Frank said, hugging his mom. "Where have you been all day?"

"We went out to lunch with some friends and went to meet with a realtor," his dad said.

"A realtor?"

His mom nodded. "We've been talking about selling the house for a while. It's just too big. And we spend so much of our time in Florida anyway. It's become a financial drain. What we want to do is sell the house and split the money we get from it between you and Katherine."

Frank noticed Quynn slip quietly from the room. He wanted to lean on her, to have her there for him, but he knew whatever they had wasn't something that allowed for that. One dinner, a few conversations, and a handful of kisses didn't mean she'd be there for him. Hell, the last woman he liked half as much as he liked Quynn was his ex-wife, and the ex part made it clear how much she was there for him.

"You're selling the house?"

His parents exchanged a look and nodded. "We are. It's time. And this time of year is still good for selling. We just need to get it on the market."

"Where are you going to go?"

They exchanged another look, but that one said he wasn't going to like their answer. "Florida."

"What?"

"We have friends there, and we enjoy it. We have trouble with the winters here. We'll still come back to visit you, but we're ready to move."

Frank's head spun with the information. He understood they liked Florida, but he didn't like that they would just pick up and leave. For good.

"What... Wow. Um, okay." Frank turned to leave the room, but his mom stopped him.

"Talk to us, honey. What are you thinking?"

Frank shrugged. "I don't know what I'm thinking. I never saw this coming. Maybe I should have, but I didn't."

It wasn't the first time Frank had been blindsided by someone he loved. He was sure it wouldn't be the last. Especially if he kept pursuing Quynn.

"We aren't trying to hurt you. We're already gone half the year. We've developed relationships with people there. You work so many hours we barely see you, and your sister is rarely here. We feel like it's time. And if we give you half the money, then you can get a place for yourself."

The selfish side of him wanted to complain that he didn't want to go back to paying bills, but that wasn't fair to his parents. They weren't responsible for him. He needed to be responsible for himself. If he could get out from under the debt Anna left him in, he would be okay.

"It'll be fine, Mom. You guys should be happy."

She walked to him and cupped his jaw. He forced a smile for her. There wasn't one thing about the conversation that he liked, but it wasn't his decision to make. It was theirs.

"Thank you for understanding. We were going to tell you and Katherine together, but since she's not here, we thought we'd go ahead and tell you."

Frank nodded, wondering what his sister was going to say.

"Have you spoken to her?"

"Not today."

"I hope she's okay."

Frank took a deep breath and nodded. He hoped so, too.

15

---

Katherine sat on the picnic table outside Dillon's house with his guitar on her lap. She took her time tuning it until it sounded almost like the one she played on stage.

Katherine went through some routine chords, warming herself up, before she dove into what she really wanted to play. The chords Dillon played days earlier were simple enough for her to easily pick up the melody of the music. She added her own spin to it, slowing down the tune until it resonated inside her.

She closed her eyes and played, humming with the guitar until she knew it was perfect. Katherine glanced around to make sure no one was nearby, then strummed the guitar again and jumped into the song that wouldn't leave her mind.

She sang the verse that came to her first. The one she heard in her head when Dillon played the night before.

*Falling for you was like breathing*
*Love came easy*
*Your hands on me, your heart in mine*

*Your laugh, your smile, your kiss*
*You loving me, I felt so safe*
*I fell for you so fast*
*Like being on a roller coaster*
*Out of control*

Katherine smiled to herself, the music feeling more and more like what she'd been searching for. Something was missing from her music. It had been for a while. She went through the motions, but she knew she wasn't the same person she'd been when she started singing. The appeal, the desire, was fading away.

But a few days with Dillon and it was coming back.

*Lost and scared with nowhere to go*
*You took me in*
*Frozen pizza, fabulous wine*
*My soul began to heal*
*You told me I was beautiful*
*Made me believe it too*
*Dinner and dancing in your arms*
*Under the stars*

She smiled as she thought about her first few days with Dillon. It made sense that he was the one thing she was passionate enough about to write a song. Her music was made from love. Every song she sang spoke of finding love, holding on to love, or losing love.

Katherine kept playing, repeating the verses until she knew they were perfect. She altered the tune as she played, and the bridge fell from her lips.

*Your love helped me, gave me the strength*
*I faced my fear*

*The one who never showed me love*
*Undeserving of my trust*
*Abused my heart and made me doubt*
*You showed me what love should be*

The chorus eluded her as she sang. She knew it was there, but something was missing. An element to the song that she knew had to come.

Katherine kept playing, her calloused hands caressing the guitar the same way she caressed Dillon overnight. She was falling for him. It was a bad idea, but she couldn't stop herself. He was a good man, and it was time she found a good one. One who wouldn't destroy her the first chance he got.

Katherine went back to the first verse and sang loudly as she played.

*Falling for you was like breathing*
*Love came easy*
*Your hands on me, your heart in mine*
*Your laugh, your smile, your kiss*
*You loving me, I felt so safe*
*I fell for you so fast*
*Like being on a roller coaster*
*Out of control*

"Is that the music I was playing?" Dillon asked from right behind her.

Katherine jumped, nearly dumping the guitar off her lap. "Sorry. I was just fooling around."

Dillon shook his head. "Don't be sorry. It sounded amazing. Is it bad to say I didn't realize you were so talented?"

Katherine laughed and shook her head. "We really don't know each other that well. I'm kind of funny about singing in front of people, too."

"You want to be a singer and you don't like to sing in front of people? I'm not sure you'll have a very successful career."

Katherine laughed again. "That's not what I mean. It's hard. Especially with someone I really care about."

Dillon's eyebrows went into his hair. Katherine didn't expect him to say anything about her confession, but she hoped he wouldn't just brush it off.

"I really care about you, too. Which is why I want to hear you sing. Will you play that song for me?"

Katherine shook her head. "It's not finished."

"Yeah, yeah. It sounded amazing."

"It was your song."

Dillon sat on the picnic table next to her and nudged her with his shoulder. "Then you have to play it for me."

Katherine huffed a laugh and focused on the guitar. She strummed it a few times, then jumped into the song.

*Lost and scared with nowhere to go*
*You took me in*
*Frozen pizza, fabulous wine*
*My soul began to heal*
*You told me I was beautiful*
*Made me believe it too*
*Dinner and dancing in your arms*
*Under the stars*

*Falling for you was like breathing*
*Love came easy*
*Your hands on me, your heart in mine*
*Your laugh, your smile, your kiss*
*You loving me, I felt so safe*
*I fell for you so fast*
*Like being on a roller coaster*

*Out of control*

*Your love helped me, gave me the strength*
*I faced my fear*
*The one who never showed me love*
*Undeserving of my trust*
*Abused my heart and made me doubt*
*You showed me what love should be*

"That's all I have so far," she said.

"Is that about me?"

"Um, yeah. I mean, I'm not saying I'm in love with you or anything. I know it's too soon for something like that, and I'm not some crazy stalker-type who's going to say I love you after just a few days. Just, you know, it fit the song."

Dillon leaned in for a kiss. His lips were soft against hers, a caress of skin on skin. She sighed happily, letting herself fall into his kiss. There was no outside world when she was with Dillon. Just the two of them, and that was exactly what she needed.

Dillon finally pulled back, his lips wet from hers. She wanted to dive into him again, to kiss him until she forgot about everything waiting for her outside the gates of Amavita.

"I think…I think you should sing this song on your next audition. Then when you're rich and famous, I can get credit for the song and be rich with you."

Katherine's smile faltered, her heart sinking. She didn't want to believe Dillon would be after her for a quick buck, but maybe he was. Was it possible he knew who she really was? That he was just pretending?

"Yeah, if I ever get famous, I'll make sure everyone knows you wrote the music," Katherine teased, hoping the smile she forced to her lips fooled him.

He laughed and kissed her once more. "Sounds good. I have some expensive equipment to buy. All those royalties will come in handy."

Dillon stood and dragged her up with him. Katherine numbly followed him to the house. She had no idea what she was going to do.

———

DILLON TALKED THE ENTIRE TIME HE FIXED DINNER. HE DIDN'T know what was going on with Katherine, but she was definitely bothered by something. He just didn't know what.

She was happy when she was outside singing. She was beautiful when she sang her song, but ever since they came in, something was off. Dillon couldn't put his finger on what it was.

"Wine tonight?"

Katherine nodded and gave him another one of those fake smiles. She'd given him a bunch of them since he got home. What the hell was going on.

"Are you okay?" he finally asked, knowing he would hate himself for it. He should know what was wrong. She shouldn't have to tell him.

"Yep. I'm good."

The only thing worse would have been if she said she was fine. Dillon didn't do relationships, but he knew women. And if a woman said she was good or fine, she was anything but.

He poured them each a glass of wine and handed hers over. She took it without looking at him, something that bugged him more than it should. She said she cared about him. Sang a song about loving him. But she couldn't meet his eyes?

Maybe that was it. The song. She was upset that he knew how she felt about him.

"You know I'm not upset about the song, right?"

"What do you mean?"

"Your song said you were in love with me. Nothing has to change between us. I know you're leaving in a few days. I wouldn't mind if you came back to visit or something, but I'm not going to get all weird on you just because you said you're in love with me."

"I didn't say that," she sputtered. "It fit the song."

Her cheeks went pink, but she still didn't meet his eyes. Okay, she was not mad about the song.

"What's going on?"

"Nothing," she said, sipping her wine.

Dillon wanted to force her to talk, but she would talk when she was ready. And if she wasn't ever ready, she was leaving in a few days.

*Damn, that hurt to think about.*

"I talked to Kristen about doing another weekend event. I think we're going to do something for Labor Day."

"Good," she said.

"Kristen has a lot of ideas about how to do things. Sometimes I think she should be the CEO instead of me."

"Why?"

Dillon shrugged. "I don't know that I'm really cut out for this. A lot of women think I'm the one with the money since I'm in charge, but we all own the same share. It's one of the reasons I don't date much and only pick up women outside Bereton."

"Do you think that's why I'm here?"

Shit. Not what he was trying to say. "No. Of course not. I wasn't thinking that at all." *My siblings and cousins were, though.*

"You do. You think I'm here for your money. Do I need to remind you that *you* picked *me* up in that bar?"

"Katherine, I know. I wasn't trying to say that at all."

"First, you tell me I need to make you rich and famous and now you complain that I'm a financial drag. It can't be both, so which is it?"

"Neither," Dillon said with a sigh. "I wasn't trying to say anything. I'm sorry. Let's not fight, okay?"

Katherine took a deep breath and nodded. "I'll be back in a few minutes."

She left the room before Dillon could say anything. Not that he had any clue what to say.

Dillon racked his brain for what the hell to say to her as he started dinner. Cooking always calmed him, so he threw himself into the task, hoping it would bring some answers.

He added pasta to boiling water and stirred the ground beef and vegetables in the sauté pan. He'd almost finished dinner when Katherine finally came back out.

Dillon immediately went to her. "I'm sorry. I was an ass. I want you to use the song because you sounded amazing. It's not mine. Sing. Enjoy it. Don't let me joking ruin this. We only have a few more days together."

She smiled at him, but her eyes were sad. "Do you think I'm here for your money?"

He shook his head and dragged her into his arms. "No. It never even crossed my mind. A lot of women are, but you didn't know who I was any more than I knew who you were when we met."

She stiffened briefly, enough that Dillon noticed it, then sank into him. She curled her body around his, taking comfort from him that he was more than happy to give.

Dillon brushed her hair back from her face and kissed her forehead. She looked up at him from beneath her lashes, her desire plain for him to see.

"You can't look at me like that. I'll forget about dinner so I can have you right now."

She grinned and pulled back from him. "I'm pretty

hungry so I can't interfere with that. Maybe I can steal a kiss, though?"

She moved into his arms and went up on her toes as he ducked to meet her lips. The kiss was over far too quickly for him, but her stomach growled loudly, telling him he needed to feed her.

They sat on the couch with the TV on. Dillon flipped channels to find something interesting when he caught a glimpse of Kate Maddox. He paused and went back to the channel.

"...still hasn't shown up for her appearances. Fans are beginning to speculate about Ms. Maddox's concert this weekend. If she isn't going to show up for the events planned all week in the area, is she going to be around for the concert? Word from her publicist is that she's spending time with family. We hope that's true, and that she'll reschedule her interviews."

"I'm starting to wonder if she doesn't care about the little people and just wants the money. A local TV show isn't going to bring in much attention for her, but a concert will. I think maybe Kate Maddox has forgotten where she came from."

"I wonder where she is," Dillon said when the newscasters went on to other stories. "She's always seemed pretty reliable, but if she doesn't want to be bothered with little people like us, then maybe I don't want to go to her concert."

He looked at Katherine with a smile, but it faded when he saw how pale she was.

"Whoa. Are you okay?"

She nodded, but her eyes were focused on the TV, not on him.

"Katherine, what's wrong?"

She shook her head then smiled at him. "Sorry. I'm good. I think I waited too long to eat something."

"Sorry. I just couldn't resist joining you outside when I heard you play earlier. I should have started dinner."

"No, no. It's fine. I liked having you there."

"It's the little things, and little people, that make life worthwhile. It's sad to me that people like Kate Maddox don't see that."

"They said she was with family."

Dillon snorted. "Yeah, after she vanished for days. This is what I worry about with famous people. Promise me you won't end up like her. That you'll stay in touch with the people you care about. And honor your commitments to where you're from."

Katherine gulped. "I promise."

———

KATHERINE WASN'T SURE SHE COULD EAT HER DINNER. SHE WAS dying to run off and call Quynn, but she couldn't without Dillon wondering what was going on. She should have called Quynn when she was in the bedroom earlier instead of getting mad and packing all her stuff.

She was ready to leave, just get the hell away from Amavita and Dillon, but he apologized. She couldn't leave him because of a misunderstanding. She liked him. No, she loved him. It wasn't fair to either of them to run off when they only had three days left.

Katherine ate most of her dinner, but she barely tasted the food. When Dillon took her plate and brought her back a second glass of wine, she was ready to relax.

"If you didn't work here, what would you do?" she asked him.

"Huh. That's a tough question," Dillon said. He leaned back against the couch and draped his arm over her shoulder, pulling her to his side. "I've never thought about working anywhere besides here. It's been my plan forever."

"You never had a moment of teenage rebellion where you wanted to defy your parents and go work somewhere else?"

Dillon laughed and shook his head. "No. I think I'm pretty boring."

"Really? Not even some girl who tried to talk you into following her to someplace far away?"

Dillon froze for a second, half a second, then sucked in a breath. "I learned a long time ago not to let someone else make up my mind for me."

"What do you mean?"

"There was a girl once. In college. We were together for almost a year, but she decided to jump ship and find the guy who made more money. Or, whose family made more money. I wasn't a big enough fish for her."

"Really?"

Dillon nodded. "I thought we were in love, she thought I was a meal-ticket."

"That's why it's so hard for you now. You still worry that women see you that way."

He sighed and dropped his head to the back of the couch. "Maybe. I guess. I'm the CEO. I'm the one most people think is in charge. All of us own an equal share of the vineyard, but not everyone knows that."

"I'm sorry, Dillon. It's not easy not knowing who likes you for you and who likes you for what you can do for them."

He nodded.

"I think you're doing what's right. Keep your family close, make sure you know who your real friends are, and protect yourself."

"I know. I don't think I'm very good at any of those things, though."

"What do you mean?"

"I should have told them about Perry. I didn't say anything at the meeting this morning about him being at Amavita over the weekend."

"Why not?"

He shrugged, dislodging her head from his shoulder. "I don't want them to worry. They all have jobs to do, and tracking him isn't part of it. That's my job."

"You just said that Kristen could be running the place. And the rest of your cousins and your siblings all have a hand in things. You all own an equal share, you should all have equal responsibility."

"We do," he huffed. "That doesn't mean they should have to deal with this kind of stuff."

Katherine rubbed his cheek. "It doesn't mean they shouldn't either. Let them in."

"I don't keep them out."

She smiled. "You do. You keep them out, and they don't know you. You're afraid they're after you for the wrong reasons also."

Dillon closed his eyes. "I'm not sure I know how."

"Sure you do. I'm here. I'm sitting on your couch. You trust me. Trust your family. They want the same things you do."

"To get you naked?"

Katherine laughed and slapped his arm. "No."

Dillon shook his head. "I think Sean and Leo might want that."

Katherine crawled on his lap and pressed her body to his. "They'll find other women. There's only one man that's going to see me naked this week."

"This week?" he asked with a raised eyebrow. "Are you saying next week you'll move on to some other guy?"

She shrugged. "I do enjoy sex. And if you won't be around, I might have to find someone else to help me out."

Dillon stood, holding her thighs so she didn't fall. "The next guy you're with is going to know my name."

"Why?"

"Because when I'm through with you, the only name you'll be able to say during an orgasm is mine."

Katherine squealed as Dillon carried her to his room.

16

Katherine buried herself under the covers the next morning, smelling Dillon on the sheets. She wondered if he'd notice if she took something of his so she could remember him. Maybe if she asked, he would give her something.

The thought of leaving weighed heavier and heavier on her mind. She was not looking forward to going back to her life. She loved being Kate Maddox, but she didn't want to have to give up Dillon. She knew she couldn't have both, though. He didn't want her life, and she did. Which meant she either had to give up the career she'd worked hard for, or she had to give up Dillon.

She wasn't sure which would be harder.

Katherine heard a buzzing noise as she tried to go back to sleep. It stopped after a few minutes, but started right back up again. She finally dragged herself out of bed and searched for her phone.

"Quynn," she breathed when she finally found it.

"Katherine," her friend said, her voice shaky. "Katherine, where are you?"

"Quynn, what's wrong? Do you need me to come get you? Where are you?"

"I'm at your parents' house. Christian just showed up here. He's going to tell everyone."

Dread sank low in Katherine's gut. She knew better than to ask, but she had to know. "Tell everyone what?"

"Who you really are. He said if you don't come out of hiding and tell everyone that you were really with him, he's going to tell the world your real name."

"He can't do that," Katherine whispered.

"He can. He never signed an NDA like the rest of your staff. He's free to tell anyone anything."

Katherine sank to the edge of Dillon's bed. She tugged her hand through her hair, still knotted from Dillon's hands the night before. She knew their time together was ending, but she didn't want it to end like that. It hadn't been that long since he'd been inside her. He woke her up before he went to work so they could be together.

And instead of enjoying that for the day, she was stressing about Christian.

"He promised me he would never tell anyone. Isn't that a verbal agreement or something?"

Quynn sighed heavily into the phone. "No. It won't hold up. Besides, once he tells everyone, it won't matter what kind of anything you had. It'll hurt you more than him."

Katherine stood and paced the room. She was still naked so she grabbed a t-shirt Dillon left on the floor and put it on. She had to think.

"I tried to tell all the reporters that you were spending time with family, but when they pushed for even phone interviews, they didn't believe me. I'm sorry. I've made a mess of everything this week."

The phone rustled on Quynn's end. Before Katherine could reassure her, Frank was on the phone.

"What did you say to her?" he demanded.

"Are you talking to me?" Katherine asked.

"Yeah, I'm talking to you. She's practically crying right now. What did you say to her?"

"Um, first, hi. Nice to hear your voice, big brother. Second, I didn't say anything. I'm trying to figure out how to keep my life from blowing up in my face."

"And that means you can trash Quynn?"

"Back off, Frank. I didn't say anything to her. None of this is her fault. And if you hadn't taken the phone away from her, I could have told her that."

"You're damn right it's not her fault."

"Hey, I'm your sister, remember? Aren't you supposed to be on my side? You're sounding like you care more about Quynn than you do about me. What's going on with you two?"

"Nothing," Frank said way too quickly. "I just don't want you upsetting her."

"Uh huh. Sure. Let me talk to her, Frank. She's my assistant, and we need to figure out what we're going to do."

"I'm taking a few days off work. I'm not going to take the chance that I'm not here when that piece of shit comes back."

"Why would he come back?"

"He told Quynn he would. After he told Mom and Dad that he would ruin their lives, too."

"He said that? Give Quynn the phone," Katherine demanded.

"I'm sorry, Katherine. I really am. If he didn't see me, he probably would have thought he had the wrong house. Your parents told him he did, but then he saw me hiding on the stairs and he barged in. I'm so sorry."

"Okay, first, you need to tell me what's going on with you and my brother. But that can happen later. Second, none of this is your fault. I'm the one who ran off. I'm the one who didn't stick around to face him. I'm the one who pissed him off. You didn't do any of that, so relax. And third, you've been holding everything together for me. Between rescheduling the interviews and Christian. I know he's not easy to deal with."

"I should have just stayed out of sight. I heard voices when your parents answered the door, and I was curious because the voice was familiar. When I realized it was him, I wanted to storm down there and tell him to go to hell, but your dad said he had no idea what Christian was talking about. He really pulled the whole thing off."

"He's good like that."

"He was. I still don't even know how Christian heard me on the steps, but he looked up and stared right at me, and we couldn't deny it. He said he wanted you back, and that he always gets what he wants."

"He's not going to get me back. I don't want him, and I refuse to be with him."

"What are you going to do?"

"I don't know."

---

A knock on the door had Dillon's head lifting from the invoice on his desk. The events over the weekend were expensive, but the added business more than made up for it.

"Sean," Dillon said when he saw his brother at the door. It was rare that Sean sought him out. They hadn't spoken much since Katherine arrived, and Dillon felt a little guilty for stealing her out from under his younger brothers.

Except for the fact that she was his first.

"Got a sec?"

Dillon nodded and waved his brother into the office.

Sean took a seat on the opposite side of the desk and handed over a stack of papers.

"What's this?"

"New equipment options. I know there isn't really a good one, but I wanted to make sure you had all the information."

Dillon flipped through the first few sheets, each one detailing a different possibility for Amavita Estates.

"What's your recommendation?"

"I think that's your call."

Dillon shook his head. "I want to know what you think."

Sean held his stare for a minute before he reached for the papers. "Leasing holds merit because it's the most affordable option. With the different wines we make, it'll take some scheduling to do, but it's possible. Fixing our current equipment doesn't seem like a reasonable investment to me because it'll cost about seventy-five percent of the cost of all new equipment, and there's no guarantee it'll last half as long. New stuff would be great, but it's obviously the most expensive option. We could go with one of the used sets out there, but there's no telling what condition any of it is in. Plus, we would be responsible for getting it here, and that could make the whole thing close to the same price as new."

Dillon leaned back in his chair. He'd done the same research as Sean and come to the same conclusion it sounded like his brother had. That didn't make it easy, though.

Dillon took the sheets from Sean and flipped through again. The refurbished equipment option was one he hadn't dug into. He was impressed with the things Sean found. There were three that had complete systems. They were a little out of date compared to what they could get new, but they were leaps and bounds better than what Amavita was using.

"My guts says new," Sean jumped in.

Dillon looked up at him, hoping his brother would expand on his decision.

"I know it's a lot of money, but it's the best investment. Having to lease equipment means working around the clock when it's here. And with the different wines we make, it would mean bringing equipment in at least twice each year. At the current lease rates, we'll end up paying almost as much in the long run. It's cheaper on paper, but once you add in all the other factors, like overtime and waste because we'll be rushing, I don't think it'll be the best choice. What we have is shot. It'll hold out for another year, at the most, but we need to make a decision this year."

"I agree with you. Shit, it's a lot of money. We're going to need a new loan from the bank for this. We don't have this kind of capital just laying around."

Sean swung his foot and chewed his lip. "What about the weekend?"

"The weekend?"

Sean nodded. "This past weekend. It was a success, right?"

"Yeah, but it wasn't enough to pay for this."

Sean shook his head. "No, I know that. But we're going to do something around Labor Day, right?"

Dillon nodded.

"What if we plan another event around Christmas, and maybe something at a few other times during the year? Boost sales, bring people in, and help pay for these big things. It won't help now, but it could allow us to pay down the loan faster."

Dillon picked up the invoice he was looking at when Sean walked in and handed it over.

"What's this?"

"That's the invoice for the band from the party. It's already paid, but that was just one. Pulling the weekend together was pricey. We made money, but it wasn't cheap."

"What about one day events instead of full weekend events?"

Dillon nodded slowly, thinking about Sean's suggestion. "Some day time, some evening. Keep the full weekend events to Memorial Day and Labor Day, but do smaller things throughout the year. Still draw in people, but reduce the commitment and expense on our end."

"If we do it right, we might be able to do some of these completely in house. That way we're not really spending any extra cash to get it done, but we bring in a little boost."

"That's a great idea, Sean. Genius. Kristen's been working on a few ideas. Why don't you stop by and talk to her about this?"

"Do you want me to run with this?"

"That's up to you. If you want to be involved, you can be. If you want to hand it all over to Kristen, she can handle it."

Sean nodded. "I'll work on it with her a bit. She's definitely the genius behind all this, so she'll take lead, but I want to get involved in other things."

Dillon smiled. "I know what you mean."

"You?"

Dillon's eyebrows rose. "You think I want to sit in this office all day?"

Sean snorted. "Well, yeah. You've always wanted this office. When we were kids, you'd come to work with Dad and spend all night talking about how one day you were going to take over."

Dillon sighed and ran a hand through his hair. "I know. I thought it would be different."

"Different how?"

"I guess I thought it would be more fun. Dad always loved it."

"We all thought you did, too."

Dillon shook his head, thinking back to his conversation

with Katherine. She was right. If he was going to get closer to his family, he had to let them in. "I wanted to, but there are times I wish I could get outside. Be in the fields and get my hands dirty."

"Why don't you?"

Perry's smirking face flashed in Dillon's mind.

"What happened?" Sean demanded.

"Nothing," Dillon said quickly.

"Don't give me that. Something's going on. What is it?"

"Perry."

"What does he have to do with anything?" Sean asked, his face a question mark.

"He was here over the weekend. He's trying to steal Michele."

"Why didn't you say anything at the meeting Tuesday?"

"Because I don't want you guys to have to worry about it."

"Do you have a deal with the aunts? One the rest of us don't know about?"

"No, of course not. Why would you even ask that?"

"Do you own more of this place than we do?"

"You know I don't."

"Then why the hell do you think you need to take on more than the rest of us? I know you're in charge, but that's just how it all shook out. It doesn't mean the rest of us aren't willing and able to help. We're not kids anymore. You're still the oldest, but that just means you're old."

Dillon barked a laugh. "Yeah, yeah. You're still an infant."

Sean smiled. "You need to let the rest of us take some of this on. How about tomorrow you get out in the field and I'll handle whatever comes up here?"

"Here?"

"I'll do your job. Unless you don't trust me."

Dillon grinned, feeling better than he had all day. "You're on."

Sean reached to shake Dillon's hand, then tugged him in and slapped his back. "We're telling everyone else about Perry. And you're going to get the hell out of the office more."

"I can handle that. But I'm not sure about Perry. He's—"

"Nope. Nonnegotiable. If you get out of here, everyone knows. We all need to be on the lookout for him. If he ends up in the vines again, he could do some real damage. Ryan and Henry need to know. And Zach should know he's trying to steal Michele. And—"

"Okay, fine. I get it."

"Good," Sean said with a smirk. "I've gotta get back to work." He looked around Dillon's office with a grin. "I think I might redecorate tomorrow. Maybe pink walls."

"Don't you dare," Dillon growled. All his siblings knew he hated the color pink.

Sean walked toward the door laughing. "Definitely pink. Maybe a few pillows for your chairs. Pink curtains. I'm sure Andie could help."

Dillon couldn't help but laugh when Sean was gone. One sibling down, two siblings and five cousins to go.

---

Quynn parked her rental car in the driveway outside the Price's house. She grabbed the bags from the backseat and slammed her door shut, turning toward the house.

Someone stepped out from behind a column as she walked up the porch stairs.

"Aah!" she screamed, dropping her groceries on the steps. "Christian? What are you doing here?"

"We both know what I'm doing here, Quynn. Where is she?"

"I don't know."

Christian smiled, that creepy sneer he always gave her. His eyes scanned her curvy figure before settling on her breasts. She wanted to tug her jacket tighter around herself, but she knew that would only make it worse.

"She's not here. These are nice people. Leave them alone, Christian."

"They're not so nice if they're keeping me from the woman I love."

"You only love yourself," Quynn snapped.

Christian's eyebrows winged up. He recovered quickly, but the sneer was replaced by a snarl. "You don't know anything about my relationship with Kate. And if you did, you wouldn't be standing in our way. We're good for each other. Especially after this week."

"What are you talking about?"

A smirk settled on his lips. "You haven't been doing a good job of keeping the sharks at bay. Kate's disappearance has gone national. It's no longer a little local news story that she's not showing up for interviews. It was all over the national programs this morning."

"You're lying," Quynn whispered. There was no way word had gotten out that Kate Maddox was MIA. If it did, her career could be over. Celebrities who vanished were usually painted with addiction issues and never recovered from it.

"I'm not lying. But see, if you would tell me where she is, then she and I could straighten things out. I could help her."

"I really don't know, Christian."

"And I really don't believe you," he spat. "She's destroying herself. If she doesn't pull her head out of her ass, she's going to take me down with her. This deal I have is good for both of us. She needs to sign off on the song so I can record it. If she doesn't, I'm fucked."

Quynn's heart pounded. He was still playing her. Christian was looking out for himself, not Kate. He was probably lying about her being national news, too.

"Screw you, Christian. You had me fooled for a second, but I won't make that mistake again. Kate wants nothing to do with you. You're a parasite, and she's done with you."

"A parasite? Really? And what are you?"

"Excuse me?"

"Well, you're living at her parents' house. Usually you live with Kate. She pays for you to go everywhere with her. Do you ever do anything for yourself? Or do you just live off her?"

"It's my job to be with her. And she was supposed to be here. She would have been if you hadn't shown up."

Christian smirked again. "She'll be here soon. And when we get back together, the first thing I'm going to do is make sure she fires your fat ass. Then she's going to get back to the gym. Hanging out with you has made her fatter. She needs to get back into some kind of shape. Shit, she was already too big. But now… You're no good for her."

Quynn's eyes swelled with tears. She hated Christian. With every piece of her fat self, she hated him. But he was powerful. If Kate took him back, Quynn knew she'd be out of a job. Because Christian wouldn't forget about his promise.

"What's going on out here?" Frank said, joining them on the porch.

Quynn watched the two men square off. Frank's smile said he had no idea who Christian was.

"This is Christian Blake."

Frank glared at Christian for half a second.

Then punched him.

## 17

Frank shook his hand and glared at the asshole who made his sister run. Not only that, but the shithead was getting in Quynn's face. He had more than one punch coming if he thought he could treat women the way he did.

"What the fuck? Do you know who I am?" Christian yelled, wiping his bloody lip on the back of his hand. "I'm going to sue you for that!"

Frank nodded. "Good. I'm a cop, douchebag. I'd love nothing more than to go to trial and tell everyone exactly what you said and how you were threatening my sister and my friend. I don't think there's a court in the world that will be on your side."

"You sucker punched me."

Frank shook his head. "Not even a little. You were trespassing. I heard her ask you to leave more than once. You threatened my sister. You threatened my whole family from what I heard earlier from my parents. So I'm well within my right, as a police officer, to remove you from this property, however I see fit. So, would you like to leave on your own, Mr. Blake. Our should I call my buddies on duty today and ask them to take you to jail for trespassing and threats and endangering the lives of my family and friends."

Frank draped an arm around Quynn, tugging her close to his side. He could feel her shaking and wondered if it was because of him or Christian. Once the dickwad left, he could find out. First order of business was getting rid of Christian Blake.

"You can't threaten me. My lawyers have lawyers. I'll bury your whole family."

"You probably will. I have no doubt that you could. But I'm pretty sure you won't risk damaging your reputation. Kate Maddox has some pretty big pockets, and she's got connections with the press that will make sure this story gets out long before you can file any kind of lawsuit."

Christian sneered. "Your sister isn't big with the media these days. Running off in the middle of a tour isn't a good idea. They like to keep tabs on people, especially people they have interviews with."

Frank shrugged, praying he pulled it off. "All that's been taken care of. And Kate will be back soon."

"I'm counting on it. I'll wait to see her. She'll be happy to see me."

"No," Frank said, stepping forward again. "You stay away from her or you'll regret ever setting foot in this town."

"Was that a threat, Mr. Police Officer?"

Frank grinned and shook his head. "Not at all, Mr. Blake. That's a promise. She doesn't want to see you. She never wants to see you again. She's met someone else. Someone who knows how to treat her. She's done with you."

Quynn sighed heavily, drawing Frank's attention. He glanced back at her, and she was shaking her head with her eyes closed.

"Met someone else?" Christian choked out. "I'm gonna fucking kill him!"

He stormed off the porch and slammed into his black car parked across the street. He tore off, leaving Frank to wonder what just happened.

"Why did you tell him that?"

"What?"

"That she met someone? Now he'll really never leave her alone!"

"Whoa, what are you talking about?"

Quynn sighed. "Christian Blake doesn't like to be beat. He has to win, at all costs. If she chose someone else, she's telling him he's not good enough. It doesn't matter that they broke up, he expected her to wait around until he was ready to get back together."

"Why would she do that?"

"She wouldn't, but he thinks she would. He's delusional."

"What did she ever see in him?"

Quynn smiled. "He was good to her at first. He was never as big of a star as her, but he'd been in the spotlight longer. He made it seem like they were friends who just became more. But the longer they were together, the more he tried to control her. And the more he tried to control her, the more she retreated into herself. She never stood up to him."

"That's not the Katherine I know."

"Yeah, tell me about it. He was the first guy she dated that was in the music industry. I think she was afraid he'd ruin her career if she pushed back."

Frank groaned. "It sounds like he's trying to anyway."

"She wrote a song with him, one song. She told me she loved doing it, but never wanted to write with him again. He broke up with her shortly after and started pimping their song around, apparently. He's found a buyer, but they recorded the demo together. We copyrighted it before he could. Christian tried. Re-recorded the song, but he can't sing for shit."

"So he needs her."

"Exactly," Quynn said with a roll of her eyes. "He thinks she'll just welcome him back."

"Instead she ran. And I just told him she's with someone else."

"He'll never find her."

"Are you sure about that?"

Quynn nodded. "She's smart. She'd never go somewhere he would think to look. She's probably somewhere from when you guys were kids. A favorite spot that she never mentioned to anyone else."

"I thought you said she was with a guy?"

Quynn finished picking up her groceries and laughed. "She is. She met him in Ithaca, but he was wherever she was. She didn't mean to see him again, which means she was going to where he was on her own. It was coincidence that they ran into each other."

"Or fate."

Quynn grinned and walked inside with Frank. "Or fate."

***

THERE WAS A KNOCK ON THE DOOR ALMOST IMMEDIATELY followed by it opening. Katherine squealed and looked around for a weapon to use on the intruder when Andie stuck her head inside.

"Hey! Are you dressed?"

Katherine looked down at her shorts and Dillon's t-shirt. "Um, yeah."

"Good." Andie pushed inside with Kristen right behind her. "We're going shopping. Thought maybe you'd want to go with us."

Katherine looked between the cousins and nodded. "Yeah, sure. Let me just change really quick."

"Take your time," Andie said. "I'm going to grab a drink. We're off the rest of the day. Is Dillon taking you out tomorrow night?"

"Out?" Katherine asked through the closed bedroom door. She did *not* want to go out with him. She was loving the little cocoon they'd created and had no interest in disturbing it with a night out.

"Isn't tomorrow your last night in town? I thought he said you were leaving Friday?" Andie said from right outside the door.

Katherine stripped off her clothes and dressed in something more appropriate for going out in public. She figured her barely there shorts and Dillon's oversized t-shirt, without a bra underneath, weren't right for an afternoon of shopping.

She had a new pair of shorts on and was pulling a shirt over her head when there was a knock on the door.

"Katherine? You okay?"

"Yeah," she said absently, letting herself remember the way Dillon made love to her the night before. She'd never had a man touch her the way he did. He was a kind and generous lover. And she was walking away from him.

"Is he taking you out?" Andie asked again.

Katherine shook her head as she opened the bedroom door. "No. I don't think so. We haven't talked about that."

"He should. You guys really like each other and you haven't had an actual date yet. I think you should see where thing can go."

Katherine forced a smile and tied her sneakers on. "What are you guys shopping for?"

"Something to wear to the concert," Kristen said. "All my clothes are all wrong. I need something new."

"Me, too. Plus, we're staying in Syracuse overnight. I need something new for then, too."

Kristen rolled her eyes. "I wish I had a guy to buy new lingerie for. God, I hate being single."

"You're always with someone," Andie argued as they all walked outside. "It's not like you're alone."

Kristen glared at her. "I might as well be. The guys I'm with are around long enough to get off then they're gone again."

"So stop screwing everyone around," Andie groaned, driving toward the highway.

Kristen shrugged. "I like sex. There's nothing wrong with that, right Katherine."

"Whoa," Katherine said laughing. "Don't drag me into this. I'll be gone in a couple days."

"Which makes you exactly the person I should ask. You're only here because you're hooking up with Dillon. If you weren't, you would have taken the room at the inn."

"Um…"

"So you know that sex is fun and not something you should eliminate from your life just because your ex is a jackass who wants to get married. How old are you, Katherine?"

"Thirty."

"See? She's two years older than me," Kristen said. "Why should I be locked into one guy? Have you ever been married, Katherine?"

"Um, no."

"Ever engaged?"

"No."

"Ever wanted to be?"

Katherine laughed and shook her head. "No. I've been focused on my career for the last few years."

"Have you been celibate?" Kristen asked.

"Of course not."

"See?" Kristen said. "She's sleeping around, too. There's nothing wrong with it."

"I never said there was," Andie defended. "Philip is the one who wanted you to get married. I think you need to do what's right for you."

Kristen groaned. "He's right for me. I need to figure out how to want to get married. This has gone on long enough."

Andie shook her head and laughed. "You should just move on. Like you said, it's gone on long enough."

"Can I offer some advice?" Katherine asked.

"Sure. God knows I have no idea what to do," Kristen said.

"Get it out of your system. If you're happy sleeping with whoever you want whenever you want, do it. You'll be miserable if you go back to Philip, right?"

Kristen nodded.

"And you still don't want to get married."

"But I love him."

Katherine nodded. "That's not always enough."

"Is it enough with you and my brother?" Andie asked.

Katherine smiled. "I wish it could be, but I don't think it is."

"So you do love him?"

Katherine nodded. "Yeah, I do."

---

THREE HOURS LATER, KRISTEN AND ANDIE HAD MULTIPLE BAGS full of lingerie and clothes for the weekend. Katherine felt weird shopping with them for clothes to wear to her concert. Even weirder was when they tried to talk her into buying lingerie to wear for Dillon.

"He's going to love what you got," Kristen said.

Andie groaned. "I finally understand how Dillon feels when Cody and Jake start talking."

Kristen laughed. "You don't really care."

Andie chuckled. "No, not really. It's still a little odd to be friends with the woman my brother's sleeping with."

"You were friends with Angela, weren't you?"

"Who's Angela?" Katherine blurted. She figured she could pretend not to know anything about Dillon's ex and find out more about him.

"Sean's wife. She died right after Emily was born," Andie explained.

"Sorry. I had no idea."

Andie shrugged. "It was a while ago. I was friends with her, but we weren't that close. She was really sweet, but we definitely never talked about her and Sean having sex."

"Well, Katherine hasn't given out any details so technically you haven't talked to her about it either," Kristen chided.

Katherine laughed. "You two are bulldogs. I don't know why you want to know about it. I wouldn't want to know about anyone having sex with my brother."

"You have a brother?"

Katherine nodded. "He's six years older than me. He's a police officer."

"Is he cute?" Kristen asked, turning in her seat to look back at Katherine.

Katherine nodded. "I think so. He doesn't seem to have trouble getting dates when he wants them."

"That doesn't sound good. What's wrong with him?"

"You really don't hold back, do you?"

Kristen shook her head.

"He's divorced. His ex cheated on him. It's a good thing they're divorced, but I think it's hard on him."

"Well, that sucks. Hell, I've only been through a break-up

and I feel like my world collapsed. I can't imagine ending a marriage."

"Not all marriages last," Andie said.

"True, but I imagine you go into it thinking it will," Kristen argued.

"Is that why you never wanted to marry Philip? You didn't think it would last?"

Kristen shook her head. "No. I'm not ready for something like that. I'm enjoying my life. I want to be able to meet a guy and spend a week with him like Katherine's doing. Or go on vacation because I feel like it. I'm too young to get married."

"What about you, Andie?" Katherine asked. "Are you and Cody thinking about getting married?"

Andie and Kristen laughed. Hard.

"No," Andie finally said. "I love him, and I'd marry him in a second, but we're taking things slowly."

"How long have you been together?"

"Six months."

"Wow. Really? I would have guessed much longer," Katherine admitted.

Andie nodded. "We've known each other forever. He said he's been in love with me since I was seventeen."

"You didn't feel the same?"

Andie huffed a laugh and shook her head. "I thought of him as my brother's best friend. I never really looked at him that way until he was right in front of my face."

"Then she was looking at him all sorts of ways," Kristen teased. "I still can't use the island in our kitchen." She shuddered.

Andie slapped her. "Whatever. I cleaned it with bleach. Every time."

"Gah! I don't want to know you're still having sex where I sit every day. Gross."

"Oh, please. You and Philip would have done the same thing," Andie joked.

Kristen's laughter faded. "Yeah. You're probably right."

"Shit. I didn't mean it like that. I'm sorry."

Kristen shook her head and faced the window.

Katherine felt bad for both of them. Andie didn't mean to hurt Kristen's feelings, but she was definitely hurting. From the little Katherine knew, Philip wasn't worth Kristen's time, but it wasn't like she could say that to her.

Andie parked in front of Dillon's house but kept the car running.

"Do you guys want to come in? Drink some of Dillon's wine?"

Andie looked at Kristen who just shrugged.

"Come on. I'll tell you *one* story."

"Really?" Kristen said, her smile back.

Katherine nodded.

"I'm in," Kristen said, jumping out of the car.

Katherine laughed with them as they all walked into Dillon's house. Katherine stashed her one bag from the lingerie shop in Dillon's room. She was going to save it for the next night and didn't want him to find it before then.

When she walked back into the kitchen, Andie already opened a bottle of wine and was pouring three glasses. She handed one to Katherine and said, "Spill."

Katherine laughed. "Dillon came home early a couple nights ago. I was outside playing his guitar."

"Wait. You were playing *his* guitar?" Andie said.

Katherine nodded. "Yeah, why?"

"He doesn't let anyone touch his guitar," Kristen supplied. "Ever. I've never even touched it. He didn't freak out?"

Katherine shook her head. "No. He told me to keep playing."

The cousins exchanged a look.

"What?"

Kristen busied herself with a healthy sip of the wine. Andie opened and closed her mouth like a fish.

"Just spit it out," Katherine demanded, getting anxious.

"My brother's falling for you."

Katherine laughed and shook her head. "No. He can't. He's not. We've only known each other for a few days."

"He's never let anyone touch his guitar."

"He's been around a lot more lately."

"He's changed. He's different with you here. You should stay."

"Ooh, yeah," Kristen agreed. "You should definitely stay."

Katherine smiled sadly. "I can't."

"Hasn't he asked you?"

"It has nothing to do with that. I have a job. And responsibilities. I can't stay, no matter how badly I want to."

"But you do want to?" Andie clarified.

Katherine nodded. "Yeah. I do."

---

DILLON STOPPED BY SEAN'S HOUSE ON HIS WAY HOME. HIS GUT churned all day after telling Sean about Perry being on Amavita. It didn't help that his father stopped by after lunch and reinforced that Dillon needed to handle shit without involving the others. Dillon had to tell his brother not to say anything before the whole vineyard found out.

"Hey Dillon," Sean said when he answered the door. "Come on in."

"Thanks."

"Hi, Uncle Dillon," Emily said from her seat at the dining room table.

"Hey, Em. Doing homework?"

She nodded then ducked her head back to her work.

"What's up?" Sean asked.

Dillon pulled in a breath. "I wanted to talk to you about our conversation before. About Perry."

"Yeah, I was thinking about that all day. I was going to call Zach later and talk to him—"

"Don't," Dillon blurted.

"What?" Sean's eyebrows tugged together, his head cocked to the side.

"Don't tell anyone what I told you."

"Why not?"

Dillon sighed. "I shouldn't have told you any of that."

"Why not?"

"You don't need to worry about it. You've got Em and your own job. It isn't something you should stress over."

"That sounds like Dad talking, not you."

Dillon shook his head, immediately denying the truth. "It's me, Sean. I just—"

"Save it. I got enough bullshit from Dad growing up. Not to worry about things. It wasn't anything for me to concern myself with. You know how that made me feel? I'm not the oldest. I'm not the favorite. So I just got pushed aside. Now my brother's doing the same thing Dad always did? That's bullshit, Dillon."

"It's not that I'm trying to push you aside. I just don't want everyone else to worry when there's nothing to worry about."

"Did Perry show up at Amavita this weekend?"

"Yes."

"And did he threaten to steal Michele from us?"

Dillon sighed. "Yes."

"What changed since this morning?"

"Nothing. I just had more time to think about it. I shouldn't have unloaded all that crap on you. This is my job. I know you think I'm being an ass about this, but my job is to handle this kind of shit. I'll talk to Michele. I'll make sure we're staying vigilant. Henry and Ryan are in the vineyard all the time. So is Jake. Perry won't step foot on this vineyard without someone knowing about it."

"Yeah, but—"

"No, Sean. I can't. This is my job. My responsibility. I need to be the one to handle these things. Everyone else has enough to deal with. This is my job."

Sean's face hardened. Dillon glared right back at his brother, wondering when they'd grown so far apart that he barely recognized the man who stood before him. Sean still had the same short, dark hair and brown eyes he'd always had, but he was older. Rougher. Angrier.

Dillon recognized that look.

"Yes, sir. I'll be in your office tomorrow morning. I'll keep my trap shut."

Dillon sighed. He wanted to fix things. Sean didn't get it, and Dillon owed him more of an explanation.

"Say good night to Uncle Dillon, Em. He's heading out."

"Good night, Uncle Dillon."

Dillon sucked in a deep breath and forced a smile for his niece. "Good night, Em."

She smiled at him then asked Sean about dinner. He ignored Dillon to take care of Emily, leaving Dillon to let himself out.

Dillon shook his head at himself on the way to his house. "And that's how you piss off your brother," he said to absolutely no one.

18

DILLON WAS LOOKING FORWARD to a quiet night with Katherine but instead walked in on her drinking with his sister and cousin.

"Hello, ladies."

"Dillon! You're home!" Andie said, getting up from the couch to hug him.

"Are you drunk, Andie?"

She shook her head. "Nope. Only had one glass. Just happy."

Dillon shared a grin with Katherine who hid her smile behind her glass. Kristen met his eyes and shook her head, telling him that Andie was not drunk.

"We were talking about you," Andie said when she released him. "Katherine should stay. You should ask her to stay."

Dillon's eyes went to Katherine, but she avoided looking at him. He was worried until he saw an adorable blush lift from beneath her collar and paint her cheeks.

"Andie," Kristen hissed. "I think we should go."

"No, stay," Katherine immediately protested. "Have dinner with us."

Andie and Kristen exchanged a glance then turned to Dillon.

"You both know you're always welcome," Dillon said diplomatically. He should get a fucking medal for it.

"What are we having?" Andie asked, pouring another glass of wine. "Can I invite Cody?"

"I don't know, and of course."

Dillon went to the fridge to search for something to cook. Andie called Cody and from the sound of it, he was on his way over. Kristen and Katherine sat on the couch and talked, but Andie leaned against the counter.

"I really like her."

"Who?" Dillon asked.

Andie rolled her eyes. "Katherine. She's really sweet. And she likes you a lot."

"I like her, too."

"Why haven't you asked her to stay?"

Dillon spun on his sister. "What?"

"I'm just wondering why you didn't ask her to stay. She said you didn't ask her to."

Dillon sighed. "She has a job. And it isn't here. I'm not going to rope her into the deal we made. This is our home. It's not hers."

"Did you know she's from Syracuse?"

Dillon nodded and turned back to the fridge. He pulled out food to get started on dinner while Andie kept talking.

"It's not that far. She could see her family. And you guys could be together."

"She wants to be a singer, Andie. I'm sure you know this already. I'm not going to stand in the way of her dreams. I can't. You of all people should understand that."

Andie sighed and nodded. When she and Cody were

dating she found out he was leaving. She was going to let him because she thought it was what he wanted. Andie always lived with her heart, and she would never let Dillon stand in the way of Katherine doing the same.

"I'd love it if she stayed, but I won't hold her back."

"Do you love her?"

"Andie," Dillon warned.

"Fine," she huffed and went back to the couch with Kristen and Katherine.

Cody knocked and let himself in. He grabbed a beer from Dillon's fridge and sat with the women in the living room while Dillon cooked. He loved having his family around, but he couldn't shake the feeling that Katherine was avoiding being alone with him. Like she was done with him already. They still had two nights and one full day together. He wasn't willing to waste them, but his family was in the damn way.

"Need any help?" Katherine asked when dinner was almost ready.

Dillon shook his head absently, unsure how to take her offer.

"I'm sorry I invited them to dinner. We had a fun day, and I wasn't sure I'd get another chance to spend time with them."

Dillon nodded. "I get it. I'm not the only one who's going to miss you."

"About what Andie said…"

"Don't worry about it. I know that was just Andie being Andie."

Katherine didn't say anything for a few seconds. Dillon finally turned and caught her eyes closed, fighting for control. She flipped them open and smiled at him. "I just wanted to make sure we were on the same page."

Dillon wasn't sure what happened, but it wasn't good. "Katherine."

She shook her head and took a step toward the living room. "I'm leaving in two days, Dillon. It's not reasonable for me to stay here."

Dillon held her gaze for a second then nodded.

She sat down on the couch and quickly joined the conversation going on around her.

Dillon wanted to kick himself. He'd fix it when everyone left. He hoped.

---

KATHERINE DIDN'T WANT DILLON TO KNOW SHE WAS UPSET, but he did. She watched him out of the corner of her eye as everyone talked and laughed and ate the dinner he cooked. She played her part and smiled, but she was counting the minutes until they left.

Or maybe she was dreading them.

"We should get home," Andie said, carrying her empty plate and wine glass to the kitchen. "Dinner was amazing. Thanks, Dillon."

The others stood with her, carrying their dishes to the kitchen. Katherine followed them, uneasy about being left alone with Dillon. She knew she couldn't ask them to stay, though. She didn't want to. She just wasn't sure she wanted to have a fight with Dillon, and she was fairly certain that's where things were headed.

"Thanks, guys," Dillon said, hugging Andie and Kristen and slugging Cody on the shoulder. "Make sure they get home?"

Cody nodded. "Yep. Their car is staying here."

Andie protested. "I'm good. I can drive."

"How many glasses of wine did you drink?" Cody asked.

Andie cocked her head to the side. "Yeah, you're right. I

can't remember so I shouldn't drive, even though I don't feel it."

"Have a good night," Dillon said as the women followed Cody to his truck. He shut the door and turned to face Katherine.

Gulp.

"I'm an ass. I know. I didn't mean I don't want you here. I hope you know that."

"It's fine," Katherine said automatically. She always gave in. No matter what, she didn't argue. It was why her career wasn't what she hoped it would be and why she stayed with Christian as long as she did. She didn't fight for herself.

"Katherine. Yell at me. Tell me I'm an ass. Hit me. Something. Don't just stand there and tell me it's fine when we both know it isn't."

"What do you want me to say, Dillon? I'm leaving in two days. Going back to my life. We don't know each other that well. It would be insane to consider staying here. Even if I wanted to, I couldn't. Not only because you don't want me here, but—"

"No," Dillon said. "Don't say that. I do want you here. I would love for you to stay, but that's not fair to you. I'm tied to this place. I love it here, but it's my home. It's always been my home. I can't imagine leaving, even if I could. I'm locked in until July, and even then, I've never wanted to be anywhere else. When you're a famous singer, you'll be traveling all over the world. I'll still be a farmer."

Katherine sighed and sank onto Dillon's couch. The soft fabric cushioned her and eased her guilt almost as much as the scent of Dillon made her feel more guilty. She wanted to tell him the truth. The words burned inside her. It would make things so much easier if he understood.

He crouched in front of her, eye level with her. "I'm happy

you're here. I'll never forget this week. And when you're famous, I'll be able to smile and say I knew you when. But I'd never ask you to give up everything you've been killing yourself for. Just like I know you'd never ask me to give up my home."

Katherine shook her head, emotion lodging tight in her throat. "I wouldn't."

He cupped her cheek and smiled. "I know, sweetheart. That's why this relationship is both perfect and imperfect. There's no easy answer."

Katherine nodded and kissed him. She poured every bit of herself into it. Kissing him was the only thing that kept her from telling him who she was. Quynn would kill her if she admitted it to him. She could hear her best friend's voice as though she was standing right there.

It wasn't fair to either of them, but Dillon would figure out who she was eventually. If it wasn't at her concert over the weekend, he'd learn when she told the world the truth. Because her week with Dillon taught her that hiding wasn't going to make things better. Christian was still out there, threatening her. He wasn't going away just because she took a vacation. She had to deal with him eventually.

And there was only one way to do it.

---

Quynn hung up the phone and slammed it onto the counter. Frank paused, one foot in the kitchen.

"Dammit!" Quynn yelled.

"Still haven't talked to her?" Frank asked.

Quynn whirled around and sucked in a breath. "I'm sorry. I didn't realize you were there."

Frank shrugged and walked to her side. He leaned against the counter and crossed his arms to keep from tugging her into them. "I've seen you worse."

Quynn snorted. "Yeah, I guess you have."

"I'm sorry she's doing this to you again."

Quynn sobered quickly. "I don't want her to be blind-sided. There's no way to know who he's going to tell or when. We only know he's going to do it."

"He won't go on TV right now."

"How do you know that?" Quynn asked, her light eyebrows pulling together.

Frank grinned. "I gave him a pretty nice shiner. I'm guessing he won't want anyone to see that so he'll lay low for a while."

Quynn's eyes widened before she laughed. "Did you do that on purpose?"

Frank shook his head. "Nah. He deserved to get hit. It was just fortunate that it had a double benefit."

Quynn sighed and poured a cup of coffee. Her slippers had unicorn horns sticking out of her toes and matched the unicorn t-shirt she was wearing. Her barely there blue shorts stretched as Quynn reached for the sugar container and Frank barely bit back a groan.

It had been far too long since he'd shared a bed with a woman.

"What are you going to do if you can't get in touch with her?"

Quynn shrugged. She opened her mouth to say something, but her phone rang. "It's her."

Frank nodded and moved to the coffee pot while Quynn answered.

"Where the hell have you been? I tried calling you all day yesterday!"

She was silent while Katherine answered. Frank poured his coffee and tried not to eavesdrop on their conversation.

Oh, who was he kidding, he was listening to the whole thing.

"Christian came back. Yes, I'm serious. He wants to expose you. He's going to tell everyone who you really are."

Frank expected screaming from his sister, but she seemed calm. What the hell?

"I agree. We should get out in front of it. Hopefully he won't say anything until next week. Frank hit him so he's sporting a nice bruise."

Quynn met Frank's gaze. For the first time in far too long, he felt a connection with someone. Like Quynn wasn't just there for his sister, but she was there for him, too. She would stand up for him. Defend him. Watch out for him.

"He won't understand," Quynn said as she pulled her eyes from his. "It's a really bad idea. Because he's nobody! He's just a guy. He won't get it. He'll get pissed off and you have no idea what he'll do. He could go to the press himself."

"What are you talking about?" Frank asked.

Quynn tilted the phone away from her lips and whispered, "Katherine wants to tell the guy she's with. She wants him to hear from her that she's Kate Maddox."

"Why shouldn't he?" Frank asked. It made sense to him. They'd been together all week. He knew his sister and was sure she'd shared more with him than she did with most people she knew. If she stayed with him, she liked him. And being honest with him was definitely the best thing.

"He's not famous. He won't understand how things work in our world. He's a nobody from nowhere. He won't be able to deal with it. He has nothing to offer her. He'll want money or his own fame. And she doesn't need that. She needs to be focused on her career. She needs to tell people in a situation that we can control and not—"

Quynn stopped talking abruptly. Frank just gaped at her. She could have been talking about him. He fit all those things Quynn said about the other guy. Nobody. Nowhere. Nothing to offer.

"You're wrong! Katherine, you can't do that. No..." Quynn walked away as she argued with his sister.

Frank sat at the kitchen table feeling like he didn't know anything. He liked Quynn. She was someone he thought he could have something with. He knew it would be hard with her traveling, but he wanted to try it. He wanted her.

But she wasn't the same woman Frank thought she was. She was cold and heartless. She wanted Katherine to keep secrets, only to tell them on TV. He knew that was what she meant by a situation they could control. Katherine shared with him more than once that Quynn liked to use TV as a sounding board. Kate would perform new songs on TV or do interviews about her personal life. She hated it, but Quynn insisted it was the best way.

Frank wanted to leave the room, but he had to know what happened.

Quynn walked back in a few minutes later with a triumphant smile on her face. "I talked her out of telling him. She really wanted to. But I told her it was better if she didn't."

"Because he's a nobody from nowhere with nothing to offer, right?"

Creases formed between her brows, and she tilted her head. "Are you mad about something?"

Frank scoffed. "Seriously?"

Quynn crossed her arms. "Yeah, seriously. Although it appears I have my answer. What the hell is wrong with you?"

"Is that really how you see me? A nobody from nowhere with nothing to offer?"

Quynn breathed a laugh. "I wasn't talking about you. You're funny."

"Weren't you?" Frank challenged.

"What is going on? I thought you'd be on my side about this. You saw Christian. He's threatening to go to the press. Every newspaper, tabloid, and TV station in the country wants to know who Kate Maddox really is. Christian isn't the first person to think of it. She had a publicist a few years ago who wrote up a press release telling everyone who she was. I found it before it went out, but it would have all been over."

"Your life you mean."

"What are you talking about?"

"Keeping Kate Maddox and Katherine Price separate is good for you, isn't it? You get to manage both of them. You have to keep everything quiet. She trusts you. You deal with all the extra crap. And if she told everyone the truth, your job would all of a sudden be a lot less important."

Quynn pulled in a deep breath and her lips trembled, but Frank was too far gone to care that she looked upset.

"You don't even know who she's with. You're assuming it's a nobody. Just like I am. No one's ever heard of me. No one cares who I am. I'm just the guy you've been hanging out with for a week. I'm not even good enough for you to screw when you're on vacation. I'm just window dressing. Isn't that what you guys call the men she takes to awards shows? Window dressing? Someone to show up with so she isn't alone, but no one of any real importance or value. Someone she can toss aside at the end of the night. You know what, Quynn. I'm not giving you a chance to toss me aside. I'm tossing you aside first." He turned to walk away.

"Frank!"

Frank spun around. "No. You don't get to try to make me feel bad about this. You just said it. I'm nobody from nowhere who has nothing to offer. Hell, at least the guy Katherine's with has his own place. I have even less to offer. But I'm sure you've already figured that out."

Frank turned and left, ignoring her cries to come back and listen. He was done listening. He'd been fooled too many times by women he thought gave a shit. He wasn't going to take a chance on one he knew didn't.

19



KATHERINE WAS STILL FEELING unsettled when she went to lunch. Kristen invited her up to the tasting room and suggested getting something to eat, which Katherine happily agreed to.

She was getting too attached to everyone. That was the only reason she wanted to tell Dillon who she really was. In only one more day, she'd be gone, and she'd never see any of them again.

Katherine looked across the vineyard as she walked to The Drunken Grape. She didn't see Dillon, but she looked for him. As big as the whole place was, she wasn't surprised she missed him. Hopefully he got a few breaks in the day, too.

"Don't worry about him, worry about yourself."

Quynn's words rang in her mind. Katherine had always been the kind of person who wanted to take care of everyone around her. Dillon was going to be hurt when he found out she was lying to him. There was no way around that.

She tried to tell herself that Quynn was wrong and that she *should* talk to him, but she didn't know.

Katherine hated the idea of her last night with him ruined with a fight. She also hated knowing she would leave and he'd end up finding out who she really was, and it wouldn't be from her.

She made it to the inn still undecided about Dillon. She forced that decision from her mind until after lunch. Kristen and Andie were women she could see herself being friends with if the circumstances were different. She knew it wasn't an option though, so she was going to make the most of the last two days she had with them.

"You're early," Andie said with a smile.

"I am?" Katherine asked.

Andie shrugged. "No big deal. Kristen said you were going to be here around noon. I'm finishing up a few things, but I'll be done soon."

"I'll go find Kristen then."

"Sounds good. You know where she is."

Katherine nodded and walked down the hallway toward the tasting room. She wondered how Sean was doing in Dillon's office for the day, and if Dillon handled letting go as well as he said he would.

The control freak in Katherine could never have let someone else take over everything she normally did, but the timid woman who struggled to stand up for herself knew there was a lot more she needed to start pushing for.

"Red or white?" Kristen asked when she spotted Katherine walk in.

"I love your pinot noir if you've got any open."

Kristen grabbed a bottle and poured an overfull glass and set it in front of Katherine.

"I'm going to be drunk by the time we get to lunch if I drink this."

Kristen snickered. "Lightweight."

"I am."

"It's okay. Maybe you'll spill all your secrets if you're drinking with us."

"Secrets?" Katherine choked out, the wine slipping into her windpipe. She coughed until she could breathe normally, then froze when she caught the curious look on Kristen's face.

"Well, I was joking, but now I think there are some secrets buried in there."

Katherine forced a grin and thanked God when another customer distracted Kristen.

Andie joined them a few minutes later, dragging Katherine to The Drunken Grape. Kristen promised to join them in a few minutes and asked Andie to order lunch for her.

"She's trying to get you to spill secrets, isn't she?" Andie asked when they sat down.

"Excuse me?"

Andie nodded to the wine glass. "She always pours heavy, but that's a bit much for Kristen. She wants to know something."

Katherine shook her head. "She said she was joking about that."

Andie snorted and sipped her water. "She said that, but she didn't mean it. Of course, Dillon's my brother, so if anyone should be fishing for secrets it should be me."

Katherine's hands were clammy, and the back of her throat tingled. She wanted to run and hide from them, but she knew it wasn't possible. That would only make them question even more.

"I'm not hiding anything from Dillon. He knows who I am."

Andie held her gaze for a second too long. "I know that. But we're protective of each other. Dillon's like everyone's big brother. He's always trying to take care of us. Kristen said she thought she saw Perry talking to both of you last weekend, but Dillon hasn't mentioned it to us. We're worried about him. And can't help but worry that you're involved with Perry."

Katherine wasn't sure whether to laugh or not. Andie was serious, but she was way off base. If she knew Katherine's real secret, they'd be having a very different conversation.

Katherine shook her head. "I don't know him. Or I didn't. But he did talk to us. I've been trying to get Dillon to tell you guys, but he thinks it's his job to deal with Perry. He said the rest of you have enough to worry about, and being the CEO means dealing with things like competitors."

"You don't agree?" Andie asked.

"Agree about what?" Kristen asked as she joined them. She grabbed her water and drained the glass. "Did you guys order yet?"

Andie shook her head. "Not yet. I'm not sure they saw us over here. We wanted to sit near the windows, and it's quieter in here."

"I'll go find someone," Kristen said. "And get some more water."

Kristen carried her glass into the other room where the kitchen was. Once she was out of sight, Andie repeated her question. "You don't agree with Dillon's opinion?"

Katherine stalled for time with a sip of her wine. It was damn good, crisp with a hint of depth that reminded her she wasn't drinking a bottle of some expensive wine that someone thought was fit for her. She was just drinking delicious wine from a family of amazing people.

"Katherine."

"Fine, no. I don't agree. I think you guys are all in this together. He's not just the CEO, he's your brother. And Kristen's cousin. You all have your jobs, but that doesn't mean you each operate in a vacuum. It would be insane to do things that way."

"That's how our dad always was," Andie admitted. "He thought no one else needed to know certain things and hid them from the others."

"You knew that?"

Andie nodded. "I overheard him talking to Dillon about it once. It kind of pissed me off. I love my dad, and we've always gotten along better than I have with my mom, but I don't like the idea of hiding things. Maybe it's necessary in some businesses, but not this one."

Katherine took another sip and nodded. "That's what I told him. If it makes you feel better, he told Sean about Perry."

"Sean? Really?"

Katherine nodded again. "Yesterday. They were talking about Dillon working in the fields today and he said something. He stopped by Sean's on the way home and asked him not to tell anyone, though."

Andie groaned. "He still thinks we're children."

Katherine chuckled. "I don't think that's it."

Andie shrugged. "Maybe not, but that's how it feels. We're family. I know he's a private person, but this is business."

"Business shouldn't be personal."

"Then we shouldn't have agreed to run it. We're family. Everything is personal."

"What's personal?" Kristen asked. "I ordered for all of us. Hope that's okay."

Andie and Katherine nodded.

"What's personal?" Kristen asked again.

"Business," Andie said. "You were right about Perry. Dillon is still trying to protect us. He didn't want us to know."

"You and me, us, or everyone?"

"Everyone. Although Sean knows."

"Why is he doing this?" Kristen asked.

"He thinks it's his job," Andie explained. "I get it, but it's bigger than one job. If I need to hire someone, I don't just deal with it, I talk to everyone. But if I need new linens, it's small, so I order them. I think it's the magnitude. He should let us help when it's something this big. Something that impacts the entire vineyard."

"I'm going to go yell at him," Kristen said, rising from her seat.

"Don't!" Katherine begged, grabbing Kristen's arm. "Please don't. He'll be mad if he knows I told you guys about this. Just let him tell you when he's ready."

"What do we do in the meantime? How do we handle Perry? And do you know him?" Kristen asked.

"Watch for Perry. Protect Amavita Estates. And give Dillon chances to talk to you. And no, I don't know Perry. I met him the night you saw us talking to him. I'm not a spy or anyone else like that. I'm just a regular person on vacation."

The lie left a bitter taste in Katherine's mouth. A taste she couldn't get rid of. Not after her wine or her lunch. The only thing that would make it go away was telling the truth.

And she couldn't do that.

---

DILLON RUSHED HOME THAT NIGHT, ANXIOUS TO SEE Katherine. One more night was not enough time with her, and he wanted to make the most of it.

He pulled up in front of his house and heard music coming from inside. He smiled to himself at the idea of Katherine dancing around his house in one of his dress shirts and a pair of socks like Tom Cruise in Risky Business.

Dillon opened his front door and froze. Katherine wasn't

in one of his dress shirts. Instead she was wearing a tight tank top and a pair of his boxers. Dillon stared as she climbed over his couch, posed on the edge of a bar stool, and ran around the room. She declared, along with Taylor Swift, that she and her ex were never getting back together. Her voice was perfectly in sync with Taylor's, and Dillon knew deep in his gut that she would one day live her dream of being a professional singer.

"Oh, shit," Katherine said, startled to see Dillon at the door watching her. Her lips curled up into a smile as he approached. "I didn't know you were home."

Dillon pulled her into his arms and started dancing along to the opening bars of the new song coming on. He knew the song well, a heartfelt love song by Lee Brice. The words seeped into his soul as he held Katherine's hand in his, his other hand splayed over her back. A woman had never felt more right in his arms and as his baritone mixed with Lee Brice's voice, he told Katherine what his life would have been like if he'd never met her.

When the song ended, Dillon and Katherine wrapped their arms around each other, holding on tight as though the other might let go. Her heart pounded against his chest, and her breath pulsed out of her, clearly as affected by the power of the song and their dancing as he was.

Dillon buried his face in her hair, desperate for every part of her. He ached for her, not just in his shorts, but in his heart. As he held her tight, her curvy figure molding right into him, Dillon knew he couldn't ever let her go.

With his lips against her ear, he couldn't stop from whispering, "I love you, Katherine."

She squeezed him tighter and buried her face in his neck. Tears soaked into his skin. "I love you, Dillon," she whispered.

He smiled against her neck and let out the breath he'd

been holding. His lips found hers in a soft kiss. His tongue caressed hers while his hands covered her body, not frantic, just exploring. Dillon knew he could be with her every day for the rest of his life and still not feel as though he had seen, kissed, or touched enough of her.

Katherine melted into him and gave back everything he asked for. Her tears slipped between their lips, leaving behind a salty taste. Dillon wanted to kiss her forever, to take away all her tears and to leave her with only joy in her world. He wanted her to be his forever.

When she left, he would never be the same again, and he knew it.

When Dillon pulled back he clasped the sides of her head and stared deep into her chocolate eyes. "I'm so happy to hear that. As much as I hate to stop what we've started here, I'm starving. And we're both going to need fuel because I have big plans for you tonight."

Katherine laughed and pecked him on the lips. "I made dinner already. I hope that's okay. I figured you would be hungry after working the vines all day. I still can't believe you did it."

Dillon grinned as he uncorked a bottle of Amavita pinot. "I could just hide in my office, but I hate being cooped up in there. I spend too much time in there. Today was amazing."

Katherine smiled. He hadn't been so excited about work the entire week she'd known him. He finally sounded like he enjoyed what he did. Like he wasn't just a talking suit. The man she met in the bar, and the guy who invited her into his home, were the man she fell for. The guy she'd watched go to work all week was a different person. A person Katherine knew all too well because she was surrounded by them. People who thought they were doing the best thing for Kate Maddox but never bothered to ask what she wanted. Katherine liked the real Dillon better.

"What did you do today?"

Dillon poured two glasses of wine and handed her one. He kissed her lightly on the lips and pulled back with another grin. "I didn't do anything special. I trimmed vines and ran some tests and enjoyed being outside. I need to see if Sean will do this more often."

"I'm sure he will. I think we all need a change from the every day once in a while."

Dillon set his wine down and nodded. "Unless you were my every day. I'd never need a change from you."

Katherine forced a smile even though it hurt to hear him say that. She wanted to tell him who she was, but she kept quiet. He kissed her again, then they sat and ate the dinner she cooked. The whole time, he talked about how great it was to be outside, and she kept quiet. Her heart told her she was making the wrong decision and to confess everything. Her head said to shut up.

She listened to her head.

"Are you okay?" Dillon asked after the cleaned up dinner and were sitting on the couch watching TV.

Katherine nodded.

"Are you thinking about leaving tomorrow?"

She nodded again, trying to hold back the tears that threatened to ruin their night.

"If it makes it better, I don't want you to go either."

She breathed a laugh and leaned into his side. He tugged her closer and held her as they watched TV.

Katherine didn't see the screen. She tried to focus on whatever he was watching, but she couldn't. She warred with herself until she gave herself a headache.

"Are you ready to go to bed?"

Katherine nodded and stood. They went into his bedroom together, and she nearly burst into tears. She had one more night. One night to be with him. One night to hold on to as many memories as possible. Then she'd never see him again.

It was for the best.

It just didn't feel like it.

---

DILLON WANTED THE NIGHT TO LAST FOREVER. HE STRIPPED slowly, as though he could delay the inevitable. When he was down to his briefs only, he pulled Katherine into his arms. She trembled against him, her tears soaking his chest.

"Don't cry, sweetheart."

"I don't want to leave you."

He nodded and kissed her neck. "Don't think about that now. We still have tonight. Tonight it's just you and me. There's no tomorrow. Just tonight."

"Just tonight," she whispered.

She tilted her face up to his for a kiss. He cupped her jaw delicately, committing the feel of her skin to his memory. Her tongue brushed his lips, prompting them to part. He loved her. And her leaving wouldn't change that. Nothing would.

They moved to the bed together. His muscles ached as he stretched out over her, reminding him of the labor he did all day. It felt good, but not nearly as good as the woman writhing beneath him.

"I need you inside me," Katherine whispered, reaching between them to wrap her hand around him. "I can't wait."

Dillon pushed off her and kicked out of his briefs. He released the clasp on her bra and eased her panties down her legs, leaving nothing between them. He rolled a condom on and settled between her legs again.

"I love you, Katherine."

She cupped his jaw and drew him down to her. "I love you," she whispered against his lips.

He slid into her, her channel slick and ready for him. He groaned, his eyes falling closed against the sensations rolling through him.

They made love slowly, their bodies moving together. He drew her knee up to his side, running his hand down her soft thigh. Her breath hitched as he went a little deeper, her body opened more to him. She dug her heel into his lower back. He squeezed her thigh and trailed his fingers down to her ass. He tilted her hips up and filled her even more.

She moaned softly, her arms tightening around his neck. He kissed down her damp cheek to her ear and nibbled the lobe. As he stroked inside her, he kissed her skin, sucking and licking and nibbling her as they built to orgasm together.

"Dillon," she whispered, begging.

He knew what she wanted, what she needed. He knew everything about her. Everything that mattered. He eased his hand between them and slid his thumb over her clit. She stilled for a second, then shivered and dragged her nails down his back.

"Yes, Dillon. Oh, yes."

He pushed up so he could slide deeper into her. He looked down to watch his cock disappear into her body. It was the most erotic thing he'd ever seen. He captured her clit between two of his fingers and tugged on it, and she moaned.

"Dillon. Oh, God. Dillon. I need to kiss you. Please."

He flattened his hand and crashed his mouth onto hers. She clawed at him, holding him tight until her channel clamped down on him and she broke their kiss with a scream.

"Yes! Dillon, yes! Oh, God. Oh, shit. Fuck, Dillon!"

He was close. Close enough that the feel of her coming tipped him from painfully aware of how badly he wanted to come to unable to hold back for another second. He pounded into her, his cock in control of his body. She locked eyes with him and cupped his jaw, right there with him as his orgasm shook him to his core.

His balls pulled up tight and erupted into her. He yelled her name as he emptied himself. He couldn't fathom the thought that it was one of the last times he'd be inside her. It wasn't an option. It wasn't okay. She was his, and he was hers.

Dillon collapsed on top of her and buried his face in her neck. He knew nothing would ever feel as good as being with Katherine felt. He never thought he'd find someone who was there for him and didn't see him as a money train. Someone who loved him because of who he was instead of who he was related to. But he found her.

And she had to leave him.

He rolled off a few minutes later and threw the condom away. When he crawled into bed with her, Katherine curled up against his side.

"Am I ever going to see you again?"

Dillon ran a hand down her back and squeezed her hip. "We'll find a way."

"Will we?"

Dillon nodded. He had to believe they could figure things out. He wasn't ready to let her go, and she felt the same. "It might not be easy, but we'll make it work."

"No matter what. Do you promise me? No matter what, we'll always love each other and try."

Dillon tugged her tighter against his side. "I promise, Katherine. I promise."

# 20

Dillon stirred before the sun the next morning. He did not want to get up and leave Katherine. They were up almost the entire night, and he wasn't ready to let her go.

He sat up and grabbed his phone on instinct. He was surprised to see a missed text from Sean.

> Stay home today. Enjoy the day with
> Katherine. If I could have one more day with
> Ang, I'd do anything to have it. I'm giving you
> yours. I've got the vineyard.

Dillon smiled and thumbed a quick *Thanks* back, then burrowed under the covers to wake Katherine up in the best way he could think of.

With his mouth between her sexy thighs.

They both fell back to sleep fully satiated and exhausted after a few orgasms for her and a teeth-rattling one for him.

Hours later, Katherine stirred beside him. Dillon tugged her against his side and kissed her head. "Don't go."

She froze.

"Sorry," he mumbled sleepily. "I meant right now. Stay in

bed with me a little longer. I'd never ask you to give up your dreams."

"You know I would, right?" she asked, her fingers slipping over his chest.

"Would what?"

"I'd give it all up for you."

Dillon shook his head. "You'd resent me. Live your dreams. When July rolls around and I can leave this place, I'll visit you. Everyone says long distance is hard, but we'll find a way to make it work."

She nodded. "I hope so. Just remember what you promised me."

"I will love you even if you become a diva superstar and change your name to something ridiculous."

She didn't laugh with him.

"Hey, I'm joking. You'd never be a diva."

She shrugged. "You never know."

Dillon shook his head. "I know you. That's not the kind of person you are. I love you. We'll make this work. Stop worrying about it."

She nodded and pushed out of bed. When she got to the door to the bathroom, she looked back at him. "Up for a shower?"

He grinned and ran after her, kissing her as they let the water heat up, then made her scream his name under the spray.

***

QUYNN WOKE UP LATE. LATER THAN SHE EVER DID. HER EYES were still puffy from crying all night, and her head pounded like someone was driving a train through her skull.

She checked her phone even though she knew he

wouldn't call. Frank said what he needed to say. They disagreed, but it was unforgivable to him.

She got it, in a way, but he didn't know how things were for Katherine. He didn't get that Quynn was just trying to protect her friend. She could care less about Kate Maddox and the secret. She wanted Katherine to be happy, and that meant keeping her secret because it was what Katherine wanted.

Quynn called room service to send her up some breakfast and checked her email. Kate Maddox's show was the next night. Katherine would be at the hotel later that day. Quynn had to be on top of everything.

While she waited for breakfast, she confirmed the interviews she scheduled for the following week and called Kate's lawyer.

"I need to speak to Mr. Powers," Quynn told the receptionist.

"I'm sorry. He's unavailable right now."

"This is Quynn O'Hara."

"I'm sorry, Ms. O'Hara. I didn't realize it was you."

"It's fine," Quynn said to the dead line. She was already being transferred.

"Ms. O'Hara. What can I do for you today?"

"Hi, Gary. We're in a world of shit."

"You mean besides Kate Maddox falling off the face of the earth? I assumed that wasn't a family thing like the press said. Then again, they all assumed it, too."

"Yeah," Quynn said, rubbing her temples. "But that's not why I'm calling. Christian Blake is threatening to tell everyone who she is."

"Christian Blake?"

Quynn sighed. "Yeah."

"Jeez, Quynn. How did that happen?"

"He wants her back, and she's not interested."

"So he's going to tell the whole world who she really is?"

"Apparently. And they say a woman scorned is the one to watch out for."

Gary snorted. "No woman has anything on Christian Blake. He's a sniveling twerp. What did she ever see in him?"

Quynn shook her head. "I wish I knew. Thankfully, she's come to her senses, but now we have to deal with it."

"Are you in town?"

"Yeah. I've been here all week."

"Okay, good. Come in now. I'll clear my schedule for the day. We'll figure this out together. Bring any paperwork you have."

"You mean bring my laptop?"

Gary snorted. "Yeah, bring your laptop."

"I'll be there in an hour."

"Great. It'll be nice to finally meet you."

"You, too."

Quynn hung up and felt better. It was good to know she had someone in her corner. Katherine hired Gary as her lawyer before she and Quynn met. He was a family friend that Katherine knew she could trust. He'd become a friend of Quynn's over the years also, but they'd never been in the same city.

Quynn ate her breakfast and took a quick shower. She was out the door in thirty minutes and on her way to Gary's office. When she walked in, the receptionist immediately fawned over her, asking about a lunch order and bringing her a cup of coffee and a bottle of water as she showed Quynn into Gary's large office.

"It's nice to finally put a face to the voice," Gary said when Quynn walked in. "It's been far too long since we've met."

Quynn walked straight into Gary's embrace and welcomed his brief hug. "It has been. There aren't many people who know both sides of her. I wish we'd met a while ago."

"I do as well. And thank you for the tickets to the show tomorrow. I'm assuming there's still going to be a show?"

Quynn nodded. "She promised me she'll be here. How excited were the girls when you told them you had tickets?"

"Not just tickets, but back stage passes. I'm not sure who screamed louder, the girls or my wife."

Quynn laughed. "Will I get to meet them tomorrow?"

Gary nodded. "Absolutely. Nancy wants to thank you for everything."

Quynn waved her hand. "Oh, please. It's the least we can do."

"We still appreciate it, Quynn. Now, let's figure out what we can do about this Christian Blake situation."

Quynn took the seat he gestured to at the table near the window. He had a nice view of the city. Quynn saw a police car fly down the street, lights flashing, and had to close her eyes. She'd never look at another cop without thinking about Frank.

"Are you okay?"

She forced a grin and nodded. "Good. Let's get started. We need to bury Christian Blake before he has a chance to hurt her. She deserves more than this."

"Especially from him."

"Agreed. So what can we do?"

"Show me what you've got and we'll figure it out."

---

Katherine packed in silence. She felt Dillon watching her, but she refused to look at him. She'd lose it if she saw his face.

When she woke up and he was still there, she wasn't sure

if she was happy or sad. She said her goodbyes when they made love all night long. Every kiss, every orgasm, every touch was in love. She loved him.

Which made it that much harder to keep her secret from him.

Maybe it really was for the best. If she told him, he wouldn't want to see her again. He would tell her to her face that he was done. If he found out another way, she could convince herself that their week together wasn't what she thought it was. That she was in love with him, but he was just saying it.

Then he could move on and be happy. And she could go back to her lonely life.

More songs danced in her mind all night long. Songs she wanted to write. Dillon was an inspiration to her that she never realized she was missing from her life. As the week wore on, she imagined settling at Amavita with Dillon. Maybe even writing songs with him. She'd been looking for a new place to settle. Having a home in New York was a good idea, but the city never appealed to her. Syracuse was too far from New York City, but Amavita and Bereton wasn't as bad.

She couldn't decide any of that until she knew how Dillon really felt, about all of her.

"Will you call me when you get to wherever you need to go today?"

Katherine nodded. "I will." She wanted to tell him where she was going, but even that tiny bit of information would trigger more questions than she was willing to answer. If she heard from him after the concert, she would know he was willing to take her for who she was.

She zipped up her suitcase and straightened to face him. Dillon was watching her, his eyes locked on hers. He opened his arms and she walked right into them, holding on to him tightly.

"We'll see each other again soon," he whispered into her hair.

She nodded.

"Do you need a ride?"

She shook her head. "I called a ride."

"You did?"

"Yeah. My friend is going to be here any minute."

Quynn was more than a little shocked when Katherine called and asked her to pick her up from the vineyard, but she agreed without questioning it. She knew Quynn would be there soon.

"I could have taken you wherever you needed to go."

She smiled. "I know. But I might not have been able to say goodbye."

"Then don't. We'll see each other soon. July is only a month away."

A horn beeped outside. Their time was up. Quynn was there.

"Remember your promise."

Dillon chuckled softly and pulled her into his arms. "I promise you, Katherine. I love you."

He kissed her slowly. She gave him everything she had, hoping it was enough when he learned the truth.

"I love you," she said when she pulled back.

He grabbed her suitcase and carried it outside for her. Quynn popped the trunk but didn't get out of the car. Katherine knew why. There were times Quynn was more easily recognized than Katherine was. If Dillon realized who Quynn was, it would blow Katherine's cover.

He slammed the trunk and hugged her again. "I'll see you soon."

She nodded against his chest. "I know," she said, then got in the car.

Quynn didn't say anything as she drove away. Katherine

watched Dillon in the mirror until he disappeared, then she cried.

"You love him, don't you?" Quynn finally asked.

Katherine nodded. "I do."

"Did you tell him who you are?"

Katherine shook her head. "He'll find out tomorrow."

"How?" Quynn asked, her brows drawing together in question.

"Because I wrote a song while I was there."

"You did? That's awesome. Congratulations!"

"Thanks. I have so many ideas for songs. I feel like I could release a new album with songs for Dillon."

"You should. You've always wanted to play your own music."

"I'm going to play the song I wrote at the concert tomorrow night."

Quynn nodded. "Good. Put it out there. Don't sit on it and risk someone taking it. If he heard the song, he could always take it to a studio and try to sell it. Of course, he could anyway. He won't know you're singing it at the concert."

"He's going to the concert."

"Shit. Really?"

Katherine nodded.

"So he's going to know who you are?" Quynn asked, his voice rising in panic.

Katherine nodded again. "I trust him Quynn. He's not like Christian. He's a good person."

"But you didn't tell him who you were."

Katherine shook her head. "I was too scared. He doesn't want my life. This way I can walk away and tell myself it's not me, it's Kate that he doesn't want."

Quynn sighed heavily. "I know exactly how you feel."

"What do you mean?"

Quynn glanced over at her. The weariness in her friend's eyes his Katherine hard.

"Who?"

"Frank."

"Frank? My brother?"

Quynn nodded. "Yep. I'm telling myself it's not me he doesn't want, it's Kate's assistant."

"What happened, Quynn?"

She shrugged. "He overheard me talking to you the other day about Dillon. He's hot, by the way, from what I could see."

"Yeah, he is," Katherine said with a sad smile.

"Anyway, Frank heard me telling you not to tell Dillon about Kate, and he got pissed. Said he thought I was a different person and that lies and manipulation weren't the way he wanted to live his life."

"Ah, shit, Quynn. Are you okay?"

She sniffed and shook her head. "No, but I will be."

Katherine reached over and grabbed Quynn's hand. "Love sucks, doesn't it?"

Quynn laughed and nodded. "Oh, yeah. Absolutely."

They talked and laughed the rest of the drive to Syracuse. Quynn filled Katherine in on everything that happened with Frank and Christian, and Katherine shared how she fell for Dillon. By the time they walked into the hotel suite, they were ready for dinner and a bottle of wine.

"I wonder if they have Amavita Estates wine here," Quynn said.

Katherine shrugged. "Doubtful, but we can ask."

They ordered room service and were told that no, the hotel did not serve Amavita Estates wine. They ordered a bottle of pinot from a different vineyard to go with their dinner and changed into the plush robes the hotel provided while waiting for their food to arrive.

"Are you going to sing the song for me?" Quynn asked.

Katherine sighed. "I don't know. Do you want to hear it?"

"Of course. I loved the song you wrote with Christian. I know this one will be a lot better because it's actually someone you love."

Katherine nodded. "I do love him. It was really hard to leave him."

Quynn hugged her and rested their heads together. "Yep, I'm right there with you."

"Well, my brother is an idiot. I know he was hurt, but that doesn't mean you're going to hurt him."

Quynn shrugged. "In his mind it does."

A knock on the door saved Katherine from answering. Quynn let the server in while Katherine hid in the bathroom so he didn't see her. When he was gone, Quynn called out that Katherine could come out.

They focused on dinner and found an old romantic comedy on the TV.

"Do you think he'll call me?" Katherine asked softly.

Quynn look at her and shrugged. "I don't know. I hope so."

"Should I have told him who I was?"

Quynn shook her head. "No. I know you don't like that answer, but you don't know who he really is. It's possible he'd be just as big of a threat as Christian."

Katherine scrunched up her face. "He wouldn't have been."

"Listen, I'm not the one who wants you to keep this secret. But it is my job to make sure it's kept."

Katherine nodded. "I know. I don't know what I'd do without you."

"Lucky for you, I have no one else in my life."

Katherine laughed sadly with Quynn. "I'm right there with you."

DILLON STARED AT HIS PHONE ALL NIGHT. HE GOT A TEXT from Katherine earlier, but it was just a quick *I'm here.* No details about where she actually was. It came less than three hours after she left him, so she was still close, but there were a lot of places she could be.

He thought about calling her but didn't want to come across as desperate. He'd never been the one left behind and wanting more. He knew Katherine didn't want to go, but that only made it worse. If she didn't want to leave, why did she have to? She said she was working on her music career. She was talented, sure, but she didn't tell him what was so pressing that she couldn't wait for July so he could go with her.

Dillon paced his living room, an idea forming in his mind. He looked at his phone again and was about to make a call when there was a knock on the door.

He rushed to it, a grin already in place.

It slid off when he saw Sean, Jake, and Cody on his doorstep.

"Nice to see you, too, asshole," Cody said, pushing his way inside. "Got any food?"

Dillon sighed and stepped back to let Jake and Sean in. "Where's Em?"

"Andie, Kristen, and Alyssa are having a girls' night in. Em and Summer are staying the night."

"Gianna's not with them?"

"Date night."

"You mean sex night," Cody said around a mouthful of something. "I need one of those. Someone needs to find Kristen a guy so Andie and I can have the house to ourselves sometime."

"Ugh, stop!" Dillon and Sean said. They looked at each other and laughed.

"I don't know how you put up with that," Sean said. "I'd throw up thinking about them having sex all the time."

"I try not to think about it," Dillon admitted. "What are you guys all doing here?"

"They're having girls' night. Where else would we be?" Jake said.

Dillon nodded and grabbed a beer. Cody and Jake were already on the couch, arguing about what to watch. Sean hung back in the kitchen with Dillon.

"You okay?"

Dillon shrugged.

"Have you heard from her?"

Dillon nodded. "She's wherever she was going."

"She didn't tell you?"

"Nope."

"You think something's going on that you don't know about?"

"I think a lot is going on that I don't know about."

"Think she's seeing someone else?"

Dillon shrugged again. "I have no idea. Anything's possible."

"Don't give up on her already. She said she'd stay in touch. We'll go to the concert tomorrow night and have a good time, and you can figure it out after that."

"I guess." He laughed. "One day I'll be going to Katherine's concert and saying I used to know her."

"Or maybe you'll be backstage with her."

"Yeah, right."

Sean shrugged. "You never know. Anything is possible."

Dillon laughed. "If she ever hits it big, I won't be a part of it. I couldn't handle that life, but more than that, I can't imagine leaving here."

Sean lowered his voice. "We can handle things. You don't have to be the only one working."

"It's not fair to walk away. We've all worked too hard for this."

"Yeah, we have. But if she's the person you want to be with, do whatever you need to do to be with her. We can always hire someone to do our jobs. There's no reason you have to be the only one in charge."

"I can't do that to everyone."

"Yes, you can. I wouldn't still be here if Ang lived and wanted to move somewhere else."

"She grew up here. Where would she have wanted to go?"

Sean shrugged. "We talked about moving a lot. She didn't have a good relationship with her parents, and she always wanted to travel. I don't think we would have stayed here."

"Wow. I never knew that."

Sean sipped his beer and nodded. "She was like Alyssa. She wanted more than Bereton had to offer. When we found out she was pregnant, she was depressed for a long time. She saw all her dreams going away. By the time we found the cancer, she was head over heels for Emily and would do anything for her. That's why she refused treatment. She wanted to live, but she wanted Emily to live more."

"Shit. How did I not know any of this?"

Sean clapped him on the back. "Because you think you need to protect us. There's nothing you can protect me from that's worse than losing the woman I loved."

Dillon took a deep breath and let Sean's words sink in. He'd treated his cousins and siblings like they were children for a long time. He knew things needed to change, and the only way they would was if he changed them.

Then he could go to Katherine, and nothing would stand between them.

## 21

Frank sipped his coffee and pretended he didn't miss Quynn. He was still pissed off that she would lie. There was never a situation where lying was okay. Especially if you loved someone.

"Good morning, honey," his mom said as she walked into the kitchen. "Are you coming to lunch with us?"

Frank shook his head. "First I'm hearing of it."

"Katherine called last night. She said she and Quynn wanted us to join them for lunch today. I just assumed Quynn told you."

"Why would she tell me?"

Kelly shrugged. "Why wouldn't she? Aren't you two seeing each other?"

Frank huffed a laugh. "Nope."

"Well, what happened?"

Frank loved his mom. Really loved her. But he was not willing to discuss his relationships, or lack thereof, with his mother. If she knew anything, she'd hold it over him forever. It took him months to convince her that calling Anna to reconcile was not a good idea. And that was only because he finally admitted she'd cheated on him.

"We live in two very different worlds, Mom. Two worlds that aren't going to cross over again."

"Well, sure they will. If you go to lunch."

"Mom," he warned.

"Oh, don't 'Mom' me. I worry about you and your sister. Neither of you has found anyone worthy of your time. This Quynn woman is very sweet and your sister adores her. I know you liked her, too. I saw you two kissing."

"You were spying on us?"

Kelly shook her head, her graying bob swinging into her face. She swept the stray hairs back and leveled Frank with her green eyes. "I was not spying. You were kissing in *my* kitchen."

Frank ducked his chin and avoided her eyes. "Sorry."

Kelly patted him on the shoulder. "I thought she was different. I thought she was good for you."

"Yeah," Frank agreed. "I thought so, too."

"I'm sorry, Frank. You're still coming to the concert, though, right?"

He nodded. "Wouldn't miss it."

"Good," his mom said. She patted his shoulder again, then carried her coffee out of the kitchen.

Frank closed his eyes for a moment and listened to his parents' mumbled voices upstairs. When he and Katherine were little, they would make up conversations they thought their parents were having, especially when they were in trouble.

He smiled at the memory and looked around. He couldn't imagine the house without his parents. He understood why they wanted to sell it, but it was hard to imagine it not being a safe place for him. He could always ask his parents if he could have it, but he'd already gotten enough charity from them. Plus, Katherine deserved her share.

Frank thought about going to lunch. He couldn't lie to himself and say he didn't want to see Quynn again, but he wasn't sure he could face her without getting upset. Or forgiving her for something he believed was unforgivable. The best thing was definitely to just stay away from her.

He finished his coffee and went down to his room. He'd already started looking for a new place. He felt like he was stuck. He didn't like any of the options he found for new places to live, and even his work felt like another thing to do. He admired his sister and the way she'd chased her dreams. She had her own set of problems, but Frank wished he had something in his life that brought him half the excitement that singing always brought Katherine.

Maybe one day.

---

"ARE YOU SURE? YOU CAN STAY WITH US NEXT WEEK. WE know it's not as nice as one of these fancy hotels you like to stay in."

Katherine shook her head at her mom. "It's fine, Mom. I don't always stay in nice places like this. Around a show it's almost a requirement. When we're paying this much for a suite, we know they'll be discrete."

"Your privacy is very important. I'd hate for more men like that Christian fellow to show up," her dad said.

Katherine nodded. "I agree. I'm sorry you guys had to deal with him."

"He was fine," Kelly said. "A bit of a jerk, but nothing we couldn't handle. I felt badly for you, Quynn. He was not happy to see you."

Katherine hugged her friend. "She never liked him. Told me a lot not to trust him."

"But she never listened," Quynn said.

Katherine shook her head. "Nope. I didn't. I thought I was in love with him. God, I was so stupid. If I had any clue what love was really like, I never would have spent so much time with Christian."

"It sounds like you have an idea. Does that mean you met someone?" her mom asked.

Katherine nodded slowly. "I did, but I'm not sure it's going to work out."

"Well, if anyone can figure out how to make things work, it's definitely you, Katie."

"Thanks, Dad. I hope so."

"Is he another famous person?" Kelly asked.

Katherine and Quynn both shook their heads.

"No. His family owns a vineyard."

"Oh, no. Don't tell me you're moving to Italy or something."

Katherine laughed. "No, Mom. The vineyard is on Cayuga Lake."

"That's only a couple hours from here. How did you meet him? Wait, you were with him, weren't you?"

Katherine nodded.

"Where is he? Why isn't he with you today?"

"Because he doesn't know the other side of her," Quynn supplied.

Katherine's parents swung their eyes to her and recognition dawned.

"You didn't tell him?"

Katherine shook her head. "After Christian... I don't know him that well."

"Well, if you love him, you'll work it out."

Katherine nodded and stepped into her father's open

arms. "I hope so."

"We gotta go," Quynn said. "I'm sorry."

Katherine hugged her parents and apologized.

"No need to apologize. We're glad we could see both of you for lunch. Quynn, we hope you'll stay with us next week also. You're always welcome."

"Thanks, Mr. and Mrs. Price. I appreciate it."

They hugged Katherine and Quynn again then left. Katherine offered to get them a room at the hotel for the night since the concert was a short walk away, but they said they'd rather be home for the night. They were going to wander around the city for a little while and do some shopping, then meet Katherine at the concert.

"You ready to change?" Quynn asked her.

Katherine took a deep breath and nodded.

They gathered everything they needed for Katherine to become Kate Maddox and walked to the convention center arena.

Quynn flashed her badge at the security guard at the door, and they found the dressing room she'd requested for Kate. With the door locked, they got to work.

"I'm so sick of this," Katherine admitted as Quynn struggled to clip one of her extensions in the right spot.

"Then tell everyone who you are."

Katherine sighed. "Am I going to get mobbed constantly?"

Quynn nodded. "Yes. You will. But you also won't have people like Christian threatening you."

"Have you heard from him lately?"

Quynn shook her head but didn't meet Katherine's eye.

"What happened?"

"What do you mean?" Quynn asked, her focus on Katherine's hair.

Katherine yanked her hair out of Quynn's hands and forced her to meet her eyes. "What happened?"

"I went to see Gary."

"Okay. Why didn't you want to tell me that?"

Quynn took a deep breath, then blurted, "Because we sent a cease and desist letter to Christian's attorney. Gary said we have a case if he says something, but we wanted to make sure he won't. We also have some questions prepped for you to answer next week in your interviews about him."

"What kind of questions?"

Quynn shrugged and moved to the other side of the room. "Nothing big, really."

"Then why won't you tell me what they are?"

Quynn sighed and faced Katherine. "I was going to tell you before you went on. Nothing is bad. Just questions to tell the truth about your relationship. He's not good for you. I want you to tell everyone the truth about who he is."

"What are you talking about? He doesn't have a secret identity."

Quynn grinned. "Yeah, he does. It might not be a new name like yours, but he's different when he's with you. He's not the guy that's managed to charm half the country."

"Quynn, I can't."

"Actually, you can. And you will."

"Quynn—"

"No, Katherine. You've put up with shit from him long enough. You don't deserve this. You need to tell everyone how you two worked together and he stole the song. And how he's threatening to tell everyone who you really are if you don't give him the rights to it. He shouldn't be able to do this. Nothing you say will be stretched or embellished. Just the facts. People should know who he is."

"I'll think about it."

Quynn nodded. "That's the best I could hope for right now. Now, let's get these extensions in and your makeup done so you can go on stage."

DILLON REALLY DIDN'T FEEL LIKE GOING TO THE CONCERT, BUT he didn't have a good excuse. They all drove up together in two vehicles, which meant Dillon didn't get a second of peace in the ninety minute drive.

"I heard this is the hotel Kate Maddox is actually staying at," Kristen gushed when they parked. "How cool would it be if we saw her here?"

Kate Maddox. Dillon smiled to himself. When they bought the tickets, he had fantasies about Kate Maddox. She was his ideal woman until he met Katherine. Before her, he'd have jumped all over the idea of seeing Kate Maddox. But after Katherine, not even Kate Maddox tempted him.

"I doubt she'll be anywhere near any of us. They probably have big suites that take up a whole floor for her and her entourage," Ian said.

"True," Kristen said with a pout.

"Still, it'd be pretty cool if we saw her," Andie said. "I always wondered what she'd be like. I picture her as this down to earth person. Like she doesn't tell anyone who she really is because she wants to be real when she's not on stage. You should tell Katherine to do that if she ever becomes famous."

"That's who she reminds me of," Cody blurted. "I've been trying to figure that out since I met her. She reminds me of Kate Maddox."

"Who does?"

"Katherine."

"They don't look anything alike," Andie argued. "Kate has that long hair, and Katherine's was kind of short. And Kate's so flashy. Katherine isn't like that at all."

Dillon listened to the conversation around him trying to

figure out if Cody could be right. He tried to imagine the two of them together, and his friend had a point.

They were nearly identical.

"Shit," Dillon said.

"What?" Andie asked.

"I think he's right. I think Katherine is Kate Maddox. It makes sense. She had to leave. Kate Maddox was MIA. She wants to be a singer. She never told me much about herself. She's from Syracuse. I'm an idiot."

"No, you're not," Cody argued. "How many people would think their one night stand was really a famous singer? Or that a famous singer would show up at Amavita? It's not her."

"You said it was."

"No," Cody corrected. "I said she reminded me of Kate Maddox. I didn't say Katherine was Kate Maddox."

"Yeah, but she is. I know she is," Dillon said.

---

KATE DID HER BREATHING EXERCISES AND WARMED UP HER vocal chords. She listened to the faint hum of noise from the crowd as her opening act left the stage.

"All clear," Quynn said.

Kate nodded. She'd practiced her new song for Quynn, and Quynn cried. She said it was the best song she'd ever heard. She talked Kate into playing it to close out the show during her second encore.

She was terrified.

And excited.

Kate was sure Dillon and the others were in the crowd. As soon as she played that song, their song, he would know who she was. She arranged for backstage passes for all of them, if they wanted to join her. She wasn't sure any of them would take her up on the offer, but she didn't want to hide behind herself. Not with them.

Kate ran through the song list in her mind. She knew her cues and her songs and how to get the crowd engaged. It was going to be a great show.

A knock on the door gave her the warning she needed. She locked eyes with Quynn and nodded.

"Kick ass out there," Quynn said, hugging Kate.

Kate squeezed her friend then smoothed down her top and headed for the stage.

The opening bars of her first song played. She tapped her toe with the beat, slipping effortlessly into her persona. Her extensions swung with her movements. She spotted her guitar on stage, in the center where she liked it by the drum set. She was ready.

The crowd roared as she stepped on to the stage. She couldn't stop her smile, forgetting all about Dillon and what she was getting ready to do.

***

DILLON WATCHED KATE MADDOX MOVE ACROSS THE STAGE. She danced, she sang, she talked to the audience. He studied her, barely listening to the things she said as much as he did the way she said them. Around him, everyone sang with Kate Maddox, the crowd perfectly in sync with her. But Dillon just watched.

When she left the stage for the first time, Cody leaned over to him. "I don't think that's Katherine, do you?"

Dillon nodded. "She does a good job of masking it, but yeah. I think it's her."

She came back out and played one of her biggest hits. Dillon watched the way she moved her hips. Their seats weren't good enough that he could see her face well, but the screens on both sides of the stage helped. They never got too close to her, probably so no one could recognize her, but there were subtleties that reminded him of Katherine.

They had the same eyes. Kate's lips were coated in lipstick, but Dillon studied them for a week. Hell, even her hands were Katherine's.

There was only the slightest doubt in his mind when she left the stage the second time. Dillon wanted to run up there and ask her, but he'd never get anywhere near her.

Then she returned.

"I know a lot of you are wondering about my last week."

The crowd shouted their agreement as Kate picked up the guitar behind her.

"I told the press I had a family emergency and had to be with them, but that wasn't really the truth. Can you guys keep a secret?"

Everyone yelled as lights flooded the crowd.

Kate smiled broadly. "Excellent. Thanks. The truth was I met someone. He's this amazing man, but he didn't know who I was. His family owns a vineyard and they're wonderful people. They took me in and welcomed me as one of their own. I've never known that before."

She choked up, pinching the bridge of her nose. The crowd cheered for her, but Dillon couldn't speak. Neither could the rest of them, all gaping at him.

"The problem now is that I've fallen for this guy, but he doesn't want to be involved with someone famous. So I left him yesterday. I'm hoping I'll see him again, especially because he's here tonight, but I have a feeling I screwed all this up. You guys know my track record with men isn't that great."

The crowd laughed. Dillon wanted to leave, but he was frozen in place.

"I wrote a song for him. A few of them actually, but only

one is finished. I was wondering if I could play it for you tonight."

Cheers and whistles echoed through the massive space. Kate's smile widened.

"Thanks guys. This is called Walk Of Fame."

She sat on a stool and played the first few chords. The chords he wrote. The song he'd played for her.

Then she sang.

*Lost and scared with nowhere to go*
*You took me in*
*Frozen pizza, fabulous wine*
*My soul began to heal*
*You told me I was beautiful*
*Made me believe it too*
*Dinner and dancing in your arms*
*Under the stars*

*I loved you true with all my heart*
*but couldn't go beyond our start.*
*I suffered through my walk of shame*
*to keep you from a walk of fame*

*Falling for you was like breathing*
*Love came easy*
*Your hands on me, your heart in mine*
*Your laugh, your smile, your kiss*
*You loving me, I felt so safe*
*I fell for you so fast*
*Like being on a roller coaster*
*Out of control*

*I loved you true with all my heart*
*but couldn't go beyond our start.*

*I suffered through my walk of shame*
*to keep you from a walk of fame*

*Your love helped me, gave me the strength*
*I faced my fear*
*The one who never showed me love*
*Undeserving of my trust*
*Abused my heart and made me doubt*
*You showed me what love should be*

*I loved you true with all my heart*
*but couldn't go beyond our start.*
*I suffered through my walk of shame*
*to keep you from a walk of fame*

*I couldn't put you through the fame*
*Life on display*
*Inside my head I said goodbye*
*I kissed you one last time*
*I knew it was the best for you*
*Even though my heart broke*
*I couldn't put you through the fame*
*I walked away*

*I loved you true with all my heart*
*but couldn't go beyond our start.*
*I suffered through my walk of shame*
*to keep you from a walk of fame*

When Kate played the last chords of the song, the entire arena was silent. Less than a second later, it erupted with noise from the crowd. Andie, Cody, Kristen, and Ian stared at Dillon. He shook his head and left.

2 2

KATE LEFT the stage with tears in her eyes. The crowd loved *Walk Of Fame*. She did, too. Singing it out there, just her and her guitar, the way she always imagined she would perform, felt better than anything she'd done on stage in a long time.

Quynn was waiting for her in the dressing room. "It sounded like the crowd loved it as much as I did."

Kate nodded. "They did. It felt so good to do it that way."

"You should get back to that."

Kate grinned. "I've been thinking the same thing."

They shared a smile but were interrupted by a knock on the door.

"Do you think it's him?" Kate asked.

Quynn shrugged. "One way to find out."

Quynn went to the door and stepped back when she saw who was on the other side. "Can I help you?"

"We were on the list, apparently. We're looking for Kath — um, Kate."

"Let them in," Kate said.

Andie and Kristen walked inside, looking amazing in the outfits they bought with Katherine just days before. Kate forced herself not to look behind them to see if Dillon was there, too.

"Wow. It really is you," Andie breathed.

"Shit. We took you shopping. You must have thought we were such idiots," Kristen said.

Kate shook her head. "No. I meant what I said on stage. Spending the week with your family was one of the best weeks of my life. When I'm like this," she gestured to her shiny pants and bedazzled top, "I'm not me, but everyone wants to know me. That's why I've never told anyone who I really was."

"We weren't important enough. We get it," Kristen said.

"It wasn't like that, Kristen."

She shook her head. "I've been lied to enough over the last year. I know how things like this work. And as hurt as I am, I can't even imagine how Dillon feels."

Kate's eyes flipped between the cousins. "Is he here?"

Andie shook her head sadly, but Kristen looked like she was going to kill someone.

"He left after your last song," Andie said.

"So he knows."

Andie nodded. "He figured it out on our way here. Cody said you reminded him of...well, you. And Dillon put it together. When you sang that song, he left."

"I never meant to hurt him," Kate said, reaching for Andie's hands.

She nodded. "I know. He has a lot of issues with trust."

Kate pulled in a breath. "I wanted to tell him."

"But you didn't," Kristen said. "You didn't tell him and he had to find out with thousands of other people that you're not who he thought you were. If you really loved him, you would have told him. I guess things work differently in your world, but in our world, the one you were slumming in for the last week, we talk to people. We tell people the truth. We don't hide massive parts of who we are."

"I didn't hide," Kate said, his voice trembling. "I'm exactly who I said I was."

"Yeah, except we all thought you were Katherine Price, aspiring singer. Not Kate Maddox, superstar."

"I am Katherine Price. That's my legal name. The name I grew up with. It's me. Kate Maddox is a stage name. Maddox was my mother's maiden name. It was close enough to my name that I didn't feel like I was hiding everything. Dillon, and you guys, you know me. Katherine is who I really am."

Kristen huffed a mirthless laugh. "Funny, you don't look like the Katherine I thought I knew. Come on, Andie."

Andie flashed Kate a sympathetic grin and followed her cousin out the door. It clicked behind them with finality that Kate knew meant she'd never see Dillon again.

"Are you okay?" Quynn asked.

Kate shrugged. "Just get me out of here. There's no sense hanging around. He's not coming."

---

Frank didn't know what it was, but something was telling him to stay close to his sister. He tried to brush it off as his cop sense working on overdrive, but the feeling wouldn't go away.

He saw a guy hanging around backstage that looked familiar in a way. He couldn't place him since he couldn't see his face, but there was something about the guy that had him thinking his instinct was right.

The door to Kate's dressing room opened and Quynn stepped into the hallway. She turned the opposite direction from where Frank was standing so she didn't see him. Fuck, it hurt to look at her. He wasn't that broken up when his ex-wife left him, but one fight with Quynn and he felt like someone took everything that mattered.

It would pass, he told himself.

He hoped.

He was so busy staring after Quynn that he almost missed the guy duck into Kate's dressing room.

Frank moved to the door and listened. If it was someone she knew, he wasn't going to break in there like a crazy, possessed ex. He was her big brother, not some guy who was going to be jealous of another guy in her dressing room.

"I said get out," Kate said firmly.

Laughing followed, but it got closer to the door. If she asked him again, Frank would go in. She didn't need him fighting her battles. She was strong.

The door opened, but no one walked out.

"I should have known you'd be off fucking some loser. It's even better that he doesn't want you. He knows you're used goods. And that song? You're never going to get another contract if you keep singing things like that."

"Go away, Christian."

Frank's head snapped up. Christian. Sonofabitch.

"Haven't I punched you somewhere before?" Frank asked, stepping into the room.

Christian Blake whirled on him, his eyes scanning Frank. His lips pulled back into a scowl, and he absently rubbed his cheek, a faint bruise visible beneath his makeup.

*Seriously? The guy wore makeup?*

"We were having a private conversation."

Frank shook his head. "It sounded to me like she asked you to leave. And your name wasn't on the list. So how did you get back here?"

Christian smirked. "Please. It doesn't take much to bribe a backstage security guard. Especially when I can tell them so much about Kate here."

"Guard!" Frank shouted, knowing there were a few lurking nearby. Kate never wanted full time security, but it was time she started thinking about it.

A massive man stepped in the room. His shoulders nearly brushed the door frame. So did his head.

"This man is not on the list, and he's harassing Kate. He needs to be removed. Unless she wants to press charges."

All eyes swung to Kate. She shook her head.

"You can file a restraining order, Ms. Maddox," the man said, his voice deep and authoritative. "If he's harassing you, it might be a good idea."

"Thank you, Rich. I appreciate the advice. And I think it's a good idea."

He reached into his pocket and handed her a card. "If you need someone to testify for you, give me a call."

Kate nodded and tucked the card into her pocket. "Thank you."

"Any time, Ms. Maddox. We love you around here. Our own hometown superstar. Would hate to see anything happen when it could have been prevented. I'll dispose of this trash for you."

He grabbed Christian by the elbow and half-dragged him out of the room.

"Thank you," Kate said, throwing herself into Frank's arms. "I didn't know what he was going to do."

"I think he's relatively harmless," Frank assured her. Christian was definitely a pain in the ass, but he wasn't dumb enough to be dangerous.

At least, Frank didn't think so.

"He's just an ass," Kate said.

Frank laughed with her. "I'll definitely agree with that one."

"What happened?" Quynn asked, rushing into the room. "Are you o— Sorry. I didn't realize you were here."

Frank wanted to sweep her up in his arms, but he couldn't.

He looked away from Quynn and focused on his sister. He saw the sadness in Kate's eyes and knew it wasn't because of Christian. It was the guy she was seeing. Kate added his name to the list of people who were allowed backstage. His and those of his family. He didn't go see her, though. Which means he was pissed off.

Because she lied to him.

"I was just leaving," Frank said.

"You don't have to. Everything is set. Stay with Kate. I'll meet you back at the hotel."

Quynn turned and left the room without another word.

Kate was silent for a minute, then said, "I know you're mad at her, but—"

Frank shook his head. "No. You don't know anything."

Kate raised her eyebrows. "Then tell me. What happened?"

Frank sat and dropped his head into his hands. "Shit, Katherine, I don't know."

"Want me to tell you what I think happened?"

He lifted his eyes to hers. "What?"

"I think you got scared."

Frank snorted. "No. I was fucking terrified."

Kate laughed. She sat next to him and patted his leg. "You know what, big brother? Me, too."

"Why didn't you tell Dillon about," he waved his hand at her, "all this?"

Kate shrugged. "We talked. A lot. He said he didn't want to be in the limelight. His family vineyard was pretty well known in the area. They're a big vineyard and really good. He has some local fame, so to speak. Women throw themselves at him to get a piece of the vineyard. He said he couldn't imagine how it would be to be really famous."

"How in the world did that come up?"

Kate laughed. "I told you we talked. I told him I wanted to be a singer. That I was writing music to jump start my singing career."

"So you lied to him."

Kate shook her head, her long hair brushing Frank's arm. He wasn't used to seeing his sister as Kate Maddox. She was Katherine to him. But this other person she was… He wasn't sure about it.

"I didn't lie. Not entirely. I was writing in order to help my career. To move toward the career I truly want."

"Which is what?"

"I want to sing songs I believe in. I want to write my own music. I want to take a week off to spend with a guy and fall in love and not have it be national news."

"Then do it. Why can't you?"

Kate shrugged. "Because that isn't Kate Maddox."

"Then be Katherine Price."

"What?"

"I've never been a big fan of you telling everyone who you are, but I was wrong. When Anna left me, lying became the enemy of everything for me. I never thought of what you do as lying until this week. You lied to Dillon, and his family. For a full week. You should have told him who you were so he didn't have to find out like this. You never should have listened to Quynn."

Kate shook her head. "Don't be too hard on her."

"Why not? You're miserable right now because she told you to lie to a guy. If you'd told him the truth, he would have been here with you."

"I don't know. He said he doesn't want fame."

"You didn't give him a chance to decide. You took it from him."

Kate sighed. "We talked about it a lot."

"You wanted to tell him. Quynn convinced you not to. This is her fault."

Kate shook her head again. "It's not her fault. She's been there for me every step of the way with Christian. She's the only one helping me stay ahead of him. She spent the day with Gary to figure out how we could stop Christian before he tells everyone who I am."

"That doesn't mean you should have lied."

"Christian and I wrote a song together."

"Yeah, I know."

"He wrote the music, I wrote the words. We argued about it, but it was a song I was proud of. We were mostly just playing around when we wrote it. Quynn recorded us playing the song and sent it in for copyright. She put both our names on it."

"So?"

"Christian was trying to sell it without me. He stole it and was shopping it around. The copyright notice showed up at his agent's office. He had no choice but to acknowledge that he wasn't the only one who wrote the song. He even rerecorded it on his own afterward, but he wasn't smart enough to copyright it."

"What does this have to do with anything?"

"Quynn has been there for me for years. She knows what I need before I do. She's my personal assistant, but she's also my friend. When she told me not to tell Dillon, it wasn't because she's an advocate for lying, it's because she knows how painful it was for me when everything with Christian blew up. She was protecting me from that pain again with Dillon."

Frank met her eyes. He didn't get it. "You're in pain. How was she protecting you?"

"Because if I told Dillon who I really was, he could have

exposed more than just my secret. I love him. If he'd turned on me, it would have destroyed me."

"Do you think he'd do that?"

Kate shrugged. "Yesterday, I said no. I knew it for sure. Today… He didn't show up, did he?"

"No," Frank said. "He didn't."

---

DILLON SLID ONTO THE ONE EMPTY BAR STOOL AND SIGNALED the bartender. He was going crazy sitting in his room, so he decided the bar was the next best place to be.

"What can I get you?"

"Whiskey. Double."

"You got it."

"Rough night?" the woman next to him asked.

Dillon handed the bartender cash and nodded to the blonde next to him. Her eyes were focused on a spot above the mirrored wall they faced. "Definitely a rough night."

"Right there with you."

"Buy you a drink?" Dillon asked with a nod to her empty glass.

She shook her head and flashed him a smile. "Sorry. I'm not going to your room."

A surprised laugh burst out of him. "Wasn't going there, but good to know. I'm having enough trouble with women these days."

"Women? More than one?"

"No, there's only one. Unless you count my sister and my cousin making me crazy."

"Family drama?"

Dillon smiled. "They care."

The woman faced Dillon, her green eyes painful and a

little lost. "It's nice to have someone who cares. Most of us don't have enough of that in our lives."

"And here I thought you were drinking alone because you're as popular as Kate Maddox," Dillon spat.

She snorted. "Not even close. Kate Maddox has an entourage of people who love her. I can't trash her, though. She's a really nice person."

Dillon barked a laugh. "How do you know that? She's a mirage. The person she says she is isn't reality."

She shrugged. "There's always more to a person than what we see. Kate's famous, sure, but she's real. And the people who love her truly love her."

"I thought I loved her."

"You and every man in America."

Dillon chuckled. "True. It's funny, though. Love. When you think nothing can stop you from loving someone, something stops you."

"Tell me about it," she groaned.

Dillon accepted another whiskey from the bartender and paid for that and his new friend's drink. "I'm not going to your room," he told her.

She laughed. "That's my line."

He shrugged. "I figured I should say it, too. I'm too screwed up to get another woman involved in my mess."

"I'm right there with you. I fell for my best friend's brother. He didn't agree with a piece of advice I gave her, and we were done. Before we really even got started."

"That sucks. What was the advice?"

She studied Dillon for a second then took a deep breath. "I told her not to tell someone something. Her brother took it as lying. I see it as protecting her."

"Well," Dillon said, signaling for a third whiskey, "lying sucks. Can you keep a secret?"

She grinned. "Better than you can imagine."

Dillon started on his third whiskey. "Did you go to the Kate Maddox concert tonight?"

She nodded.

"You know the guy she said she fell for? At the end. Before she sang that new song."

She nodded again.

Dillon leaned over and whispered, "I'm the guy."

Her green eyes widened. She studied him head to toe.

"You can't tell anyone. I can trust you, right?"

She nodded.

"So, I really am in love with her. And I know who she really is. Her real name and everything. But she never told me who she was. I spent a week with her, longer than a week really, and she never told me she was Kate Maddox. And I'm so dumb, I didn't figure it out either."

"You're not dumb."

He snorted. "Oh, yeah. I'm the dumb farmer she was slumming it with for a week. I guess I was just fodder for her new song or something. And I fell for it, you know. I fell for every word she said. I thought she meant it when she said she loved me. And then she left and got up on that stage and sang a song that we wrote together. Well, she wrote. But I came up with the music. That was my music. And I don't even care about the music. I just wish she trusted me."

"It can't be easy to have a secret that big."

Dillon shrugged. "I guess not. I mean, now it's my secret, right? And I have to keep quiet because I know who she is."

"You can tell me. I promise I won't tell anyone."

Dillon glared at the woman. "I'd never betray her. She might not want me, but that doesn't mean I'd ever use her for any reason. You don't do that to people you love. You don't lie and you don't use them and you don't expose all their secrets. You protect them."

She laughed mirthlessly. "You're right. She's lucky to have you, Dillon. I've got to go. Have a good night."

She was halfway across the bar before Dillon realized he never told her his name.

"Hey!" he called out, but she was lost in the crowd.

## 23

QUYNN BURST through the door to the suite into the darkness. Panic gripped her immediately. She thought Katherine would be back already.

"Katherine! Are you here?"

She moved toward Katherine's room and heard sniffles before her friend's voice said, "I'm getting ready for bed."

"It's early. We should go down to the bar for a drink."

"You go. I'm tired."

"Katherine, come on. Get some jeans on and a cute top and we'll go see if we can find some cute guys."

Katherine finally opened the door to her room. Tear stains streaked her cheeks from her red eyes to her swollen lips. She pulled one between her teeth.

"What happened?"

Katherine shrugged and walked out. "He didn't show. You know that. It just hurts, you know. I really thought he would."

"He's here."

"Here where?"

"He's in the bar downstairs. He's staying in this hotel."

"He is?"

Quynn nodded. "He is. Let's go see him."

"Did he say he wanted to see me?"

Quynn shook her head. "He doesn't know you're here. Let's go surprise him."

Quynn grabbed Katherine's arm, but she tugged it free. "No."

Quynn's pulse raced. She was ready for a fight. After the shit she got from Frank, then seeing him again, and running into Dillon and finding out Frank was right, she was pissed off. Mostly at herself, but she'd happily take her anger out on someone else.

"I can't go down there."

"Why the hell not? He's there. Sitting at the bar. Looking miserable. Why wouldn't you go talk to him?"

"He doesn't want me, Quynn. He has no use for me." Katherine's eyes welled again, tears racing down the trails to her chin. She squeezed her eyes shut and shook her head.

"He wouldn't tell me who you were."

"What are you talking about?"

Quynn sighed. "He sat down next to me. I didn't recognize him. We started talking, and he said he was in love with you. Then he said he knew who you were and that he was the guy you mentioned before *Walk Of Fame*. I asked him who you really were, and he wouldn't tell me. He kept your secret."

Katherine burst into tears, covering her face with her hands. She went to the living room and sank onto the couch.

Quynn followed her, trying to figure out what was wrong. "Are you okay?"

Katherine shook her head.

"Didn't you hear me? He wouldn't tell me who you were."

Katherine laughed. "Yeah, I'm not surprised by that. He's a good person. He wouldn't betray me, even though I betrayed him."

"You didn't betray him."

Katherine leveled Quynn with a glare. "Yeah, Quynn, I did. It was the right call to make, but I won't say I don't regret it. I have no idea if he would have reacted better if I'd been the one to tell him before I left, but I'll always wonder."

"It's all my fault," Quynn said. She felt the weight of it all on her shoulders.

"No, it's not."

"It is, Katherine. If I hadn't told you to keep it a secret, you would have told him. And if you told him, you wouldn't be sitting here crying right now. And if I hadn't told you that, Frank and I wouldn't have fought. The four of us would be out on a double date right now instead of the two of us feeling bad for ourselves and them…well, Dillon's drinking. Who knows what Frank's doing. I did this."

Katherine shook her head. "I didn't have to listen to you."

"I didn't give you much of a choice. Christian scared the shit out of me. I let him get to me. I really thought he was going to destroy you."

"You protected me. You always do. It's what you do. You make it possible for me to live this life. If you hadn't had the foresight to copyright the song he and I wrote together, he'd have sold it and I'd be hearing it on the radio one day."

"And if I hadn't, he wouldn't have bothered coming back to fuck with you. We both know the only reason he's back is because he knows he needs your approval to sell it."

Katherine sucked in a deep breath and nodded. "True. But he would have done this to another woman. And one after that. He's a asshole. Thank you for seeing it and protecting me when I wasn't willing to protect myself."

"You're welcome," Quynn said. "And speaking of which, I also sent in the copyright for *Walk Of Fame*."

"You did?"

She nodded. "Yep. Which means you're going to need Dillon's permission to officially record it."

Katherine chuckled. "Maybe I can pay him to love me."

Quynn shook her head and pulled Katherine in for a hug. "If he doesn't love you for all of you, he's not worth it. You're an amazing woman, Katherine Price."

"So are you, Quynn O'Hara. My brother's just as big of an idiot as Dillon if he doesn't see you were trying to protect me."

"We're quite a pair, aren't we?"

Katherine laughed. "Oh, yeah."

POUNDING ON THE DOOR WOKE DILLON UP THE NEXT morning. Sunlight tried to break through his drawn curtains, and when he sat up, the single streak blinded him.

"Fuck," he groaned, turning his face away.

The pounding continued so he dragged himself to the door. He yanked it open and yelled, "What!" to absolutely no one.

"Fucking kids," he growled, letting the door slam behind him.

Immediately, the pounding started up again. He stalked to the door and peeked through the peephole. He didn't see anyone in the hallway, but someone was still pounding on the door.

He took a deep breath and closed his eyes, almost falling over, and realized the pounding was not coming from the door, but from next to him.

He opened the adjoining door that led to Andie and Cody's room, but theirs was closed.

Then he heard it.

"Yes! Harder, Cody. Harder. I'm coming!"

"Oh, God!" Dillon yelled. He slammed the door and went to the bathroom. With the shower running, he couldn't hear them anymore.

Hot water beat down on his back, but nothing could drown out the revolting memory of his sister getting screwed by his best friend. And her screaming his name.

Dillon was going to throw up.

He sucked in a breath and tried to stifle the urge to vomit. When it passed, he showered quickly and got dressed. He threw his clothes from the night before in his bag and left the room before Cody and Andie went for round two.

Dillon tossed his bag into the trunk and headed back inside for breakfast. They all agreed to meet in the restaurant downstairs, but he was the first one there.

He asked the hostess for a table and sent a text to everyone else so they knew where he was seated. Sean and Emily were the first to join him.

"Morning," Sean said. "Where'd you run off to at the end of the concert?"

"Just had to get out of there."

"Everything okay?"

Dillon was saved from answering by Zach, Gianna, and Summer. They immediately jumped into a discussion about how 'awesome' the concert was.

Ian and Kristen were next, flashing him sympathetic looks. Cody and Andie came down last, giggling and holding hands.

"You look like you two had a good night," Kristen said with a grin.

"A good morning, too," Andie replied.

Cody sat next to Dillon.

"Do you two know I was in the room next to you?"

Cody and Andie shared a confused look. "Yeah. Why?"

"Your good morning woke me up," Dillon growled.

Cody had the decency to look embarrassed, but Andie just laughed with Kristen and Ian.

"It was not fucking funny."

"Language, Uncle Dillon," Emily said sternly.

"Sorry, Em," Dillon said, still glaring at his best friend.

Cody opened his mouth to say something, but Dillon cut him off. "Don't say anything. I promise you can't say anything that will make this better."

Cody fought a grin and turned to kiss Andie's neck. That definitely did not make it better.

"I tried to download the new Kate Maddox song this morning, but I couldn't find it online. I can't believe she sang a song she hasn't even recorded yet," Emily said to Summer. "I loved that song."

Half the table, the half that rode with Dillon and knew, sat silently. Sean, Zach, and Gianna had no clue anything was up, so they picked up the conversation.

"That song was really sweet. I wondered if she was with someone. It didn't seem real that she was with her family. Especially since that was the plan all along. She could have done all those interviews and spent time with her family. I wonder where she stayed," Gianna gushed.

"Closer than you think," Andie murmured.

Sean gave Andie a questioning look. She nodded her head toward Dillon, who kept his eyes trained on the menu even though he knew what he wanted for breakfast. He could feel everyone watching him.

"What are we getting for breakfast?" he asked, louder than necessary. He needed them to change the subject. Immediately.

"Em and I were thinking pancakes, but the waffles look good, too. Maybe we'll split them?" Sean said.

"Yeah," Emily agreed. "I want both."

The rest of the table jumped on the breakfast discussion, letting Dillon have his time.

The waiter took their orders and had their food out quickly. Everyone paid for their breakfast and checked out of the rooms and they were heading to the garage in no time.

"What's going on?" Sean asked, pulling Dillon from the rest of the group before they reached their cars.

"Katherine is Kate Maddox," he confessed.

"What?"

Dillon waited for it to sink in. It didn't take long before his brother's eyes widened with realization.

"Holy shit. She was talking about you, wasn't she?"

Dillon nodded.

"You wrote that song?"

He shook his head. "I played the music, but she changed it a bit and added the lyrics. It's her song."

"Damn. Too bad. If you got royalties from a Kate Maddox song, we could buy a new bottling line without going to the bank."

Dillon shook his head. "She was using me. Or us."

"Why do you think that? She said she was in love with you."

Dillon shrugged. "Stage talk. She never told me who she was. If she really loved me, she would have told me."

Sean shook his head. "If that's your logic then you should be telling everyone about Perry."

"It's not the same thing. I'm not lying. I'm just not sharing everything."

"It sounds like exactly what she did."

Dillon sighed. "I'm trying to do my job and keep the vineyard running. She didn't trust me."

"Are you saying you trust all of us?"

"Of course I do."

"Then why haven't you told anyone about Perry?"

———

KATE SAT IN THE CHAIR ON THE STAGE AND SMILED INTO THE camera. The interviewer, Monica, introduced her to the crowd, reading the bio Quynn provided.

"We're so happy you could be with us today, Kate," Monica gushed.

Local TV was always extra accommodating and generous when someone truly famous wanted to be on the show. Kate loved talking to smaller stations because they really wanted to have her there. They weren't looking for dirt that they could scoop another station with, they just wanted her on their show.

"Thank you, Monica. I'm excited to be here. I really appreciate you letting me reschedule."

"Oh, we didn't mind at all. I was at your concert last night. Can I share your secret?"

Kate laughed. "Yeah, I think it's out there now."

Monica turned to the camera. "For those of you who haven't heard, Kate confessed at her concert here in Syracuse last night that she met someone last week. I have to ask, Kate, did you see him after the show?"

Kate shook her head and let the sadness show. "Unfortunately, no."

Monica frowned. "Sorry. We were all cheering for you."

"Thanks. I was hoping it would work out, but I know being with someone like me isn't always easy. He's an amazing guy and he deserves to be with someone who can be everything he wants. With my schedule, I wouldn't be around that much. It's hard on a couple, so I get it."

"Your last relationship was with Christian Blake. Can you tell us a little about that?"

Kate smiled, knowing it was one of the questions Quynn provided. "Christian and I had a whirlwind kind of romance. We met on tour, and it was refreshing to have someone who understood this world. We were together all the time since we were touring together, and it was easy."

"But it wasn't right?"

Kate shook her head. "Not even a little. I thought I loved Christian, but he wasn't the person I thought he was. Unfortunately, what he put me through tainted my relationship with the guy I met last week. I didn't tell him some things because I worried about it."

"What kind of things?" Monica asked.

"He didn't know I was Kate Maddox until the concert."

"And he knows now?"

Kate nodded. "He knows."

"And I take it he wasn't happy?"

Kate laughed mirthlessly. "Um, no. Where Christian wanted to tell everyone who I am and make a quick buck on me, this other guy refused to tell anyone so he could protect me. That's the difference between real love and imaginary love. He'll do anything to keep me safe, even if he doesn't want to be with me. Christian wants to be with me, and threatens to expose me to get me to agree to it."

"Christian Blake threatened you?"

Kate nodded.

"Well, we're going to get that full story after our break. Don't go anywhere, folks."

Kate held her grin until someone said they were clear then relaxed in the seat.

"Can we get you some water? Or coffee? Anything Ms. Maddox?" Monica asked.

Kate shook her head. "No, thank you. And call me Kate."

Monica's grin widened. "Thank you. We really are happy you could join us today. And I'm sorry about the guy. He doesn't know what he's missing."

Kate smiled but didn't say anything.

Someone from makeup touched up Kate's face and before she had a chance to really breathe, they were going live again.

"If you're just joining us, we're live this morning with Kate Maddox. After her concert last night, the internet blew up with demands for her new song, *Walk Of Fame*. We're going to talk more about the song in a minute, but first, Kate's sharing a few things about Christian Blake. They dated for about a year, right?"

Kate nodded. "Right at a year, yes."

"And now Christian is threatening to expose who you are in order to get you to go back to him. Let me ask you, why keep your identity a secret?"

Kate had been asked that question, or a variation, many times. For the first time, she wanted to drop the act and tell the truth.

"I was scared," she admitted. "The first time I was recognized by a fan, I was still playing clubs in Nashville. He didn't know my name, but he called me Kate and came on to me. I was having dinner with a friend, but the guy sat down at our table and put his hand on my thigh and tried to talk me into going home with him. It terrified me."

Monica's face reflected the fear Kate felt that night. "How horrible."

Kate nodded. "It was. At that point, I was debating using a stage name or not, but after that, I started changing my appearance on stage. Whenever I go out, no one recognizes me. It gives me the opportunity to have a normal life."

"And now Christian Blake is threatening that."

Kate nodded again. "He is. We wrote a song together, and he wants to sell it. It was copyrighted in both our names so he needs my permission. That's the real reason he's threatening me. He wants me to give in so he can make some money."

"Are you going to do it?"

Kate shrugged. "There's a part of me that wants to draw up a contract and sign over all the rights to him and never have to deal with him again. And then there's another part of me that wants to frustrate him as much as he's frustrated me."

Monica laughed. "I can understand that part. I think every woman who's been burned by an ex can relate."

Kate nodded. "I agree. At the end of the day, I really just want Christian to stop harassing me. I want the threats to end. Part of the reason I was gone all last week was because of him. The guy I met, he gave me a reason to stay as long as I did, but Christian was the reason I ran."

"So, let's go back to him and this song. It's not recorded, is that true?"

Kate shook her head. "No, it's not. It won't be available to download anywhere for a while."

"And you wrote the song?"

"I wrote the lyrics. The guy I was with wrote the music."

"Really?"

Kate nodded and grinned. "He did. He likes to play guitar but never took it further than a hobby."

"It sounds, from the song, that you had a pretty amazing week together."

"We did. One of the best weeks of my life."

"Then I guess something good came out of Christian Blake."

Kate laughed. "I guess you're right."

DILLON TURNED OFF THE TV AND SHOOK HIS HEAD. HE shouldn't have watched her interview. He knew it wouldn't make things better, but he was a glutton for punishment.

And desperate for any small piece of her he could have.

Him and every other man on the planet.

He went through his house and collected all the things that reminded him of Katherine and put them in the closet in the guest room. He wasn't willing to get rid of them yet, but he definitely didn't want to stare at Katherine constantly. It was bad enough he had to keep her secret and pretend he didn't care that she lied to him.

Dillon was about to fix dinner when there was a knock on his door. He cursed his traitorous heart for leaping at the thought that it could be Katherine. He rolled his eyes at himself and opened the door to find Kristen.

"Hey. What's going on?" He stepped back to let her in.

"Do you have a minute?"

Dillon nodded. "Always. Definitely now. Want a drink?"

Kristen nodded. "Whatever you have open is good with me."

Dillon poured Kristen a glass of merlot since it was her favorite. He grabbed a beer for himself. He couldn't finish the bottle of wine Katherine and he opened before she left even though it was his favorite.

"What's up?" Dillon asked when they both had their drinks.

"We saw her last night."

Dillon shook his head. "I don't want to hear it, Kris."

"She was wrong to do that to you."

"Excuse me?"

"She never should have lied. I know Andie gave you shit about giving her another chance, but I don't blame you at all. She should have told you what was really going on."

Dillon sighed. "Yeah, she should have."

"The only problem I have is that you're sitting here upset and you have people you can call."

Dillon gave her a look that said he didn't.

"You could have called me. I'm sure Sean would have come over. Cody and Jake and Zach would be here if you need them. Henry, all of us. Why don't you lean on us?"

Dillon smiled. "Because I'm supposed to take care of you guys."

Kristen snorted. "Last I checked, I could wipe my own ass, cuz."

Dillon laughed. "That's good because I'm not doing that for anyone."

Kristen laughed and nodded. "You and me both." She paused. "When are you going to tell everyone about Perry?"

Dillon's head snapped up. He rolled his eyes and swore. "Sean shouldn't have told you about that."

"He didn't."

"Crap. That's right, you saw him, didn't you?"

"It doesn't matter. You should have told me. You should have told all of us. I was managing that event and never thought to pass out photos of him to all the staff. I forget that they don't all know who that lying sack of shit is. It's my fault he was there."

"No, Kristen. It's not your fault."

She glared at him. "It's not your fault either, but you're allowed to beat yourself up about it. Why shouldn't I?"

Dillon wrapped her up in a hug. "You know I love you, right?"

Kristen nodded. "Love you, too."

"Good. If I learned one thing this weekend it's that lies and omissions of information don't do anyone any good."

"So you're going to confess?"

Dillon nodded. "Yes, dammit. I'll confess."

"It's the right call, Dillon. We're all in this together.

Besides, if another superstar comes along and sweeps you off your feet, the rest of us need to be able to fill in for you when you're gone."

Dillon snorted. "Yeah, that'll never happen."

"It's nice to dream about, though. I'd love to have someone sweep me off my feet."

"Philip's an idiot."

Kristen smiled. "No argument from me."

## 24

KATHERINE WOKE up the next morning to a string of pissed off phone calls and texts from Christian. She expected it and forwarded all the messages to Gary to review.

*Guess he saw the interview.*

She did the right thing. He didn't like having his shit aired on television, but it was the only way he'd ever back off. He was using her, and he would keep using her if she didn't put a stop to it. So she did.

Katherine tossed her phone on the nightstand and sighed. It was mostly empty, like all nightstands in hotels. An alarm clock, a lamp, and a notepad. Nothing personal. Nothing like being at Dillon's. Staying in the hotel was a rude awakening after being with Dillon for a week. For someone who had a life in hotels, Katherine was feeling twitchy after just a couple nights back in them.

It definitely wasn't home.

Wherever that could be.

It was part of why she was thinking of getting a place near her family. She wanted to go home more often.

Whether home was in Nashville or home was in New York, she wanted to have her own stuff with her.

And maybe one day she'd find a guy to share her life with also.

Or maybe she'd just live with Quynn forever.

"Coffee?" Quynn asked, offering a cup.

Katherine took it gratefully. "Thank you. I need this today."

"Still no word from him?"

Katherine shook her head. "No. He won't call me."

"Have you called him?"

"Have you called my brother?"

Quynn clamped her mouth shut.

"What time do we need to get moving?"

Quynn glanced at her phone. "Two hours."

"Good. So I can enjoy this."

Quynn nodded. "Yep. You might even get to enjoy your shower, too."

"Ooh, endless hot water and two bathrooms so I don't have to rush out for you. There are perks to living in hotels."

Quynn laughed. "Yeah, if you can afford a suite with separate bedrooms and bathrooms."

Katherine nodded. "True. It wasn't always like this for us."

"Remember the first tour we did?"

"Oh, God," Katherine groaned. "Those hotels were horrible."

"We had so much fun, though. I almost wish we could go back to then. As much as it sucked, I loved it. We were in it together, and it was all about the music. Those hotels almost felt like home."

Katherine nodded. "That's why I went to Amavita Estates."

"Why?"

"I've been thinking about finding a place around here to

buy a house. I didn't really want to be in Syracuse, or New York City, but I wanted to be close to my family. I went there when I was a teenager and remembered it. I wanted to get a better idea of the area and maybe buy a place there."

"Why didn't you tell me that?" Quynn asked.

Katherine shrugged. "I knew you'd try to talk me out of it."

"Really?"

Katherine nodded. "Yep. I can see it right now. The argument is on the tip of your tongue. You know you would, but you're trying to figure out how to tell me you wouldn't have even though you still think it's a horrible idea."

"Well, isn't it?"

Katherine laughed. It started as a giggle and built every time she met Quynn's eyes. Within seconds they were both laughing so hard tears ran down their cheeks.

"You're right," Katherine said through her tears. "It would be a horrible idea. God, can you imagine if I settled in the same town as Dillon? What a disaster."

"I'm so with you. Two weeks ago I didn't even know you had a brother and now I'm in love with him and wondering how quickly we can get the hell out of town so I never have to see him again."

Katherine nodded. "Yep. Dillon was a stranger in a bar I slept with one night. Now I have a head full of songs and am so in love with him that I can't imagine ever wanting another man again."

"Love sucks."

Katherine snorted. "Absolutely."

Katherine and Quynn drank their coffee and were both headed for their rooms when someone pounded on the door.

"What the hell?" Quynn asked.

Katherine looked around the room for something they

could use as a weapon. "Did someone find out who I am? Oh, shit. Do you think it's Christian?"

Quynn sucked in a deep breath but jumped when the person pounded on the door again.

Katherine moved toward the door wearily. When she got close enough she peaked through the peep hole and sighed. "It's just Frank."

Quynn bolted for her room and slammed the door just as Katherine let her brother in.

"Hey. What are you doing here?"

Katherine hugged him, but his mind was obviously somewhere else.

"What's wrong? Are Mom and Dad okay?"

"What? Yeah. Why?" Frank scanned the room, barely sparing Katherine a glance.

"You're acting all weird. What's wrong with you?"

"I'm just… I need some help."

"Help?"

Frank paced to the living room and dropped onto the couch. "I screwed up with Quynn. I really like her, Katherine. A lot. And I thought she was being ridiculous, but I haven't been able to stop thinking about what you said the other night. She's a good person."

"I know she is. She's amazing," Katherine said, joining him.

Frank huffed a laugh. "She is. I know it's insane because you're leaving, and she'll go with you, and it doesn't make any sense, but I don't want things with her to be over."

"So what do you need from me?" Katherine asked, an idea forming in her mind.

"I need to apologize to her. In a big way. I need her to know I mean it when I say I was wrong and I'm sorry. But I don't know much about her or what would really matter to her."

Katherine smiled. "I think the truth would matter a lot to her. She'd want to know you were scared and that you're sorry and that you aren't ready for things to be over. Empty promises aren't going to make things better, but if you show her that you've really changed, and agree that she gave me the best advice, then you might get another chance with her."

Frank nodded. He stared past Katherine out the window, then met her eyes. She saw the pain her brother held deep inside. He was too good of a man to have to deal with the crap he'd been handed. He deserved someone like Quynn.

"Is it worth it, Katherine?"

"What? Quynn?"

He shook his head. "I know she's worth it. I'm just not sure apologizing and trying to see her again is worth it. I know it won't last because we'll never see each other. And the idea of falling in love again terrifies me, but…"

"But what?"

"But I don't want to imagine what my life will be if I never see her again."

Katherine smiled. "Then I think it's absolutely worth it."

"What about when it ends? I don't want to come between you two."

"First, don't plan for it to end. And second, I'm not worried about you coming between us."

Frank sighed heavily. "I want her to be happy, Katherine. Am I going to be in the way of that if I talk to her?"

She shook her head. "Not at all. I think you're going to make her happier. She's just as lost as you are. She misses you, Frank. And I think you two would work really well together."

"For a few days at least. Shit, it's going to be hard to say goodbye to her."

"What if you didn't need to?"

"What?"

Katherine shrugged. "I've been thinking of hiring someone. I want to tell everyone who I am. If I do, I want to hire someone to be in charge of my personal security."

"Okay?"

"You know there's no one else I'd rather work with."

"You want to hire me?"

Katherine shrugged again. "If you're interested in the job. I trust you more than anyone else to keep me safe. And if you're with me, I'll know you're safe."

"Do you really think someone would go after us to get to you?"

Katherine shook her head. "No. I don't. But it sounds good."

Frank laughed. "I think you should ask Quynn before you make a decision like this. I don't want her to feel uncomfortable if I'm around all the time."

"I think she'll be okay with it," Katherine said with a grin.

"What makes you so sure?"

"Because she's standing behind you nodding."

Frank spun around. Quynn had her hands up to her mouth, crying silently. Frank stood and went to her, wrapping her in his arms.

"Don't cry."

"It's…happy…tears," Quynn choked out.

"Did you hear what I said?"

She nodded.

"What do you think?"

She smiled up at him. "I think we need some privacy."

They grinned at Katherine then kissed their way into Quynn's room and closed the door.

"Guess I'm going to my interview alone," Katherine said with a smile.

"I THOUGHT YOU WERE GOING TO TELL EVERYONE," KRISTEN hissed when she walked into Dillon's office after the meeting and slammed the door. "What the hell, Dillon?"

Dillon sighed. After Kristen left the night before, he saw an older interview with Kate Maddox. She was dating Christian Blake at the time and said something about a song they were writing together. The way she looked at him made Dillon sick. He couldn't stand to think about her with that jackass.

And then he thought about all the other lies she told him, and he couldn't trust himself.

He couldn't trust himself about anything anymore.

"It'll be fine, Kristen."

"How do you know that?"

"Because it will," Dillon yelled. "I'll handle it."

Kristen threw her hands up and backed up. "Got it. Understood. I won't bother you again."

"Kris, don't," Dillon said, but she was already gone.

Dillon stared at the closed door and swore. He hated feeling like a pariah in his own family. All he was doing was trying to protect them. They were his family. He owed it to them to keep them safe. And that meant keeping the vineyard safe as well.

Dillon paced his office and tugged at his hair. He was frustrated in ways he hadn't been in weeks. Not since the night he met Katherine.

He considered going to Ithaca for the night and finding another woman to lose himself in, but he didn't want a random woman. He wanted the one he couldn't have.

Dillon left his office and walked through the vines. He didn't see anyone as he walked, going up and down lines absently. When he found himself in front of the bottling building, he almost laughed. He went there frequently as a kid. It was one place his dad rarely went into, so Dillon often chose it as a hiding place.

He walked into the room and stared at the equipment. It hadn't changed in his lifetime. He'd followed countless bottles down the rolling conveyor, mesmerized as they were blasted with air, then filled with wine, corked, and labeled automatically. As a child, the entire process fascinated him, that things could happen without a person doing them. As he grew up, he understood how it worked, but the whole thing still amazed him.

It was a perfect dance that made him realize not everything in life required interference.

"Hey," Sean said, stepping out of the office he had in the bottling building.

"Hey," Dillon replied. "Sorry. Just needed an escape."

"I bet. Office getting too small?"

Dillon nodded. "I promised Kristen I'd tell everyone about Perry this morning."

Sean's eyebrows winged up. "I must have missed that part of the meeting."

Dillon shook his head. "Katherine wanted me to tell everyone."

"And now you think since she lied that you shouldn't do anything she said to do."

Dillon nodded. "That's about it."

"Angela knew she had cancer before I did."

"What?"

"She knew about it. I didn't find out until after she was gone, but she wrote me a letter. She was explaining why she died."

"Explaining?"

"Her oncologist told her she wouldn't survive without treatment since she was so bad when they found it. She told them not to do any treatment. The only reason she ever told me was because it got worse and she had no choice."

"Shit."

Sean nodded. "Yeah. When I found that letter...I was so angry with her. I couldn't believe she left me like she did. But I still love her. Through the lies and everything, I love her. I'll always love her, because you can't just forget about the people you love. They never leave you."

"Katherine left me."

Sean shook his head. "You left her. She wanted you to go see her after the concert, but you skipped out."

"Can you blame me?"

Sean shook his head again. "Not a bit. But you've had a few days. You have to decide if what happened is bad enough for you to never forgive her, or if she's the person you always thought she was and she made a choice to protect you, even if you don't agree with it."

Dillon thought about it for a few minutes. Sean let him have his silence.

"What does this have to do with Perry?"

Sean smiled. "If you won't tell us because she told you to, and you can't ever forgive her, then you'll never tell everyone else. If you can forgive her, then I hope you'll let us help you. With Perry, and with Katherine."

"There's nothing to help with when it comes to Katherine."

Sean smiled. "We'll see."

---

Quynn still couldn't believe Frank was there. Not only was he there, but he was staying.

"You don't have to take the job," Quynn said carefully, running her hand down his chest.

They were in her hotel room. After Kate's interview, they went to lunch and filled Frank in on everything that had been going on with Christian and Dillon and Katherine's thoughts about finding a new place to live. They had dinner with Kelly and George, who were thrilled that Frank and Katherine were going to work together.

Frank laughed. "I know. I've been feeling like I'm in a rut, though. I've wanted to do something else for a while but didn't know what. When Katherine said something about it, it felt right."

"As long as you're sure."

Frank leaned away to look at her. "Do you not want me to take it? I said I wouldn't if you'd rather I'm not around all the time. I'm not trying to force myself into your world. And—"

"Frank, stop. I love the idea of you being there all the time. Tonight was amazing, and I can't wait to do it again. I just worry about Katherine."

Frank nodded and settled back on the pillow. Quynn snuggled up to him, resting her head on his bare chest.

"She has really bad luck with men. I know us being together is going to be hard on her."

Frank stroked his fingertips down Quynn's spine then back up. He kissed her forehead and whispered, "You're a good friend. She's lucky to have you."

Quynn shrugged.

"I mean it. I feel the same way about my sister. I hope things work out for her one of these days."

"The way she talked about Dillon was different than any other guy. I really thought he was going to be someone she could let in."

"I think she did. That's why it's so hard for her. She let him in, and he ran. He decided he didn't want all of her."

Quynn sighed. "I can't imagine what it's like for her. Do you think she'll be okay going public?"

Frank nodded. "She's strong. She'll be okay with everything. We just have to make sure she knows we're here for her."

Quynn burrowed in closer. "I hope she knows that. Did you find out anything else about him?"

Frank sighed. "Do you really want to talk about this now? We just had sex for the first time and we're discussing my sister's sort of ex-boyfriend."

Quynn felt guilty for about a second, but she pushed through. "I need to know he's a good guy before I try to talk her into getting in touch with him."

"Why are we doing that again?"

"Because she loves him. And I think he loves her, too. But he's scared. He's going to find out soon enough that his name is on the copyright for the song, but I think it's better if she tells him in advance. Gary has a contract for him to sign before she can record the song, but she's afraid to call him."

Frank laughed and nuzzled against Quynn's neck. "I was afraid to come over here. I was sure you'd slam the door in my face."

"Hotel room doors don't slam very well."

Frank tickled her until she squealed then crawled on top of her. "That wasn't very nice."

Quynn laughed and shook her head. "Nope. But it got you where I wanted you."

He lengthened against her belly. "Oh, really?"

She nodded and drew him down to her then kissed him again and showed him just how much she wanted him.

SHITTY DIDN'T EVEN BEGIN to describe Dillon's mood, but he didn't care. Nothing felt right. Nothing felt good.

He got out of the office Tuesday around lunch time and headed into town to get something to eat. It was a nice enough day that he could walk around with his burger and get some fresh air.

"Do I know you?" a guy asked him.

Dillon looked the guy up and down. Fancy shoes, expensive clothes, and hair that was too perfect for anyone in Bereton.

Dillon smiled and shook his head. "Don't think so, dude."

"No, no. I do. Aren't you the guy that was with Kate Maddox?"

Dillon flinched just enough to tell the guy he was right.

"I knew you were. See Katie isn't very smart. And all it took was a quick search through social media to find pictures of her. Then I just had to find out where those people were and bam. Here you are. Saves me a trip out to your vineyard."

"Who are you?"

"Oh, who I am isn't important. You're the one that matters right now. See Katie needs to know you aren't going back to her. That cute little song will be the last one you two write together. She has other people in her life she can write songs with."

"You're Christian Blake, aren't you?"

"How the hell do you know my name?"

"You're not the only one with a cell phone and an internet connection. It was really interesting to read all about your relationship online. I think mine was a lot more fun, but then again, I'm not after her for what she can do for me."

A laugh bubbled out of Christian and grew until he doubled over. He laughed for a good minute, then straightened and glared at Dillon.

"I'm not as dumb as you look. See, I know a few things about you and your vineyard. Like the contract you signed and the financial struggles you're having right now."

"What the hell are you talking about?" Dillon growled.

Christian chuckled. "You're not the only one who can do some homework. I know a lot about you. And if you don't back off Kate, it's all going to be public knowledge."

Dillon shrugged. "So? It's all public anyway."

"Really? Even you screwing Kate Maddox?"

"You leave her out of this."

Christian grinned and shook his head. "See that's the thing. She's right in the middle of this. If you don't stay away from her, I'll ruin you. I'll tell everyone that you tricked her, and we both know Kate isn't going to challenge me. She runs and hides when I'm around. So you stay away, and I'll stay away."

Dillon shook his head. "I'm not so sure I can do that."

Christian's face twisted with anger.

"What you don't know is that you'd be doing me a huge favor if you told the world that I wrote that song. And that I was the guy it was about. I mean, you know how people are. You grew to fame because you were dating her. I have expenses. Stuff we need to buy. Sounds like you know about all that already. So I think you should go ahead and tell everyone who I am. Make them curious. Send them my way. It's a great idea."

Christian glared at Dillon then stormed off. Dillon watched him go, getting more and more angry with each step. Someone was feeding Christian information, and Dillon was pretty sure he knew exactly who it was.

***

KATE HAD ANOTHER INTERVIEW WEDNESDAY. MORE questions about Christian and Dillon, except she couldn't answer the ones about Dillon. She wanted to call him. Even if it was just to hear his voice. It was hard not talking to him after having him as such a huge part of her life.

It didn't help that she barely slept with Quynn and her brother up all night having sex.

Time to start investing in two hotel rooms instead of one big suite. Two rooms on opposite sides of the hotel would be best.

Quynn was trying to be considerate, but she was happy. Katherine wanted Quynn to be happy, but it was a constant reminder of how unhappy she herself was.

The worst part was she made the mistake of reading one of Christian's texts. She saw Dillon's name in it and froze, her eyes scanning the entire message.

It didn't make sense that Dillon would protect her secret and then tell Christian to share it with the world. He could have easily told everyone he wrote the song and he was the one she spent the week with. God knew others had made the same claim. But Dillon didn't say anything. Hell, he didn't even say something to Quynn the night of the concert. He was a good guy, which was what made it harder to accept that Christian was telling the truth.

She called Gary. She needed some assurance about the whole situation. It couldn't blow up in her face before she was ready to tell everyone.

"Mr. Powers' office."

"Hey Molly, it's Katherine. How are you?"

"Ms. Price. Good to hear from you. I'm well. Do you need to speak to Mr. Powers."

"I do, please. I need an appointment, too. Can you schedule me for his next available spot?"

"He'll see you whenever you can be here."

"Oh, no, Molly. Whenever he's free. I don't need to bump anyone."

"How about three o'clock?"

"Perfect. Thanks."

"Any time. Hang on and I'll transfer you."

"Thank you."

A few seconds later, Gary answered, "I wondered if I'd hear from you. We have an appointment today?"

"Yeah. Molly just scheduled it for me."

"Are you going to give me an idea what it's about?"

"Christian and Dillon."

Gary sighed. "I figured. Anything in particular I can have ready for you?"

"Have you gotten the copyright notice yet?"

"Just the digital confirmation."

"Is it enough to draw up a contract?"

"It should be. Want me to get started?"

"Yes. I'll have all the information you need when I get there."

"See you soon, Katherine."

Katherine hung up the phone and felt better. At least

Dillon would know she wasn't trying to screw him out of any money. Then he could go on with his life and not worry about her or anyone else bothering him again.

---

ANDIE WALKED INTO DILLON'S OFFICE THURSDAY AFTERNOON with an official looking envelope in her hands.

"What's that?"

"No clue. It was just delivered by messenger. From a lawyer in Syracuse."

"Who is it addressed to?"

"You."

"Not the vineyard?"

Andie shook her head and handed over the package. She waited while Dillon tore the envelope open and scanned the first page.

"It's a contract. Katherine registered the copyright for *Walk Of Fame* and put my name on it as the composer."

"Really?" Andie asked, moving closer to read over his shoulder.

"That's what it says," Dillon said absently, reading the rest of the contract quickly. "She wants to give me royalties for it. If I approve this contract, I agree to let her record the song and all iterations and she gives me fifty percent of any profits from the song."

"Holy shit, Dil. That's amazing."

Dillon nodded. He couldn't process the whole thing. It seemed like a lot of money for her to hand over, but he'd never been offered a contract like that before. Was she being generous, or did her boyfriend tell her Dillon wanted everyone to know who he was so he could make some money off her?

He hadn't meant it, although it had crossed his mind. He

was angry with her, but he'd never actually use her for his own good. He just wanted that asshole out of his face. Dillon knew if he told him not to do it, he'd be on the phone as soon as he walked away, telling the world. But if he acted like he didn't care, Christian wasn't likely to tell anyone.

Except maybe Katherine.

"Are you going to sign it?" Andie asked, bringing Dillon back to the present.

Dillon shook his head. "I don't deserve it. She took a few chords I played and turned them into a song. She made that song her 'next great hit.'"

"We could really use the money, Dillon." Andie crossed her arms, but she wasn't the tough woman she used to be. She'd gone all soft and mushy since she and Cody got together.

Dillon loved seeing his sister happy, but she made him want to laugh. She was like a puppy trying to intimidate him. And it wasn't working.

Besides that, he had no interest in taking anything from Kate Maddox.

"I loved her, Andie. And all I am to her is a contract. She doesn't even have the decency to call me. To talk to me about this. She has her lawyer deal with it. A bunch of money won't make this whole thing better."

"I'm sorry," Andie said. "You're right."

"That's the worst part of all this. If I'd gone to see her after the concert, I would have said things I'd regret. I'm still so angry with her, but all I've gotten from her is radio silence. She's going on with her life like I was never a part of it, and I'm left here, seeing her everywhere, knowing I was the only one who meant it."

"How do you know she didn't mean it?"

Dillon met Andie's eyes. "Could you have let Cody go to

Florida? Would you have left things the way they were and never called him again?"

She paused for a second. "I…" She shook her head, her auburn hair catching in her lipgloss. "No. I had to see him."

"She has no interest in seeing me. I'm a fucking contract. Someone she can pay off to keep quiet."

"Do you really think that's what she's doing?" Andie's eyes narrowed at the accusation.

Dillon laughed mirthlessly. "I ran into her boyfriend in Bereton yesterday."

"Boyfriend?"

"Christian Blake."

"He was in Bereton?"

Dillon nodded. "Looking for me, it seemed. He threatened to tell everyone about Katherine, I mean Kate, and me. He said he'd tell everyone who I was so we'd be flooded like I don't want. I told him to go ahead. That I was considering the same thing and that it'd be great for business. And today this contract shows up. Meaning I get paid for keeping my mouth shut."

Andie sighed. He could see her warring with herself over her next words and knew before she spoke that he wasn't going to like what she had to say.

"Are you sure? Because all the interviews she's been doing said she hasn't spoken to Christian. She's trashing him pretty hard on TV right now."

"Imagine what she'd say about me if I actually told everyone about us."

Andie shook her head. "I really don't think that's what's going on. I know you're hurt and I know you're mad, but I really think she's trying to do the right thing with this contract. I think she's saying she's not stealing the song from you. She wants to give you what she thinks you earned."

"That's not better, Andie. I'm a work horse. Someone else for her to hire."

"Dillon."

"No," he said. "You're not going to talk me into this."

"How about Perry? Can I talk you into that?"

"Dammit. Is there anyone who doesn't know about that? Why do I have to say anything at all if you all know?"

"Because we don't all know. And we haven't heard it from you."

"Did Sean tell you to talk to me about this?"

Andie grinned. "Nope. And before you ask, neither did Kristen. Henry, Ryan, and Jake are out in the field blind right now. They have no idea that Perry could be hanging around. They need to be prepared. Our staff needs to be prepared. He never should have gotten into any of our events."

"Legally, we can't keep him out."

"Maybe not, but we can assign someone to stay on him the whole time."

Dillon pulled in a deep breath. "We definitely need to do that."

"Good," she said, moving toward the door. "I'll call a meeting for tomorrow morning so you can tell everyone about it. You get a plan together."

Andie was gone before he could argue any more.

FRANK SAT ON THE COUCH NEXT TO KATHERINE AND KISSED the side of her head. Ever since she was little, he adored her. He could still remember when his parents brought her home from the hospital. He was in kindergarten and told his teacher that he was getting a baby sister. When he got home that day, she was there. Sitting in his mom's lap and screaming.

"You doing okay?"

She shrugged.

"I saw you writing earlier. Are you working on a new song?"

She nodded.

"About Dillon?"

She nodded again.

"Want to talk about it?"

She huffed a laugh. "With my big brother who probably wants to kill him? Not a great idea."

"I don't want to kill him. I understand him. I am him."

"What do you mean?"

Frank smiled and wrapped his arm around Katherine's shoulder. She moved her head to tug her hair from under his forearm then settled against him like she did when they were little and would watch scary movies.

"I resisted anything with Quynn because she's basically famous, too. She might not have the same recognition you do, but she has your life. It's terrifying to imagine having to share the woman you love with everyone else in the world. Especially when you're a private person."

Katherine sighed. "I guess."

"You told me once that you were Kate Maddox on stage but still Katherine Price inside. I always took that to mean that at your core, you hadn't changed. You still had the same values as you always had."

"I do," Katherine said defensively.

"Good. But it took you a while to get there. You had to do some serious soul searching to accept that you could be both rich and famous and still ordinary. It took you a long time to trust that. Dillon has had a few days."

"He's not going to be famous for writing one song."

Frank laughed so hard he choked. When he calmed down and sat back, he looked at Katherine closely. She was exhausted, her eyes weary with bags under them. Her frown tugged her lips down and made her look like a child again.

"He's going to be famous for dating Kate Maddox."

"What?"

"If you come out, which you said you want to do, he's going to be Kate Maddox's boyfriend. If you don't come out, he's going to end up on tour with you, or at an award show with you, or somewhere with you eventually. You're either going to need a disguise for him, or he's going to end up just as famous as you are."

Realization dawned in her eyes, but sadness quickly followed. "He's never going to want to be with me."

Frank shook his head. "I didn't say that."

"You didn't have to. I know him. We talked about what would happen if my music career took off. He said he couldn't imagine living in the spotlight like that."

"I know. I heard *Walk Of Fame*," Frank said.

Katherine smiled at him. "I know. So did he. And it said all he wanted to hear from me."

"I think you should call him."

Katherine shook her head, fear flooding her wide eyes. "No. I can't. He doesn't want to talk to me. I can't hear his voice and know how mad he is. I can't do it, Frank."

"Okay," he soothed, drawing her in for a hug. "You don't have to. I don't think it's as bad as you do, but you don't have to. If it were me, I wouldn't have the guts to call the famous woman that I was in love with. I'd feel like a fake calling her."

"I'm still the same person I was last week."

Frank shook his head. "Not to him. Last week you were Katherine. Today you're Kate Maddox."

"I'm still me."

Frank knew she wouldn't understand, but he tried again. "In your mind, you are. In reality, you are. But he's never been faced with this reality before. For him, you were just an ordinary woman who wanted to be a singer. I'm sure he was supportive, but he wasn't likely to believe you'd make it. Then he finds out that not only did you make it, but you're one of the most popular and famous singers out there. And he didn't even realize who you were. You slept with him, kissed him, cooked together, talked, sang together, and he never realized you were you."

Katherine closed her eyes and sank back against the couch. "I really screwed up, didn't I?"

Frank shook his head. "No. You didn't. But you need to reach out to him. Apologize for deceiving him. Tell him you trust him and that you want another chance. Don't make him do all the work."

Katherine sucked in a deep breath and nodded. "What if I go there tomorrow? Try to see him. Can I tell him all this in person?"

Frank nodded. "Even better. Quynn and I are going with you."

"I don't need a babysitter."

Frank grinned. "Not a babysitter. We want to meet this guy."

"Oh, no. Maybe I should call and warn him."

Frank laughed. "Then you'd have to talk to him."

"Dammit. I'm out of choices, aren't I?"

Frank grinned and hugged his sister, happy to see the smile back on her face. He just hoped it stayed put.

## 26

"Didn't we just do this Monday?" Kristen whined when she sat down next to Andie.

Dillon noticed she didn't look at him. He felt like an ass, but he knew Kristen would forgive him. They were family. You had to forgive family.

"I know. And I'm sorry. I wanted to meet again because there's something you all need to know. Zach, talk to Michele after this. I know she's covering the kitchen. And we need to make sure everyone else who works on this property knows what I'm about to tell all of you."

He had the undivided attention of everyone in the room. His brothers and sister, his cousins, the significant others who were in the room, everyone. Even his grandmother stood at the back of the room.

"What's going on?" Andie asked.

"Perry has been on Amavita property. A couple weeks ago, Memorial Day weekend."

"Shit."

"Seriously?"

"Why are you just telling us now?"

"All right, I know," Dillon said, raising his voice above the others. "I should have told everyone when I saw him, but I didn't. I accept responsibility for that."

"Why are you telling us now?" Jake asked.

"Because I know I was wrong to keep it from everyone. My reasons for doing so are irrelevant, but I wanted all of you aware of it."

"What was he doing?" Ryan asked. "Was he in the vines again? I haven't seen him. Neither of us have."

Ryan looked to Henry who nodded his agreement.

"He was at the parties. He told me he's trying to steal Michele so he can open a restaurant. In general, he was just being an ass, but I thought I could handle it instead of telling everyone. It wasn't a big deal, so I didn't make a big deal out of it."

"We need to step up our observation," Henry said to Ryan. "I'll take the north side in the mornings and the south side in the afternoon, you can do the opposite. Keep your phone on you at all times. We'll set up a text code to alert everyone if we see him out there."

"Hold on," Dillon said. "Let's take a breath. He's a vindictive son of a bitch, and I don't trust him, but I also think we need to go on with our jobs."

"We need to watch for him," Henry said.

Dillon nodded along with the others. "We do. Absolutely. But we have work to do. None of us are sitting on our asses around here. Mix things up a little. Walk a different way than you normally would. Or take a break at a different time. If he's out here, he's trespassing. Get a photo of him on our vineyard so we can go to the cops with proof."

"What do you think he's doing?" Alyssa asked.

Dillon shook his head. "I have no idea. It doesn't matter

what he's doing, though. We have to treat it as though he's threatening our livelihood because he is. He's on our property."

"Tell them what he said to you," Kristen urged.

Dillon met her gaze and nodded. "He knows about the contract with the aunts. He made it sound like he thinks someone is going to sell him Amavita."

"What?" the others echoed around him.

"Calm down," Dillon said sternly. "He only said I couldn't kick him out because I wasn't the owner yet and even when we take over, I won't be the only owner. He thinks he has something, but we all know he's just trying to get to us. No one likes him."

"I hate to say this, but do we know Katherine wasn't working with him?" Leo asked.

Dillon glared at his brother, but Leo didn't back down until Sean told him to drop it.

"Why? Golden boy says she's not a spy so she's not. She wouldn't tell anyone what she does for a living. She was jumpy. And she didn't give up any personal information. She could be anyone."

"She's Kate Maddox," Dillon spat.

Leo's eyes went wide before he cracked up. "You're full of shit. You almost had me. Kate Maddox. At Amavita. And none of us realized it. Did she tell you that? Maybe she really is a spy and that's her cover."

"Shut up, Leo," Andie growled.

Leo shot her an annoyed look. "Listen, she liked me. He fucked up my chances with her, and I'm supposed to think she wasn't trying to hook the big fish so she could get more dirt for her boss. Screw you."

"She really is Kate Maddox, Leo. She basically confessed at the concert. Except the only one who knew was Dillon. She wrote a song for him."

Leo dropped to his seat, shaking his head. "There's no way. I had Kate Maddox in my hands and he stole her?"

"She was never in your hands. She was mine before you ever met her."

"I gotta tell—"

"No," Dillon roared. "You are not going to tell anyone. Ever. Until she wants the world to know her real name, none of you will utter a word of this. And she'll never be yours, Leo. Don't let me hear you say it again."

Dillon stormed from the room and closed himself in his office. When a soft knock came on his door a few minutes later, he still had his fists tightened into balls, ready to punch something.

"What?"

"Is that any way to talk to your grandmother?" Nonna said, stepping inside.

"I'm sorry, Nonna. I didn't realize it was you."

"And that makes it okay? You shouldn't be talking to any of your family that way."

Dillon nodded. "You're right. I'm sorry. What can I do for you?"

"You can tell me why you haven't gone after Katherine."

"You mean Kate?"

Nonna shook her head. "No. I mean Katherine. That's the woman you fell in love with. Kate is a mirage. Katherine is the real woman."

"Did you miss that part of the meeting? They're the same person. Katherine is Kate. Kate is Katherine. And I'm the fool who thought she actually loved me."

"Did you ever think about why she lied to you?"

Dillon groaned.

"Shut up and humor an old lady. Why do you go to Ithaca to find women to sleep with?"

"Nonna!"

She raised an eyebrow at him and patted his cheek with her wrinkled hand. "I know more than you think, my boy."

Dillon laughed and shook his head.

"Answer my question."

Dillon met her eyes and said, "Because I don't want anyone to know who I am and see a meal ticket."

"How much does this vineyard earn in a year?"

Dillon shrugged. "I don't know an exact number."

"Do you think it's more than Kate Maddox makes in a year?"

Dillon snorted. "Not even close."

"So if you find the need to hide who you are so you can get laid, how hard do you think it is for her?"

Dillon huffed. "Yeah, but what about after she got here? I mean the night we met was one thing, but what about when she was staying with me and meeting the family? Why didn't she tell me about it then?"

Nonna shrugged. "I'm sure she had her reasons. Judging by that song, I'm guessing it has something to do with you not wanting to be famous."

"What?"

Nonna leveled him with a look that said exactly how stupid she thought he was. "Did you listen to the song?"

Dillon nodded. "I was there when she played it, Nonna."

"That's not what I asked. I asked if you listened to it. Did you hear the words? Really hear them?"

"I don't know. Sort of."

"Pull it up on your phone and listen, Dillon. Really listen. She's telling you how much she loves you. The least you could do is listen to the woman."

Nonna left Dillon to stare after her with that parting shot. It took him a few seconds to think back to the concert and realize he was so angry with her that he barely heard anything she said that night. The music was so familiar to him that he could have sang along to every song, but he was numb watching her on stage.

When she started talking about the new song, he was simply angry. He told her she could use his music, and he meant it, but it was different when it was Kate Maddox singing the song. It was a slap in the face because he couldn't see what was right in front of him.

Dillon went to his desk and pulled up one of the cell phone videos of Kate singing *Walk Of Fame*. He listened, really listened, to every word.

*Lost and scared with nowhere to go*
*You took me in*
*Frozen pizza, fabulous wine*
*My soul began to heal*
*You told me I was beautiful*
*Made me believe it too*
*Dinner and dancing in your arms*
*Under the stars*

*I loved you true with all my heart*
*but couldn't go beyond our start.*
*I suffered through my walk of shame*
*to keep you from a walk of fame*

*Falling for you was like breathing*
*Love came easy*
*Your hands on me, your heart in mine*
*Your laugh, your smile, your kiss*
*You loving me, I felt so safe*
*I fell for you so fast*
*Like being on a roller coaster*
*Out of control*

*I loved you true with all my heart*
*but couldn't go beyond our start.*
*I suffered through my walk of shame*
*to keep you from a walk of fame*

*Your love helped me, gave me the strength*
*I faced my fear*
*The one who never showed me love*
*Undeserving of my trust*
*Abused my heart and made me doubt*
*You showed me what love should be*

*I loved you true with all my heart*
*but couldn't go beyond our start.*
*I suffered through my walk of shame*
*to keep you from a walk of fame*

*I couldn't put you through the fame*
*Life on display*
*Inside my head I said goodbye*
*I kissed you one last time*
*I knew it was the best for you*
*Even though my heart broke*
*I couldn't put you through the fame*
*I walked away*

*I loved you true with all my heart*
*but couldn't go beyond our start.*
*I suffered through my walk of shame*
*to keep you from a walk of fame*

By the time she finished singing, Dillon knew what she was saying. And he knew what his answer was.

He just hoped he wasn't too late to tell her.

***

"ARE YOU SURE THIS IS A GOOD IDEA?" QUYNN ASKED FROM the passenger seat.

"She needs to go to him. As Katherine, not Kate, and tell him she's sorry. Saying it on stage in front of thousands of people and having it broadcast all over the world isn't personal enough," Frank said.

"I never would have done this."

"Then I guess it's a good thing I couldn't let you walk away without giving us a chance."

Quynn grinned and brushed her hand down Frank's cheek. Katherine watched the exchange from the backseat of Frank's SUV. She wanted what they had. Sweet, normal love.

With any luck, she'd get it.

The closer they got to Amavita Estates, the more nervous Katherine was. She trusted her brother, but they could all be wrong about Dillon. He might just not want to see her. Or he might have been telling her he loved her because he knew he'd never see her again. Or any number of things. She just hoped he didn't laugh in her face.

"Turn left at the next road," Quynn told Frank, taking over for Katherine since she couldn't find her voice. "Are you ready for this?" Quynn asked her, turning in her seat to face Katherine.

Katherine shook her head.

Quynn laughed. "You'll be fine. Do you think he'll be home or at the office?"

"Office," Katherine choked out.

Quynn pointed to the inn that loomed on the horizon. From the road they could see the entire property, the inn sitting midway between the road and Cayuga Lake. It was stunning, just like Katherine remembered from when she was a kid. She could feel the inspiration swirling inside her as they drove the short distance to the inn. If she lived there, she'd never stop writing music.

Frank parked and turned with Quynn to look at her. "Do you want us to come in?"

Katherine shook her head but made no move to get out of the car.

"Come on," Quynn said, opening her own door and then Katherine's. She half-dragged Katherine out of the car and urged her toward the door.

Katherine stopped, took a deep breath, then walked up the steps. She said a quick prayer before she opened the door and walked inside.

---

DILLON SAT ON THE PICNIC TABLE OUTSIDE HIS HOUSE WITH the guitar. He listened to *Walk Of Fame* more times than he could count. He was trying to pick up her chord changes and almost had them down. He just hoped he didn't miss her. Andie said she had another interview that day so he was banking on her still being in town, but he had to hurry. One last run through and he would go see her.

*Lost and scared I hid my heart*
*I took you in*
*Frozen pizza, fabulous wine*
*My heart began to heal*
*I've never seen such beauty*
*Inside and out*
*Dinner and dancing in your arms*
*Under the stars*

*I love you true with all my heart*
*we never went beyond our start.*
*You suffered through a walk of shame*
*I'm ready for my walk of fame*

*Falling for you was like breathing*
*Love came easy*
*Your hands on me, your heart in mine*
*Your laugh, your smile, your kiss*
*You loving me, I felt so safe*
*I fell for you so fast*
*Like being on a roller coaster*
*Ride of my life*

*I love you true with all my heart*
*we never went beyond our start.*
*You suffered through a walk of shame*
*I'm ready for my walk of fame*

*Your love helped me, gave me the strength*
*I faced my fear*
*The ones who never showed us love*
*Undeserving of our trust*
*Abused our hearts and made us doubt*
*You showed me true love*

*I love you true with all my heart*
*we never went beyond our start.*
*You suffered through a walk of shame*
*I'm ready for my walk of fame*

*You wouldn't put you through the fame*
*Life on display*
*I never thought it was goodbye*

*I kissed you one last time*
*I watched you walk away from me*
*Even though my heart broke*
*I couldn't put you through the shame*
*I'm here to stay*

*I love you true with all my heart*
*we never went beyond our start.*
*You suffered through a walk of shame*
*I'm ready for my walk of fame*

Dillon played the last chord and took a deep breath. He set the guitar in the case and turned to go and found Katherine watching him, Andie and another couple right behind her. His breath stuck in his throat. She was even more stunning than he allowed himself to remember in those damn jeans he loved and a purple top that had his fingers itching to reach out to her.

"How long have you been there?"

Tears streaked down her cheeks. He ached to wipe them away, but he didn't know what they meant.

"The song…" Katherine began.

Dillon nodded. "I know it's yours. I'm not a recording artist. I'm not going to steal it or sell it or anything. I…I wrote that for you. What are you doing here?"

"You wrote it for me?"

Dillon nodded again and ran a hand through his hair. He set the guitar case down on the table and took a step toward her. "I was going to come see you."

"You were going to come see me?"

He laughed slightly, moving closer to her. "Are you going to repeat everything I say?"

She shook her head. "Did you mean it?"

Dillon glanced at the guitar case. "Every word."

"The song is yours. The music. You wrote it. I… Did you get the contract I sent you?"

Dillon scowled. "Yeah."

"Why the face?"

"Did you mean what you said to me last week? Before you left. Our last night together."

Katherine glanced away for a second, her eyes unfocused as she tried to remember. "When I said I loved you?"

Dillon nodded.

She stepped closer to him. Her brown eyes melted as she looked up at him. She reached for him, cupping his cheek. "I love you, Dillon. I've never loved another man the way I love you. I didn't know what love was until I met you."

He wanted to drag her against him, but he had to know. "Why did you send me a contract?"

"Why?" she asked, taking a step back.

He immediately missed the feel of her palm on his skin.

"You wrote the music. It wouldn't be right for me to take credit for it when it was your song."

"Did Christian tell you I wanted him to tell everyone who I was?"

She rolled her eyes. "He sends me texts every day. I forward them to my lawyer. I did read that one, but I didn't believe it."

"I just wanted him to leave. I wasn't going to tell anyone."

Katherine grinned. "I know. And I should have known that before I left. I should have told you when I was here."

"Why didn't you?"

Katherine glanced behind herself to the woman. Dillon looked closely at her and recognized her.

"Didn't I meet you at the hotel bar?" he blurted.

She smiled and stepped forward. "You did. I'm Quynn O'Hara, personal assistant to Kate Maddox."

"Shit."

Quynn grinned. "I should be the one saying that. Katherine didn't tell you who she was because I told her not to. We were in the middle of Christian threatening to expose her, and I wasn't sure if you were someone she really could trust. She wanted to tell you, but I talked her out of it. Don't be upset with her for that."

Dillon laughed softly. "Thank you for telling me that. Lucky for me, my sister forced me to see things from your perspective. I don't blame you for not telling me," he said to Katherine.

"You don't?"

He shook his head. "You deserve your privacy. I don't blame you a bit."

"You need to answer one more question for me."

Dillon nodded for her to ask.

"Why aren't you kissing me yet?"

Dillon grinned and stepped forward slowly. He took his time wrapping an arm around her waist and hauling her against him. She chuckled softly as he leaned down and pressed his lips to hers.

It didn't take any coaxing at all to get Katherine to part her lips for him. He kissed her until he worried he was going to pass out from lack of oxygen. He didn't care. It would be a hell of a way to go with Katherine in his arms.

She broke their kiss when the others started cheering and whistling. Dillon kept his focus on her, kissing her neck as she turned back to smile at their audience.

"I guess I should introduce you to my brother. Dillon, this is Frank. Frank, meet Dillon."

Frank stepped forward and shook Dillon's free hand. "Don't hurt her."

Dillon nodded once, keeping one arm around Katherine. "Not a chance. She's mine for as long as she'll have me."

"She deserves the world."

"I can't give her the world, but I'll give her everything I have."

Frank grinned. "Good enough."

## 27

"You don't have to do this," Dillon told Katherine.

She rolled over in bed and smiled at him. "I know, but I want to. I've been thinking about it for a long time."

"Really?"

She nodded. "I have. I know they couldn't control it, but when they first said something, I felt guilty."

"You can't feel guilty about stuff like that."

Katherine grinned. "It's part of my charm. I feel guilty about a lot of things."

"Like Christian's demise?"

Katherine snorted and shook her head. "Um, no. I don't feel guilty about that. He tried to ruin me."

Dillon rolled on top of her. "Well, I'm happy he's gone. I don't want him showing up here and messing with us any more."

"He won't. Gary took care of that."

"He's a good person to have in your back pocket."

Katherine laughed. "The only one I want in my back pocket is you."

Dillon nuzzled her neck and nibbled his way to her ear.

"I'm always going to be in your back pocket. And I've been talking to Sean. If you go on another tour, I'm going to try to go with you."

"You are?" she asked, pulling back. She couldn't believe he was willing to give up everything he knew for her. "But you have to be here."

Dillon shook his head. "Sean can handle it. And I really want to be with you."

Katherine smiled and melted into him. "I want to be with you, too. Right now I'm taking a break from touring. I feel so inspired when I'm here. I want to record some new songs and get back in touch with my fans. After next week, everyone is going to know who I am and things are going to be different."

"This place is going to be a madhouse. The guests at the inn are going to go nuts."

Katherine laughed. "They are. I can't wait to see them. I don't know how you guys kept the secret about today this long."

Dillon kissed her softly. "It wasn't easy."

"How much time do we have?"

Dillon glanced at the clock. "Enough for me to make you scream a few times," he said as he slid into her.

---

QUYNN WAS STILL AMAZED BY HOW KIND ALL OF DILLON'S family was. Between Dillon giving her and Frank a place to stay for a while to his cousins pulling together for Kate's reveal party the following week to the private concert they arranged that day, they were the kindest people she'd ever met.

"What can I do?" Andie asked as she met Quynn outside Dillon's house.

"Kate's getting ready now. I was going to walk down and see Alyssa. Since she has no idea what we're doing, I want to make sure she's okay with us invading her for a little while."

Andie nodded, her hair catching the sunlight. She and Quynn had become fast friends, their shared love of Dillon and Katherine an easy bond.

"I talked to her yesterday. I think she's going stir crazy since she isn't working much."

Quynn looked out over the vineyard. "I don't think I'd ever go stir crazy in a place like this. It's so peaceful. I'd actually get some reading done and sleep in and enjoy the fresh air."

Andie turned to walk along the water. "I love it here, but I think being forced to relax is what's making her nuts. Jake doesn't want Alyssa doing much of anything. She gets outside and walks regularly and comes up to the inn, but he won't let her do a lot. He insists she only works about four hours a day, if that."

"That's really sweet. I know all your aunts and your grandmother are thrilled to have a new baby in the family. The first boy."

Andie laughed. "There was a war before the reveal party. Nonna insisted it was a boy, but everyone else was positive it was a girl."

Quynn smiled. She was an only child so having so much family around and involved in your business was definitely an adjustment. She could tell how much they all loved each other, though. That made her want to stay, especially since they accepted her so quickly.

"Are you and Cody going to have kids?"

Andie snorted a laugh. "Not any time soon. We're taking things slow. I've known him forever, but I never thought of him as anyone other than my brother's best friend. I wonder what the hell took me so long to realize he was right in front of me, but I have him now. And kids will come eventually."

"Have you talked about getting married?"

Andie nodded. "A lot. I'd say yes today if he asked me. He knows that."

"He seems like the kind of guy who will make a proposal really special."

Andie laughed. "Yeah, he is. You need to see how special he made my house before you leave."

"Your house?"

"He remodeled it last fall. He took every little thing I ever said and put it into the house. It's my dream house."

"Wow. That's awesome."

Andie nodded. "Yeah, it still amazes me. Frank seems like he'd be the same. Always looking out for what you want."

Quynn grinned. "I think we both got pretty lucky."

"Absolutely."

Andie knocked on the door to Alyssa and Jake's house, then let herself inside.

"Alyssa! We're invading you and dragging you outside."

"Thank God," Alyssa groaned from the living room. "I need a break from these four walls, and Jake won't let me go outside unsupervised."

"Holy shit," Andie said when Alyssa stood. "Did you get bigger overnight?"

"Screw you. I'm due in two months."

"And you look like you're going to pop tomorrow. Just promise you won't have the baby today."

Alyssa rolled her eyes, making Quynn laugh. "I make no promises. I can't see my feet. Help me get my shoes on."

"Wear flip flops," Andie argued.

"Jake's afraid I'll fall in them."

"You're not running a marathon in them. We're going outside. Knowing you, you'll be barefoot before long."

Alyssa grinned and shrugged in agreement.

"We're not going far. Let's get out there."

The three of them went outside and sat at the picnic table overlooking the water. They talked about Alyssa's pregnancy and the men in their lives. When Quynn got a text from Kate, she nodded at Andie.

"We have a little surprise for you."

Alyssa looked at her warily. "What kind of surprise?"

"The kind where you have to promise to breathe and not go into labor."

"What the hell did you do?" Alyssa demanded.

"It's a good surprise. Jake should be here soon, and then you'll see what the surprise is."

Jake appeared a minute later and walked over to Alyssa. He kissed her and asked how she was doing before he turned his attention to Andie. "I was told to be home. What's going on?"

"We all wanted to have lunch, so Zach's on his way here with food. And we have a little surprise since you guys couldn't make it to the Kate Maddox concert."

Alyssa gasped. "Kate Maddox." She slapped Jake and pointed. "Kate Maddox. Am I dreaming or is she really there?"

Jake stood up straight and stared at Kate and the others. Quynn grinned at the shocked expressions on their faces. Kate was holding hands with Dillon. They were followed by Frank and the rest of the family.

"I get why Dillon would like her, but what the hell is he doing with her? He's in love with Katherine," Alyssa hissed at Andie.

Andie grinned, but Quynn burst out laughing. They both shook their heads and waited for the group to get closer. Not all of them knew Katherine was Kate Maddox, but Dillon was going to tell everyone before they walked down. Quynn noticed the whispers of some of the family she hadn't gotten to know well and smiled.

Kate stepped forward, guitar in hand, to speak to Alyssa and Jake.

"Hey, guys. Since you weren't able to make it to my concert, I wanted to give you your own version. I hated that you missed it, but I'm sure they all filled you in."

Alyssa nodded absently.

"I have to ask you to keep my secret for a little while longer, though. We'll be telling everyone soon."

Alyssa finally found her voice. "Secret? Don't tell me you stole Dillon from Katherine. I really liked her."

Everyone laughed except Alyssa.

Kate shook her head. "That's the secret, Alyssa. I am Katherine."

Alyssa's brows tugged together, and she tilted her head to the side. Katherine smiled at her, letting Alyssa look. When she finally saw the truth, Alyssa gasped.

"Oh, my God. We had a superstar staying here and I never even realized it! How did you let me look so dumb?" she asked, slapping Jake's arm.

He laughed. "I didn't know either. I'm just as shocked. And think I need a night with your cousin to understand how the hell this happened."

Alyssa nodded. "I feel so stupid."

Kate shook her head. "No reason to. I do this," she gestured to her outfit and hair, "so people won't recognize me. I never wanted to be Kate Maddox all the time. I wanted to have a real life, one that didn't involve cameras trying to catch every time I left the house without makeup or wearing sweatpants or being normal."

Quynn went to Frank as Kate and Alyssa talked about the perils of being recognized. Quynn didn't realize she was married to a governor for a while. Alyssa really did get it.

"How is she?" Quynn asked Frank.

Frank nodded. "She's good. She's ready for this. And for the next one."

Quynn smiled. "I'm glad someone is. I'm still freaking out."

Frank kissed her cheek and settled her back against his front as Kate sat on the picnic table next to Alyssa and Jake. Kate started to play, enchanting the entire crowd. Frank swayed to the music then spun Quynn so they could dance together. As he moved her around the space between the vines and the house, Quynn knew everything was exactly how it was supposed to be.

***

DILLON NEVER THOUGHT HE'D FIND SOMEONE WHO MADE HIM feel the way Katherine did. She was everything to him, and knowing she wasn't going to rush back out on tour made him happier than he'd been in years.

Kristen looped her arm through his and rested her head on his shoulder. He squeezed her hand and smiled at her. "You okay?"

She nodded. "It's awesome that she's doing this for them."

"She really wanted to. She felt bad that they couldn't make it to the concert."

"A private concert just for them is a pretty great way to make it up to them."

Dillon grinned. "They're lucky I have connections."

Kristen laughed. "They're lucky you're the one who picked her up in the bar that night."

"No, I'm lucky."

Kristen nodded, but there was a sadness in her eyes that Dillon hated seeing.

"What's going on?"

Kristen shook her head.

"Talk to me," he urged.

"I'm fine. I just keep thinking Philip would have loved this."

"So it's really over between you two?"

Kristen shrugged. "I haven't heard from him since Alyssa's wedding. At all. I'm guessing it's safe to say it's over."

"I'm sorry, Kris."

She shrugged again and tossed her hair over her shoulder. "I'm making the most of it. Maybe get everyone else out of my system before he comes crawling back."

Dillon heard the false bravado in her voice but didn't call her on it. If she wanted to pretend it was business as usual, he wasn't going to be an ass about it. "He always does."

Kristen chuckled softly. "Yeah."

The stood together, watching Kate sing some of her more popular songs. Kristen clung to him like she was afraid to let go. He followed her gaze to Jake and Alyssa swaying slowly together, trading soft kisses and words no one else could hear. When he looked back at Kristen, there were tears in her eyes.

"Are you okay?" he asked, pulling her to the side.

She shook her head. "I want that. I thought I had it, but I know he's done with me. It's hard, Dillon."

Dillon wrapped her in his arms and held her as she cried. Andie shared that Kristen hadn't cried at all since she and Philip split up. It worried Andie and Dillon, but there wasn't anything they could do to help her get over him.

As Kristen cried in his arms, Dillon hoped it meant she was finally saying goodbye to Philip and moving on. He didn't deserve her attention or love. Of course, Dillon couldn't tell Kristen that. She'd always defended Philip. Through their break-ups and reunions for years, she was always quick to forgive him and take him back.

But she'd never cried for him.

Kristen finally eased back and dried her eyes. She looked up at Dillon with grateful eyes. "Thank you."

He smiled. "Any time."

Kristen snorted. "I hope to not make a habit of crying on my cousin's shoulder. Usually I use Ian for this."

"Aw, Kris. You can always come to me."

She nodded. "I know. Katherine's made some changes in you in a short time, and I'm happy you have her, but it's hard to talk to any of you when you're all so happy. Girls' nights used to be Andie, Emily, and me being silly. Now it's a love fest of happily married women. Ian's the only one I really feel like I can talk to."

Dillon pulled her back in for a hug and kissed the top of her head. "I'll put my happiness aside and we can hang out, okay? You just have to promise you won't tell me about your sexcapades."

Kristen laughed and nodded. "I might hold you to that."

"I hope you do," he told her honestly.

***

Kristen stood at the outskirts of the group once Kate was finished playing. Dillon went to her, as he should, leaving Kristen without a person to lean on.

She was not a mopey, weepy kind of woman. She never was. All the times she and Phillip broke up, she rarely cried or got upset at all. He always came back before she had much of a chance to miss him.

But this time was different. It had been months since she'd heard from him. She never told anyone, but she called him a few times. He never answered her calls and never returned them, but she knew he saw them. She sent him a text a few days ago asking if they could hookup.

Then hated herself for it.

Phillip made it clear he didn't want her, but she was holding on. He'd been her first everything, from her first kiss to the first boy she fell for to the first person she slept with. She kissed and slept with plenty of other guys since she did them with Phillip the first time, but he was still the only guy she'd ever loved.

It bugged her that he could dismiss her so easily. They were young, only a few months past turning twenty-eight. She had no interest in getting married. Not yet. But he was anxious for a wife, and when she said no to his proposal, he left.

She never told anyone that part either. She was too embarrassed. They all thought of her as a party girl. They'd say she was also irresponsible, selfish, and stupid if they knew she'd refused to marry Philip.

Kristen got a plate of food and sat on the steps to Jake and Alyssa's house alone to eat. When she was done, she was ready to leave the party, but her cousin stepped in front of her.

"You good?" Ryan asked.

He was the youngest of all the cousins, but always miles more mature than Kristen felt. She adored Ryan. They were close, but not close enough that she'd tell him the truth. Kristen nodded. "Always," she said with a fake smile.

"Leo and I found out about this new place on Cayuga. Based in Ithaca, but they do stuff all over the lake. We're going there this weekend if you want to come with us."

Kristen shook her head. "I'm working all weekend."

"Crap," Ryan said. "I should have realized that since Leo's off. We'll find out more about it and see if they could be a good fit for us."

Kristen nodded. "Sounds good. What's it called? I'll look it up."

"In-Zane's. The owner's a pretty cool guy. Moved here a few months ago."

"It sounds like you already know him."

Ryan nodded. "We met him out one night. Had a few drinks, met a few girls."

Kristen smiled. She'd had more than her fair share of nights like that. Getting blissfully drunk and sleeping with whichever guy piqued her interest. It was the only way she got from one breakup with Phillip to the next time he came back. That and she really enjoyed sex. There was no reason for her not to have any just because Philip was being a dick about something stupid.

She shook her head at herself. She should be celebrating. She was free. She never had to worry about Phillip telling her how to act or what to do. She had her life to herself, for the first time ever, more or less. She'd been with him for so long that losing him felt more like losing a limb than losing the man she loved.

It was time to move on for good. He clearly was.

"Next time you guys go out, let me know," she said to Ryan.

He nodded. "Absolutely."

Kristen talked to him for a few more minutes then headed back to the tasting room for the rest of the afternoon. She felt lighter, happier, more free. There was no reason she had to hold on to Phillip. He clearly wasn't holding on to her. She decided whenever she had moments of doubt, she'd do what she'd always done.

Fake it.

---

THANK YOU SO MUCH FOR READING KATHERINE AND DILLON'S story. They were one of the first couples I thought about when I decided to write this series and I had such a great time bringing them to life.

The series continues with Kristen's story. With a broken heart, she decides she's done with men. Too bad Zane has a different plan for her. Pick up Fake It Till You Break It today!

COLLEGE GRAD, PAIGE IS ON A BREAK WITH HER BEST FRIENDS. She's newly single, and the perfect way to get over her ex is with the sinfully sexy Dante. Five days is long enough, and they go their separate ways. Until Paige walks into her new job and finds Dante is her new coworker. Read In Front Of Me today.

TARA THOUGHT SHE'D ESCAPED THE PRYING EYES OF NOSY people when she left Hollywood behind. Instead, her life takes a turn she never expected in small town Winterville, and not necessarily for the better. She can't trust anyone, especially a stranger. Start Round & Ravishing now!

# ABOUT THE AUTHOR

*USA TODAY* Bestselling Author Mary E Thompson spent most of her childhood wishing she had a few less curves. She hid in the pages of books because her favorite characters never cared what size her clothes were. Now, neither does Mary, and she writes stories that celebrate women like her. Real women who have curves, chase dreams, and find love, because we should all be happy, no matter our dress size.

Mary spends her non-writing time with her husband and two kids, watching too much TV, cheering for her home-town football team (Go Bills!), and hiding chocolate from her family.

Visit https://MaryEThompson.com/ to sign up for Mary's newsletter, **Romancing the Curves**. Subscribers get free ebooks and other fun stuff, like exclusive, members only content and giveaways, plus are the first to know about new releases and sales!

www.ingramcontent.com/pod-product-compliance
Lightning Source LLC
Chambersburg PA
CBHW060749190726

48285CB00002B/356

*9781944090456*